"A S...

Le Doux Mysteries #3
By Abigail Lynn Thornton

A SIP OF MURDER

First edition. November 24, 2021.

Written by Abigail Lynn Thornton.

DEDICATION

To my oldest daughter.
I can barely keep up with your
intelligence and abilities!
You're amazing!
Keep being everything you were meant to be.

ACKNOWLEDGEMENTS

No author works alone. Thank you, Cathy.
Your cover work is beautiful!
And to Laura, for your timely and thorough editing!

NEWSLETTER

Stay up to date on all my new releases by joining my newsletter!
You can find it and other exciting news at
abigailthorntonbooks.com

CHAPTER 1
PRIMROSE

P rim paused just outside the warehouse door and took a couple of fortifying breaths. Right now she needed to be cool...collected...and completely in control. Madam Ureo wouldn't tolerate weakness. In fact, she would chew it up and spit it out before Prim ever got to her practiced speech about why she needed to be paid. She had worked the hours, it was time to see the money.

Her phone buzzed against her hip and Prim quickly pulled it out, then made a face. "Perfect timing, Nona," she muttered, silencing the device before putting it back in her pocket. She loved her friend dearly, but right now Prim needed to focus. They could always chat later.

Closing her eyes, Prim poofed her tiny fairy form into a human one and threw back her shoulders, faking the confidence that would be needed in order to convince her boss that she deserved what she was asking for, despite any financial struggles the theatre was having. After all, they shouldn't have hired her if they couldn't afford to pay her...right?

With a tight fist, Prim knocked forcefully on the wooden door.

"Enter!" Madam Ureo screeched, her harpy voice cracking enough to make fingernails on a chalkboard sound like a symphony.

Gritting her teeth against the noise, Prim pushed it open and entered with her head high. "Madam Ureo," she said calmly. Her fists stayed clenched in order to keep the shaking to a minimum.

The harpy glared with her beady yellow eyes. Although, to be fair, the look was her basic resting face, which meant Prim had no idea if her boss was angry, happy or something in between. "Ms. Meadows," Madam Ureo garbled. "To what do I owe the pleasure?"

The tone of the creature's voice let Prim know it was decidedly *not* a pleasure.

"I've been working for well over a month now," Prim began, working her way into her practice speech. "And I believe it's time for me to receive the paycheck that is owed to me."

The harpy's eyebrows shot up. "Is that so?" She folded her hands together and leaned forward onto her gnarled wooden desk. "And just what did you have in mind?" Her smile showed jagged teeth that did nothing to put Prim at ease.

Prim had to stop herself from rolling her eyes. What was it with this harpy and her tight fist on the money? "My paycheck," Prim said succinctly. "*That's* what I had in mind."

In an act of faith, Prim had taken out a second mortgage on her beloved greenhouse in order to expand her wholesale plant and flower business. Her timing, however, had been less than stellar, since there had been a shift in the market and her numbers had dropped just as her payments had increased.

At first it had been fine. Prim had some money set away, but as the months passed, her savings had whittled down to nothing and she had come dangerously close to not being able to pay her bills.

Desperate, Prim had taken on another job. A nighttime position at The Siren's Thrall Theatre. It was a place where creatures could come to watch vampire impersonators sing, as well as mingle with other cast members pretending to be famous paranormal creatures. It definitely wasn't something Prim would have ever considered before, but it had been available. And with her mortgage looming, Prim had jumped at the chance to earn enough to keep her creditors at bay.

There had proven to be two problems with Prim's decision to work. One, the harpy smirking at Prim from behind a desk. Madam Nelara Ureo absolutely lived up to her species' reputation as a rude, uncaring, demanding boss, who paid too little and asked too much. Actually...she hadn't paid at all, which was exactly why Prim was in Madam Ureo's office yet again. Prim needed that paycheck. She was tired of Madam Ureo's excuses that funds were difficult to come by. If the theatre was that hard off, they shouldn't have been hiring workers and if Prim didn't get paid soon, she would have to take desperate measures in order to save her business.

The second problem was the fact that Prim had yet to tell her best friend about the new job. Wynona had come from such a difficult background that Prim couldn't find it in herself to share her own troubles. How could she admit that she was failing as a businesswoman? Especially to someone who grew up with President and Lady Le Doux as parents? Wynona had spent thirty years being bullied and treated unfairly, she didn't need to deal with Prim's issues.

As a fairy, even a wingless one, Prim's talents definitely didn't lend themselves to stage performances. Fairies usually found themselves in pursuits that involved decorating or building of some sort. They liked to make things beautiful, which was why the interior decorating field was dominated with the species. Prim considered herself a botanist, though she didn't have a formal degree in the subject.

Her magic specialty was plants, and that had always been more than enough to fulfill her wants and desires. At least until the market had taken a turn for the worse.

Madam Ureo's dark chuckle brought Prim out of her wandering thoughts. "You think you're more important than any of my other workers?" the harpy rasped. Her laughter sounded like shattering glass. "You're nothing but a broken fairy. The little bit of money we actually have to work with goes to pay much better employees than you." Madam Ureo threw her head back and laughed so hard that she ended up coughing like a chain smoker.

Prim pressed her lips together, determined not to shout. She'd spent her entire life being mocked and bullied for not being born with wings and in the fairy world, at least Prim could understand why people made a big deal out of it. But in a job like this one, whether or not she had wings made absolutely no difference whatsoever.

"I've worked just as hard as the other actors," Prim said tightly. "I've done everything you've asked me to, and I've done it without complaint—"

"Exactly," Madam Ureo interrupted after regaining her breath. "And you'll continue to do as I say." One side of her lip curled up in a sneer. "Which is why you're now going to walk out that door and I'll forget this little incident ever happened."

"But—"

Madam Ureo placed her palms on the desk and slowly stood to her full height, which for Prim was terrifying even when she was in her human form. Eight feet of creepy black skin and boney wings was enough to make even a troll shake. "Perhaps your ears are as nonexistent as your wings," Madam Ureo snapped. "I said *get out*!"

Prim's nostrils flared as she did her best to control her anger. She wasn't usually one to work so hard to control her emotions, but she had an eerie feeling that Madam Ureo ate fairies for breakfast and wouldn't hesitate to do the same to Prim if she didn't fall back into line.

But this was important to her. She wasn't asking for anything she hadn't earned. She wasn't pressing for a raise or advance. It was within her rights to ask for what she had earned. "The contract I signed was one that included being paid for my work. I have worked for over a month now and still haven't been given a single dime. You're in breach." Prim stuck her chin in the air. "I have grounds to sue you for what is owed me, but I would rather we just solve this without the courts." The words were bitter on Prim's lips, but her business was worth the threats. Without her plants, Prim would be nothing.

Wide, leathery wings snapped out, making the large office seem like a mouse hole as they filled the expanse. "Get out or you're fired." The words were blunt and to the point and definitely not what Prim had expected her boss to say.

Her mouth dropped open. "You would really rather I bring in the authorities?"

Madam Ureo's long black fingernail pointed toward the door. "I don't deal with overeager creatures whose egos are bigger than their brains. Now, either I can have you kicked out permanently, or you can leave on your own and still keep your job. Your *silent* job."

The sting of tears hit the back of Prim's eyes, but she kept them back. After her upbringing, she'd gotten good at pretending as if nothing affected her. She stuck her nose in the air. "This isn't over." Forcing a nonchalant walk, she headed to the door and pulled it open, only to stumble to a stop.

Brell Tuall, the company's most famous impersonator, was standing at the door with her fist raised. "Oh!" Brell said breathlessly. Her plush red lips formed a perfect "O", and Prim wanted to roll her eyes with disgust.

Sirens were so annoyingly perfect.

"Ah, our star performer," Madam Ureo drawled.

Prim glanced over her shoulder to see the manager leaning lazily back in her office chair, grinning smugly. "I do believe I have a more important employee to deal with, Prim, dear. If you would?" Madam Ureo waved toward the door.

Prim's lips pinched into a tight line, and she bit her tongue to keep from telling the harpy exactly what she thought of her. The exact second something better came along, Prim was out of here, but in the meantime, Prim needed that money.

She stepped to the side to go around Brell.

"Oh, and Prim?"

Prim stopped but didn't bother looking back.

"We have a Sunday afternoon show this week. Don't miss it."

Prim spun, her mouth open to argue. That had been the one caveat she'd given when being hired. Sunday afternoons were off limits. They were the one day a week Prim got together with Wynona for tea and even with the addition of Rascal, they were a precious event for her.

Madam Ureo tilted her head and raised an eyebrow. "Problem?"

Prim snapped her mouth shut and shook her head.

"That's what I thought." The smugness in the harpy's tone was nauseating. "Now run along. I need to speak to the person who actually makes me money."

Prim spun and stormed out of the office. She didn't bother to say hello to Brell, or acknowledge the siren's shocked look at Prim's departure. How had everything gone so horribly wrong? Prim had practiced her speech for days. That money was hers! Madam Ureo had no right to keep it from her! If the theatre was bankrupt, then every employee should be told that. But as far as Prim knew, only a handful of them weren't getting paid. But why? Why was the money being held back? And why was Prim too scared to just quit?

"Because you can't afford to," she muttered to herself.

Madam Ureo, unfortunately, knew how much this job meant to Prim. Being a natural people person, Prim had come into her initial interview and shared her eagerness and troubles, which was exactly why her boss knew that threatening Prim's position would put her back in line. The harpy was as cruel as they came.

Prim's footsteps stuttered at that thought. She knew well how cruel people could be. Anyone who was raised just the slightest bit different from the norm knew. But now, as an adult, and a normally successful business owner, Prim hadn't expected her boss to be one of them.

Prim had every reason and every right to leave notice and go home. But the stubborn part of her that hadn't let her lack of wings stop her from opening a business, and the fact she had an empty bank account, refused to let someone as terrible as Madam Ureo have the last laugh. If only to spite the disgusting harpy, Prim was going to stick around. And when no one was watching, she was going to take matters into her own hands.

A slow grin crept across Prim's face as she walked down the side-walk. It wasn't much, but the thought of her rebellion helped lift the dark cloud that had been hanging over her head. No one could stop her from finding a way to win, least of all a bitter, old crone who wouldn't know a good thing if it bit her overly long nose.

Prim's walk grew more relaxed and her arms began to swing care-lessly. Yes, it was going to be fun undermining the head honcho. And if word got back to Madam Ureo and she followed through with her threat of dismissal, well...then Prim might just have to call in a favor with her best friend's boyfriend, who happened to be a police officer. Of course that would mean admitting her failure to her friends, but if it came down to confessing or losing? Prim knew exactly what she would do.

Reaching into the back pocket of her slacks, Prim pulled out her phone and dialed Wynona.

"Prim!" Wynona's sweet voice came through the line. "I've been trying to get a hold of you!"

"Well, you have me," Prim said cheerily. "What did you need?"

"Help with the flowers," Wynona said in a low tone. "I don't know what happened, but the arrangement you brought me for the pastry table completely keeled over this morning! It's like someone put something in the water, only I can't figure out what it would be."

Prim frowned. "Are all the flowers dead?"

"They're not exactly dead, just...wilted. Like, really wilted."

Prim's walk slowed as her mind worked through possible scenar-ios. "Has anyone touched it since I brought it by? It shouldn't have needed water since I only brought it yesterday."

"I moved it to the antique cabinet," Wynona said. "Other than that, no."

Prim laughed. "Nona, you put it in the sun, didn't you?"

"Well, yeah. Don't flowers like the sun?"

"Sweetie, I made that arrangement specifically for the pastry table. I knew it wouldn't see the sun, which is why I filled it with Bleeding Hearts and Lily of the Valleys. They're shade flowers."

"You're kidding."

Prim shook her head, then answered, "Nope. Just like you don't put the food near the sunny window, these flowers don't go near the sunny patches either."

"Oh my gosh." Nona gasped. "I'm so sorry. If I put them back, will they perk up?"

Prim glanced at the screen of her phone. "Tell you what. I'm free at the moment. I'll come by and give them a boost so they're ready for your opening tomorrow."

"Would you?" Wynona asked. "You're so amazing."

Prim grinned. "And this is why you're my best friend. Everyone needs someone to build their ego once in a while."

"You save these flowers and I'll build up your ego so big you won't be able to walk through the front door."

"Deal." Prim picked her pace back up. "I'll see you in fifteen."

She hung up the phone and stuck it back in her pants pocket. Seeing Wynona would be a nice break, especially since Prim wouldn't be able to come to tea this Sunday. Not that Wynona needed to know that...yet.

But between a friend visit and a planned rebellion, Prim felt as if her future had suddenly perked up just a bit. There was fun and mischief ahead, and Prim was going to come out the conqueror.

CHAPTER 2

Wynona

"Do you think orange peel and jasmine will work?" Wynona asked Violet, her purple mouse companion, who was currently eating her body weight in cake from the dining table. Wynona paused before sprinkling the two teas together and looked over her shoulder. "Well?"

Violet looked up from her treat and made a considering face, which was quite interesting on a creature that size. After a moment she shook her head and went back to the cake.

Wynona huffed. "Some help you are." She filled a tea infuser with the blend and dunked it into a hot cup of water. Gently grabbing the handle, Wynona brought the mug over to the table and sat down. She leaned down and took a whiff. "Smells good, "she murmured.

The night was quiet. The tea house was closed for the evening. Lusgu, Wynona's brownie janitor, had disappeared into the corner that he called home. Rascal was on duty and Prim wasn't answering her phone.

All in all, it was the perfect night for Wynona to do some experimenting. She had given Violet a leftover piece of cake from the day's pastries and gotten to work. She hoped to have something new to try on her friends when they came over for their normal Sunday afternoon luncheon, but so far her creative side was lacking.

Normally Wynona had a special gift with tea. She was able to custom create blends to fit any person, but tonight she just wasn't feeling it, though it wasn't from lack of trying.

She dunked the infuser a few times, then set it on a saucer to the side. Picking up the hot mug, Wynona took a deep sniff. "Hmm..." She pinched her lips in thought. "It doesn't smell too bad, but the citrus with the floral is interesting." She narrowed her gaze at the liquid. If it tasted the same way it smelled, it probably wasn't going to be a winner any time soon. The orange was nice, with a slightly bitter edge. The jasmine was also nice with the flowery back end. But the two together?

Throwing caution to the wind, Wynona took a sip and made a face. "Nope," she choked out, wiping at her mouth. "Definitely not our next house blend."

Violet snickered.

"Oh, that's rich," Wynona teased. "Coming from a lady with frosting all over her upper lip."

Violet paused and felt around on her face, confirming that what Wynona said was true.

Wynona held out a napkin, grinning as she did so. "I hate to say I told you so..."

She let the sentence drop off, smiling wider when Violet got defensive and pretended that she didn't care if she was messy.

Sighing, Wynona stood and walked into the kitchen to dump her tea in the sink. She stood staring at the drain for a moment, trying to figure out why she was struggling.

Ever since she was a small girl, she had been learning how to best use tea leaves to their advantage. The knowledge had come from Granny Saffron, whom the tea shop was named after.

It was also because of Granny that Wynona had been able to open a tea shop at all. Having been born to the ruling family of Hex Haven, the Le Doux family witches and warlocks were a proud lot and also a very powerful one. They ruled because they held more magic than anyone else. A line that had continued for multiple generations...until Wynona.

A curse at her birth meant she'd been born bound, unable to access her powers. No one knew who cursed her or why, but it had sent Wynona's life into a downward spiral with no ending until Granny helped Wynona escape on the Spring Equinox, a night which just happened to be Wynona's thirtieth birthday and the night that Granny passed away.

Saffron's passing had been the distraction Wynona needed in order to escape the abuse of her family. Having no powers meant she was useless to them, and they treated her accordingly. All except Granny, of course, who had taken the time to help a small girl find hope and purpose through tea leaves.

Leaves which were now failing Wynona miserably.

A scuttling sound caught her attention and Wynona knew Violet had joined her in the kitchen. "I can't figure it out," Wynona whispered. "Why am I having such a hard time?"

Violet climbed up her friend's side and settled onto Wynona's shoulder, nuzzling her neck. It was the rodent's favorite spot and it was a comfort to Wynona as well.

She reached up and scratched Violet's head. "Thanks," she said softly.

Violet chittered and settled down into a ball of fluff.

Depressed and frustrated, Wynona washed the dirty dishes, put away the tea tinctures and grabbed her keys. She just wasn't feeling it tonight and that was an unusual feeling for her.

"Maybe we'll just grab some dinner and go veg on the couch for a few minutes before bed, huh?"

Violet shifted but otherwise didn't answer.

Wynona chuckled. "You probably aren't hungry after all that cake." She picked up her friend and set her in the basket on the front of the mint green Vespa before strapping on a helmet and starting the engine.

Driving down the road, Wynona tried to figure out what she was going to eat. Nothing seemed to catch her attention, though the streets were crowded with revelers and patrons, all enjoying the pleasures that Hex Haven had to offer.

Friday nights were a busy time in the paranormal city and the more Wynona looked around the less she wanted to deal with standing in a line somewhere in order to get dinner.

After deciding she would just throw on some ramen, she turned left at the next light and began the trek home. It only took moments for her to be stopped again, when a bright red light flashed and she heard a single whoop from a siren.

Wynona automatically pulled over to let the police vehicle pass, but to her surprise, it came in behind her. She turned and began to smile when she recognized the large truck halfway up the sidewalk. "That's quite the parking job," she teased the large, handsome officer walking her way.

He grinned, his slightly elongated canines flashing in the neon lights. "Perks of the job," he said, coming close enough to crowd her bubble. "What's a pretty little thing like you doing out on a night like this?" he asked.

Wynona felt her face flush and she hoped it was dark enough that her werewolf guest couldn't see it, but when his grin widened, she knew she'd had no such luck. "I was doing some experimenting with different teas," she explained, "but decided it was time to go home."

Rascal nodded slowly. "And did you come up with another of your magical concoctions?"

Wynona laughed. "No magic involved and no, they were all a bust."

His smile faltered. "Really? What happened?"

She threw her hands out to the side. "I have no idea, but the inspiration just wasn't coming to me tonight."

"Huh." Rascal folded his arms over his chest. "Was Prim helping?"

Wynona shook her head. "No. I can't get a hold of her."

His frown deepened. "She's been kinda off the radar lately, hasn't she?"

Wynona nodded. "I know. I'm not sure what's going on, but something is keeping her attention and she won't tell me what it is."

Rascal leaned in and brushed his knuckle against her jawline, sending a sweet shiver down Wynona's spine. "Maybe that's why you're having a hard time. Could Prim's preoccupation have you distracted?"

Wynona huffed. "I suppose, but it still seems weird."

"Have you tried..." Rascal glanced around, dropping his voice low. "Accessing your magic again?"

Wynona pinched her lips together. Only a few weeks ago, she had discovered that a few moments of wild magic in her life, which she had assumed were Granny trying to protect her from the other side, had actually been coming from Wynona herself. But it didn't make any sense. Her powers were bound and had been that way her whole life. Why did she all of a sudden have bursts of crazy magic that sometimes proved helpful and sometimes nearly sent her to the hospital?

In an effort to allow herself the chance for research, Wynona and Rascal had both agreed not to tell anyone else what was going on. Even Prim only knew the smallest bits of information. If word ever got back to Wynona's family that her magic might be breaking free, they'd drag her back to the castle whether it caused a media storm or not.

No...Wynona needed time and she couldn't get that if everybody knew what was going on.

"I haven't tried," she whispered, knowing his shifter ears would pick it up. "I'm a little afraid to."

He scratched his chin and nodded. "Understandable. One of these days we'll have to give it a go, but don't do it without me, okay?"

Wynona scrunched her nose. "Maybe it's better if I do it alone. I don't want to risk hurting you or anyone else."

Rascal smiled, the smug smile of someone who was almost always right and in charge. "Sweetheart, what do you think you're going to do to me? A little bit of singed fur never hurt anybody."

Wynona tried to hold a straight face as she said, "What if I turn you purple like Violet?"

Rascal stiffened and Wynona lost her battle, laughing so hard her eyes watered. "Hardy, har har," he grumbled sarcastically. He glanced around at the traffic that was weaving around their little pow wow. "I hate to say it, but I probably should let you go."

Wynona felt some of her humor fade. She never seemed to get enough of his company and their relationship was so new that every moment together was still precious. "Okay," she said softly. Apparently, she didn't hide her disappointment very well because Rascal caressed her cheek again.

"Hang in there. We'll spend time together at lunch on Sunday, right?"

Wynona nodded, even though lunch wasn't quite the same. They shared the time with Prim and Violet and Wynona wanted some time with just the two of them. Still, she'd take what she could get. "Right."

He grinned. "Now, be careful merging into traffic, ma'am. The crowds are extra active tonight." He backed up and tipped an imaginary hat at her, causing Wynona to laugh lightly.

"I'll be careful, Officer," she responded.

"And no going after murderers, you hear?" Rascal teased, referring to the fact that Wynona had helped solve a couple of cases in the last few months.

"Oh my gosh, no," she gushed. "Don't even joke about it." Twice Wynona had helped bring a criminal to justice and twice she had wished she'd never been involved.

The first time, she had helped bring her landlord to justice after he killed a prominent baker in the area. The case had been close to Wynona's heart, since her shop had been the scene of the crime. Without the killer being brought to justice, she would never have been able to open and start her business.

The second time, her sister, Celia, had been accused of a murder she didn't commit. Knowing Wynona had helped once before, Celia had called on her sister for help and, bleeding heart that she was, Wynona had come to the rescue, despite the fact that her relationship with Celia was far from cordial.

Rascal chuckled, the sound deep and slightly growly. It sent sprites dancing through Wynona's stomach and she soaked in the feeling. With a wink, his signature move, Rascal hopped into his truck and waited for Wynona to leave.

Restarting the scooter, she gave her officer a little wave and headed toward home once more. Suddenly realizing that Violet, who adored Rascal, had been awfully quiet during that exchange, Wynona glanced into the basket.

A tiny ball of purple was curled up and sleeping, not at all concerned with traffic or being pulled over by the police.

"Must be nice," Wynona muttered as she drove. "No worries in the world." Rascal's words came back to her about being concerned with Prim. There was probably some truth to those words.

Prim was hiding something and it was eating at Wynona. The two had been good friends ever since Wynona had broken free from her family and they'd entered into a business contract together.

As soon as the wingless fairy and the magicless witch had started to talk, a sense of connection and understanding had settled between them. Both were outcasts, both were considered freaks of nature and both had desperately needed a friend.

An uneasy feeling churned in Wynona's gut as she parked in her small garage and carried Violet inside. After carefully setting the purple creature in her cushy bed, Wynona found herself wandering to the kitchen.

The remnants of the morning's tea were still sitting in the sink and something in her core pulled Wynona forward. With each step, she could feel a sense of anticipation mounting and the air around her began to crackle with purple sparks.

Her heart raced as she recognized the signs that her magic was in charge at the moment. These kinds of signs had preempted several frightening events in Wynona's life and she wasn't thrilled it was happening again.

"So much for waiting for Rascal," she said through gritted teeth as she continued to be pulled toward the sink. There was no stopping her progress, the pull of the magic was too strong.

With a shaking hand, Wynona reached out and picked up the dirty teacup. Fear pounded through her veins as she brought it up, knowing there would be something in the leaves she wasn't going to like.

"Dagger," she breathed, immediately seeing the sign for danger in the upper left leaves. "But for whom?" she whispered, her eyes moving to a cluster of dregs at the bottom. "Dog." Wynona jerked back. There was danger and a friend needed her help. This was worse than she'd imagined. One last section needed to be read and Wynona nearly winced as she worked to understand the shape. "Buffalo." She racked her brain, but couldn't come up with the answer.

Setting down the cup, she raced to her work room and took down her book on tea reading, flipping through until she found the correct symbol. "The buffalo," Wynona read softly. "An unexpected or unusual circumstance, creating great anxiety for all involved."

Wynona slammed the book shut and hung her head. "But who?" she asked the dark space. "Who's in trouble?"

There was no one to answer her and Wynona let her shaky legs fold, dropping to the cold, wooden floor. Rascal did a dangerous job for a living, so it could easily be him. Prim grew plants, which didn't seem like something that should be dangerous, but what about the secret she was keeping from Wynona? Could it be what the leaves were talking about?

Wynona let her head fall back, hitting the cupboards. It was too late and her friends were all unavailable for her to be able to figure this out. In other words, she would have to be patient.

"Perfect," she muttered, pushing herself to her feet. "Be patient when there's danger around the corner." Wynona shook her head as she headed back to the main part of her small cabin.

Sunday lunch was suddenly more important to her than ever. It would be the only time she'd have to talk to her friends and figure out what exactly the tea was trying to tell her.

Not wanting to eat after such an episode, Wynona headed straight to bed. She fell into her blankets, only bothering to take off her shoes. She was exhausted. Between work, anxiety over Prim and that little episode in the kitchen, Wynona knew she needed to rest if she was going to have any chance of helping the people she loved most.

It seemed no matter how often she said she didn't want to get involved in any more dangerous ventures, life just kept pulling her back in. The peaceful, quiet existence Wynona had imagined hadn't quite panned out. But if losing that meant she helped a friend, then Wynona would do everything she could to see it taken care of. She'd fought hard to be free enough to have these relationships and she refused to lose them now.

CHAPTER 3

Wynona studied her table setting. She had taken extra care in creating the mood today and wanted to make sure it was perfect.

Her antique teacups looked beautiful, the flower centerpiece was lovely, the lace tablecloth was feminine and the plate of pastries was enough to entice even the pickiest of eaters.

"I think we're ready," Wynona told Violet.

Violet squeaked from her place under the bookcase and came crawling out, her nose twitching in the air.

"No eating yet," Wynona warned her. "You need to wait for our guests."

Violet chittered angrily and put her hands on her hips.

"It's not my fault you skipped breakfast," Wynona said as she walked back to the kitchen. "Ever since I started feeding you, you've been getting pickier and pickier. If you didn't like the blueberry smoothie I fixed, you were welcome to make something yourself."

Violet huffed and disappeared as Wynona stepped through the kitchen door.

She picked up a kettle and filled it with water, keeping an eye on Lusgu's corner. The brownie had been staying out of sight lately and Wynona wanted to know why. Her shop was just as sparkling clean as ever, so she knew he hadn't left, but he didn't usually hide from her either.

She put the kettle on the stove to heat and began gathering the teas she wanted. Despite her disastrous experiments the other night, Wynona did have some new blends she wanted to have her friends try.

Grabbing a tray, she had just finished pulling out her infusers and tea canisters when the kettle began to whistle. Wynona added it to the tray and headed back out to the front room.

The kettle went on the trivet, the infusers on the saucers and the canisters within easy reach. *Now* she was ready.

She glanced at the clock and noted that it was five minutes until they usually started. A frown tugged at her lips. Prim usually arrived early. In fact, she often enjoyed helping Wynona set up.

The anxiety she had experienced the other night after the tea reading began to simmer once again in Wynona's stomach. "What is going on?" she wondered out loud, though there was no one to answer her. Prim wasn't herself and Wynona was growing more and more worried that her friend was in some kind of danger.

She pulled out her phone and prepared to shoot off a text, but forced herself to stop. "She'll be here any minute," Wynona told herself. "Plus, she's an adult. If she needs help, she'll let you know."

Wynona's hand shook just a little as she forced herself to put the phone back in her pocket. She just couldn't shake the feeling that there was more to the situation than she knew, but Prim wasn't one to be fawned over. Wynona would have to address this carefully, or she'd make the fairy upset.

The front door opened and Wynona immediately looked to the room entry, waiting for a head of bright pink hair to appear.

"Hey, Wy," Rascal said with a grin as he sauntered in, pushing a hand through his dark locks. "That wind is crazy today." He paused. "Uh...are you okay?"

Wynona bit her bottom lip. She hadn't meant to look disappointed when Rascal showed up—in fact she had been missing him all week—but she was just so worried about Prim. "No, no, it's fine." She smiled and waved him over. "I'm so glad you made it."

Rascal gave her an unbelieving look, but walked over to kiss her cheek. "What's wrong?"

Wynona shook her head. "Nothing."

Rascal tapped the side of his nose. "Try again."

She rolled her eyes. "I'm not sure anything is wrong, but I have a terrible feeling about Prim."

Rascal frowned and looked around. "Where is she? She's always here before I am."

Wynona shrugged, her hands clasped tightly together in front of her. "She hasn't arrived yet."

Rascal took Wynona's abused fists and straightened her fingers. "Hey...it's okay. Just because she's usually early doesn't mean something happened to her." He winked. "This is Prim we're talking about. She's a fighter. I'd be more worried about the other guy than her."

Wynona forced her tight shoulders to drop. "I'm sure you're right." She twisted her hand so she was holding onto Rascal and squeezed. "But after my tea reading the other night, I was sure—"

"Whoa...what? Tea reading?"

Wynona sighed. "Let's sit down and we can talk about it."

Rascal continued to look concerned after they sat down, but he didn't make a fuss when Wynona began fixing him an infuser.

The more the seconds ticked by, the more worried Wynona grew. Her anxiety was growing by leaps and bounds and was nearly a full blown panic at this point. When the metal infuser rattled for the third time in her hands, Rascal reached out and took it from her.

"Why don't you tell me what to put in," he said gently.

She gave him a grateful smile. "Add one more pinch of lemon peel and it's good to go."

Rascal's large fingers weren't quite as gentle as Wynona's slender ones, but he managed to follow her instructions and set his tea in his cup. "And for yours?"

A minute later, Rascal was pouring hot water into their mugs and the fragrance of spices and tea began to infiltrate the air. He glanced over his shoulder at the wall clock. "Why don't you give her a call?"

Wynona debated, but finally followed Rascal's advice. She held the cell to her ear and the ring droned on too many times before turning over to voicemail. "She didn't answer," Wynona said softly. "Rascal, I'm really worried about her."

"Did she tell you she was coming today?" he inquired. "Could you have forgotten that she had another engagement?"

Ever the police officer. Wynona gave him a sad smile. "She helped me out with the flowers just a couple days ago and said she was looking forward to lunch. I haven't spoken to her since then."

He nodded thoughtfully. "Okay, then what's this about a tea reading? I thought you agreed not to do magic without me?"

Wynona leaned back, deflating in her seat. "I didn't mean to do it," she explained. "And there lies part of the problem. My magic seems to control me. It comes out at odd times and I have no say in where or when." She leaned forward again, dropping her voice. "It was actually after we spoke a couple nights ago—you know, when you pulled me over?"

He grinned.

Wynona rolled her eyes. "Anyway...I went home and went into the kitchen and there were some dirty dishes in the sink from earlier that day. Naturally, I had a tea set in there and as I walked in, I could feel this electricity in the air. My whole body began buzzing and I could see purple sparkles in my peripheral vision."

She dropped his intense stare and looked down into the teacup in front of her at the moment. She was so grateful for the lavender wafting toward her face. Anything calming was welcome at this point. Even speaking about her magical encounters had the ability to set her nerves on edge. She had spent most of her growing up years not having any control over her life. Now that she was finally managing to form her own opinions, her magic seemed to be seeping through the curse and once again, things were out of her hands.

"I felt drawn to the sink and to one cup in particular." Wynona took in a steadying breath. "I knew what was happening, but an awful sense of doom invaded the space and I tried to stop myself, but I was powerless." She brought her eyes back up toward Rascal, who was beginning to look angry. "My hand reached for the cup and I turned it so I could look at the dregs in the bottom. I saw a dog, a dagger and a buffalo."

"And what exactly does that mean?" he pressed.

"The buffalo means a situation is causing anxiety for all involved." She squished her lips to the side. "The dog can mean two things. It can represent a good friend, or tell us that a friend needs our help." Wynona played with her diffuser. "In this case, I believe it's the latter."

"And the dagger?" Rascal's voice had lost all sense of playfulness.

"A dagger means danger." She forced herself to look into those golden eyes yet again. "From ourselves or from an outside source."

"So you think Prim is in danger and needs your help?"

Wynona nodded. "I do."

"Has she told you about anything in her life that might be causing that?"

Wynona shook her head. "No. In fact, she's been unusually tight lipped lately and she talks to me less on the phone than she used to. Our time in the greenhouse or over flowers has been the same, but it's not uncommon for us to have a running text thread all day long."

"When did this start?" Rascal asked, pulling out his own phone and punching the keys.

"A couple of weeks ago, I guess," Wynona answered. She picked up her teacup and took a tentative sip. "Ooh, better drink that before it gets cold. It's perfect at the moment."

Rascal nodded absentmindedly and followed her orders before going back to his phone. He paused and glanced her way. "That lemon peel is perfect. Nicely done."

Heat flooded Wynona's cheeks. "Thanks."

He went back to his phone. "So she's secretive, not as chatty, obviously not answering her phone and ditching her usual schedule." He raised an eyebrow and turned to Wynona. "Could she possibly have met someone?"

Wynona shrugged. "I guess it's possible, but why would she keep that a secret?"

"Maybe she's afraid you won't approve of the guy." Rascal snickered, then coughed. "Maybe he has a record?"

Wynona gave him a look. "Not funny."

"Sorry." Rascal cleared his throat. "But seriously. It's possible the relationship is too new and she's not ready to announce it yet."

"I guess," Wynona drawled. "But that still doesn't explain all the danger signals I'm getting."

"You said yourself that your magic seems to be in control of you," Rascal reminded her. "Perhaps you just don't understand it enough to know what it's trying to tell you. Could you have read those tea leaves wrong?"

Wynona shook her head. "I don't think I read it wrong, but I could be reading who it's for wrong, I suppose."

Rascal nodded. "I agree that we should keep an eye on Prim—she's definitely acting out of character—but until we know more, I don't see the point in getting all worked up."

Wynona sighed. "You're right."

He grinned. "Well, well, well...that's not something a shifter hears everyday."

Wynona laughed, as intended, and swatted his arm. "Don't get used to it, buddy."

He grabbed her hand and kissed the tips of her fingers. "I'm hoping to get used to lots of things where you're concerned."

That heat in her cheeks was so intense at this point Wynona was sure she could boil the tea kettle herself. "Gnox and Kyoz brought a couple new pastries," she choked out. "Care to try a pain au chocolat?"

Rascal's grin was pure mischief, as if he knew he'd embarrassed her and was pleased with himself. "We can start with that," he said slyly.

Wynona bit back the desire to fan her face. This wolf was going to be the death of her!

A chattering caught her attention and they both watched as Violet hurried across the floor, racing up Wynona's table leg and onto her shoulder, scolding Wynona the whole way.

"Sorry," Wynona said. "You're right. I should have let you know we were getting started."

Violet huffed and folded her tiny arms over her chest.

"Take it easy, little one," Rascal said, holding out his hand for the mouse to climb onto. "No harm, no foul."

Violet was apparently not in the mood to be appeased and she gave Rascal what for.

Rascal chuckled and reached across the table. "Would this make it better?" He wiggled a croissant in the air.

Violet's yelling stopped, but her look was one of suspicion and distrust.

Rascal set the treat and the mouse on the table. "It's all yours. I won't even break it in half."

Still eyeing him, Violet walked over and paused before digging into the meal.

"She's not going to be able to fit under her bookcase if we keep feeding her like this," Wynona whispered.

Rascal smiled and winked. "I think Violet's pretty proud of her figure. Not many mice are as obviously well fed as her," he responded just as quietly.

Wynona smiled and shook her head right before taking a long, long sip of her tea. She closed her eyes as the warm liquid slid down her throat. Granny Saffron always came to mind whenever Wynona enjoyed a brew such as this, and today, Wynona found herself particularly melancholy.

What she wouldn't give for her granny's wisdom and insight. Not only into the situation with Prim, but also the emerging magic. Wynona still had no idea why her magic was coming out to begin with. One of these days, she would need to do some research and figure out what was going on. She had never heard of a cursed witch suddenly getting her powers back. Of course, there weren't very many cursed witches to begin with, so maybe there wasn't much research on the topic either.

Wynona pushed the thoughts aside. Right now she had Rascal and Violet, two of her favorite creatures, sitting at her table and despite the worries about Prim, Wynona wanted to enjoy their time together. She saw far too little of Rascal as it was. She didn't want to waste the moment.

CHAPTER 4
PRIM

P rim slunk along the outer rims of the room. Her face inside the cowl was dark and silent, though the room was anything but. A couple hundred people milled about, enchanted cocktails in hand, laughing and chatting and occasionally screaming when an impersonator came up to engage in mischief.

Prim sighed, frustrated that she couldn't do more to enjoy the situation. She still hadn't been paid and today Prim had been assigned the character no one else wanted, probably as punishment for daring to want her paycheck. Carrying a scythe and pointing it at people wasn't anyone's idea of a good time.

Who the heck wanted Death at their party anyway?

A teenage boy stopped in front of Prim, facing her down with a smug grin. "You're not so scary," he said with bravado.

Prim immediately looked around, though she kept her head still, in order to find the friends he was trying to impress. She was pretty sure the five or six kids his age, most of whom were cackling worse than a witch high on bubbly, were the target audience.

Time to pull out the big guns.

Prim slowly lowered her scythe, letting it trace from the top of his forehead all the way down his abdomen. The flash of fear at her silent act wasn't lost on Prim, and although she hated that it was her role, it gave her the knowledge she needed to know that she was on the right track.

Slowly she spun to the left and began to glide across the floor toward the friends. Facing down the boy wouldn't be the best way to keep her role going, but shaking up someone he cared about? A home run every time.

"Hey! Where are you going?" the boy shouted, running after her.

Prim hid her smile. No one could miss the panic in his voice. She might be playing the world's dumbest role, but dang it, she was going to play her role well.

"I'm the one talking to you." The kid sneered, coming right up behind her. He pulled on her cloak, nearly dumping her cowl backward.

Oh, that was too much, especially when Prim was already in a bad mood. Her scythe flew through the air and she missed his nose by millimeters. To his credit, the boy didn't make a sound, but the girls in his friend group did. Swallowing hard, the teenager held up his hands and backed up a couple steps. "Sorry," he muttered.

Using that same achingly slow set of movements, Prim went back to the group of friends. She shifted her shoulders in order to reposition the stiff cowl. Death was dark and mysterious, not a grinning fairy with pink hair.

Regripping her scythe, she brought the weapon forward and pointed to the smallest of the girls. The young woman gasped and backed up, but Prim countered her footsteps.

"What're you doing?" the original boy demanded. He stepped in front of her again, but Prim spun, her cloak fanning behind her as she shifted between the boy and the girl. After all her slow walking, no one expected such a quick move and therefore no one stopped her.

Prim once again lowered the scythe, pointing at the girl, who looked on the verge of tears. A small prick of guilt ate at Prim, but she persisted. She knew this routine like the back of her hand.

No one in the group seemed to have the courage to do anything else at the moment, so Prim tilted her head to the side and slowly shifted the scythe. She felt movement behind her and began to breathe a sigh of relief. Here came the finale.

"It's not real," Brave boy said, rushing to the girl's side and wrapping his arms around her. "It's just a joke."

Prim gave one last jab of the scythe, startling the group into a few more squeals and gasps, before turning and gliding away. She didn't dare look back until she could do so without moving her head. Giving away the game always ruined it.

When she saw the girl gazing adoringly up into the boy's face and his arms were still clasped tightly on her hips, Prim let herself smile.

"You're welcome," she whispered. Laughing softly, she put her head back down and continued moving throughout the room. After that little display, the crowds parted for her without a second thought, no one wanting to get close to the scary figure who brought young love together through terror.

Prim's eyes shifted to the wall clock and she realized she was due for a break. "Thank heavens," she muttered. The crowd would need time to calm down again before she'd be able to engage anyone else. Disappearing for fifteen minutes was usually enough time for them to forget her antics and then be frightened all over again when she quietly appeared.

She slunk to the far corner and ducked behind a set of curtains that hid the back rooms of the theatre. Pushing back her cowl, Prim took her first breath of clean air that didn't stink of too many bodies and too few bars of soap.

She grabbed a cold water bottle and leaned her back into a corner, drinking heavily. Her robe was great at hiding her, but also at holding in the heat and with a party as large as this one...there was a lot of warmth.

Prim sighed and rolled the cold bottle between her hands. While she found little moments like giving that teenage boy a chance to enjoy holding a girl fun, this was not something she wanted to continue doing for the long term. Especially if she wasn't going to get paid for it.

If she wasn't in such desperate need to expand her greenhouse, she would leave this gig in the dust without even waving goodbye, but there were so few jobs for a botanist, especially ones that focused on the nighttime hours.

Her head hit the wall as she let it fall back. "What is it going to take to make her pay up?" Prim grumbled. "She can't expect to not pay me forever and get away with it."

A door slammed closed and Prim jerked upright.

"Have you seen my wife?"

Prim blinked, the irate man in front of her slowly coming into focus. "Oh, hey, Mr. Tuall."

"Brell. Have you seen her?"

Prim shook her head. "No. Sorry."

He pushed a hand through his hair, his other hand on his hip. "One of these days we won't be stuck in this dump playing for peanuts," he muttered before heading toward the entrance to the party.

Prim made a face. Being the paranormal world's most famous vampire impersonator made Brell in high demand, but it didn't mean her husband had to be a jerk. Not once had Prim ever heard him speak politely to a member of the cast. He seemed to think his wife's fame put him above everyone else and he used it to his full advantage.

She drained the rest of her water bottle, then threw it away and turned toward the party entrance, but couldn't quite get her feet moving. The idea of walking around hidden in plain sight drove Prim crazy and the discontent that had been bothering her previously came roaring back with a vengeance.

Taking a couple of deep breaths, she spun and marched down the theatre hallway. Madam Ureo was set up in an office down here, and would be for the duration of the party, since she was sometimes needed to put out fires when guests had complaints during the event. Usually that only occurred when the enchanted bar had been flowing for several hours, but still...

"One more time," Prim muttered to herself. She had to try again. She couldn't just stay quiet and keep ignoring the fact that her bills were piling up and her mortgage was overdue. Prim was a fighter, a survivor. She wasn't going to let that cheating, long-nosed harpy get away with this. No matter how terrifying she was.

Prim stood outside the office door and took one last calming breath, then raised her fist and banged on the wood several times. Without waiting for a reply, she twisted the knob and hurried inside. "Madam Ureo," Prim all but shouted. "I'm not leaving until you've given me what I'm due."

Prim's courage failed her when her boss didn't even bother to turn her chair around at Prim's bold entrance. The lights were out and Prim couldn't see the full office. She reached to her side and flipped the switch, but nothing happened. Prim flipped it up and down several times, her eyes on the ceiling, but to no avail. "Madam?"

There was still no answer. In fact, the office was strangely quiet. Prim's ears perked up, but she couldn't pick up any signs of life. Huffing, Prim realized her boss wasn't even there. She had to have gone to the restroom or something. Spinning, Prim began to leave when a noise caught her attention.

She frowned and turned back to the desk. Slowly, unsure of what she might find, she walked toward the desk, then sidestepped to the left. A long, dark object lay on the floor, looking like it had fallen from the desk area.

Prim picked it up, bringing it close to her face in order to see what it was in the dim lighting from the door.

The red stain of blood became visible just as a single drop fell onto Prim's shoe. She gasped and held the offending object away from her. Her wide eyes darted around the room, trying to figure out where the wand had come from.

Slowly, terrified of what more she would find, Prim stepped toward Madam Ureo's chair. She touched the edge with just her fingertips and spun the chair so that it was facing the light.

"No," Prim breathed. Madam Ureo lay slumped in her chair with a bleeding wound at her heart.

Without warning, light flooded the room and Prim brought her free hand up to cover her eyes until they adjusted. As she was still blinking, a scream tore through the hallway.

"MURDERER!"

Prim jumped a foot and turned toward the shout to see one of the other members of the troupe standing in the doorway, pointing at Prim.

Panic flooded Prim's system so fast she could barely comprehend the words of her accuser before the hall was filled with creatures of all kinds, fake and real. She looked down at the wand in her hand and dropped it, then automatically put her hands in the air. "No! I can explain!"

"Don't let her leave!" a voice in the hallway shouted.

"She really is Death!"

"We won't let her get away with this!"

"I didn't kill anyone!" Prim shouted as a handful of men flooded the small office and grabbed her upper arms. "Please, this isn't what it looks like!"

They began to drag her from the room and Prim struggled against their hold.

"I didn't kill her!" Prim screamed, jerking hard. "Let me explain!" The intoxicated crowd shouted over her and Prim knew she had no viable means of escape. Squeezing her eyes tight, she poofed

herself into her fairy form, becoming smaller than the men were prepared for. Without waiting to see how anyone would react, Prim
jumped out of her cloak and raced down the hallway, dodging bodies
who were still answering the panicked calls of her accusers.

An exit sign to her left had Prim changing her trajectory and
weaving pattern. She had to get out of here. She hadn't killed anyone,
but the crowd refused to listen. Prim wasn't about to stand around
for the police to come arrest her when she was innocent. If she could
just get a little time to figure this out, Prim was positive the crowd
would calm down enough for her to tell her side of the story. But not
when they had all been ordering at an unlimited bar all afternoon
and evening. Who knew what lies would come from that kind of in-
toxication.

Neon red letters brought her the reprieve she sought and Prim
put on an extra burst of speed. The sweet feeling of relief was lost
when her vision darkened and Prim tripped on some kind of fabric,
stumbling to the ground and rolling over and over against the hard
stage floor.

"Got her!"

Multiple sets of hands grasped Prim through the blanket and
wrapped her so tightly she could barely breathe. She kicked and
fought, her breathing growing more and more panicked when she
couldn't get away.

She couldn't seem to get enough air. "I can't breathe!" she rasped,
pushing at her captors. "I can't..."

Regret flashed through her mind as she thought of what she
should have been doing today. If she had just refused to work. If she
had just been willing to save slowly rather than taking out another
loan. If she had just put spending time with Wynona and Rascal at
the top of her priority list, none of this would have happened.

Prim wouldn't have been found with a murder weapon in her
hands in front of the dead body of a woman she didn't get along

with. The police were going to have a heyday with this mess and Prim knew deep down that she had never been in more trouble than right this moment.

Just before she lost consciousness, Prim felt someone begin to pull on the blanket itself. The smallest speck of light met her irises before the entire world went black.

CHAPTER 5

Wynona

R ascal licked his fingers, grinning when Wynona laughed.
"How many of those have you eaten now?" she teased, sipping her tea.

Rascal looked away in thought. "I lost count," he finally admitted, then winked. "Good thing I have a shifter's metabolism."

Wynona shook her head, but her smile remained. "Good thing," she murmured.

Rascal wiped his fingers on a napkin, then leaned forward on his elbows. "So...when are we going to go on another date?"

Wynona gave him an arch look. "I suppose when you ask."

He grinned. "It's going to be that easy?"

She shrugged, playing casual, but feeling her heart beat rapidly. When Rascal snickered, she knew he could hear her pulse, giving away the fact that she was anything but uninterested.

"Wy..." he drawled. "Do you *want* me to ask you out again?"

"Right this moment?" she said, knowing her cheeks were flaming. "Not so much."

He laughed. "Sorry. I shouldn't embarrass you like that, but sometimes it's good to know what you're thinking."

"I think you often know what I'm thinking more than I know what you're thinking." She dropped his glowing gaze and drew a random pattern on the table top. She heard a chair shift and soon Rascal was setting down his seat right next to her.

He reached out and lifted up her chin with his knuckle. "I realize not having your magic makes you feel like you're always at a disadvantage," he said softly, letting his thumb rub back and forth on her jawline. "But as you learn how to use what you have and eventually leave me in the dust, never doubt my feelings," he whispered huskily. "And never be afraid to ask... I won't hide anything from you."

Wynona's eyes widened. "You won't?"

He slowly shook his head, shifting subtly closer. "For you...I'm an open book," he whispered right before his lips brushed hers.

Wynona sucked in a shuddering breath from the touch, but eagerly leaned in, wanting more. This relationship was so new that she still hadn't gotten used to the feeling of bliss that swept through her every time Rascal touched her.

His hand slid from her jaw to the back of her head and he tilted his head, changing their angle to something more intense just as his phone went off.

Wynona gasped and jerked backward, her breathing labored.

Rascal's hand fell, but his eyes never left hers. "You okay?" he asked, slightly breathless himself.

Wynona nodded. "Sorry. I was startled." She wasn't usually so easily scared, but these emotions were fresh and she could feel her magic trying to react to her intense feelings. When she blinked, she could still see purple sparkles in her peripheral vision.

Rascal chuckled and cupped her cheek. "I guess that means we'll just have to do this more often... You know," he said in a low tone, "so you're not so scared."

"Oh, yes please," she breathed out just before he kissed her again.

The buzzing of his phone once again pulled them apart, only this time it was Rascal who pulled back. He muttered something under his breath and reached across the table for his device. "Let me just shut this off," he grumbled.

Wynona had to grin at his pouty tone. Knowing he was so eager to kiss her had her adrenaline pumping. After a second, she realized he wasn't looking away from his phone. "Rascal?"

He looked up with a grimace. "We need to go down to The Siren's Call."

"We?" Wynona blinked and shook her head. "What for?"

"There's been a murder."

Wynona groaned and threw her head back. "Not another one. I really don't want to be involved, Rascal. I've told you that. Those other cases were exceptions."

"You're going to want to be here for this," he said, standing up and grabbing his stuff. "Vi?" he gave Violet a gentle shake, waking her from her nap. "You're gonna want to come too."

Violet blinked sleepily and rubbed her eyes with her tiny fists.

"Rascal," Wynona said forcefully, standing up so she wasn't at such a disadvantage. "What's going on?"

He scooped Violet up and tucked her into his pocket. "Like I said, there's been a murder."

Wynona opened her mouth to argue, but Rascal kept going.

"And they're holding Prim as the main suspect."

"WHAT!" Wynona screeched. She threw her hands over her mouth when Rascal winced. "Sorry," she said in a muffled tone. "But how in the world do they think Prim is involved in the murder? She wouldn't hurt a fly!"

Rascal gave her a look and Wynona held up a hand.

"Okay, maybe a fly, but you know she wouldn't kill anyone."

He rubbed the back of his neck. "They must have a reason for holding onto her," he said. "But I agree, there has to be some kind of misunderstanding." His eyes were sad and resigned when he looked at her. "Which is why I knew you'd want to come along. Between the two of us, we should be able to convince the chief Prim is innocent."

"Hang on a second." Wynona marched to the kitchen. Her feelings of elation had disappeared and a simmer of anger was already starting to build. How dare anyone think Prim could kill someone!

Chief Ligurio was a smart man and usually a fair one. He should know better!

She pushed open the kitchen door. "Lusgu?" She waited a moment while he appeared from the dark corner. "I need to leave. I'm sorry about the mess, but can you take care of the food at least?" She didn't normally leave him with so much and she definitely didn't usually speak to him in such a forceful tone, but right now she couldn't get her mind off of Prim being held by the police. Her little fairy friend had to be terrified.

Lusgu narrowed his yellow eyes and then nodded. He didn't speak a word, but Wynona knew he would do exactly how she asked.

"Thank you," she made sure to say before turning and walking out of the kitchen, only to run straight into a wall of purple ribbons.

Rascal was waiting across the room as Wynona stopped and her jaw dropped. His arms were folded across her chest and she reached out to try and touch them. "I think your magic is tied to your emotions," he said.

Wynona sighed and forced herself to relax a little, the ribbons slowly fading. "It's because I don't know how to control it," she responded. "I need to take time to figure out what kind of magic I have and become the master. Until then, it'll probably always be like this."

"As fun as it is to see a physical reaction to our kisses," Rascal drawled, "I think if you want to keep others from knowing you have magic, you're going to need to figure it out."

Her cheeks were hot again, but she nodded. He had a point. "I know," she whispered. "But first I need your boss to stop accusing the people in my life of murder."

He held out his hand and together they walked to the door. "Maybe we need to work on getting the people in your life into different hobbies."

Wynona huffed, but followed Rascal to his truck. They got in and headed down the street before Wynona, musing, asked, "What was Prim doing at The Siren's Call?"

Rascal shook his head. "I have no idea. Maybe she was attending a party there? They hold conventions from time to time."

"I know, but The Siren's Call Theatre is an impersonator troupe. Isn't that where Brell Tuall works?"

Rascal scrunched his nose. "The Vampire Actress?"

"Yeah. She's a siren, I think." Wynona tucked a piece of hair behind her ear. "I don't really follow celebrities. I got enough of fame while living with my family."

Rascal grunted. "I guess we'll just have to figure it out when we get there."

Wynona waited impatiently as drove through town. The hall was downtown in the nightlife district. As they got closer, Wynona could see a long line of police cars and a couple of ambulances parked out front and her heart rate skyrocketed.

As they pulled up as close as they could get, Rascal put a hand on her knee. "Take it easy," he said softly.

Wynona nodded, doing her best to breathe through her worry. That purple haze was filtering through her vision again. "I'm okay," she finally said.

He watched her a minute, then nodded. "Okay. Let's go." He hopped out and walked around to help Wynona climb down.

She was wearing a skirt for tea and that was definitely not as user friendly for his massive vehicle. "Thank you," she said as he set her on the ground.

"You good?"

Wynona nodded. "I need to see her."

He nodded and took her hand to lead her inside.

Wynona could tell that her eyes were wide as tea saucers as she looked around the convention hall. Just because she had no experience in activities such as this didn't mean she wasn't fascinated by it all. She'd been so sheltered in her parents' castle that even pastimes that were considered less high end were intriguing.

Dark red, velvet curtains were draped across the walls, creating a mysterious feel as they entered the front entry. Couches covered in luxurious fabrics and patterns lined the walls, inviting people and couples to sit and hold an intimate conversation.

"We're in the convention room," Rascal muttered absentmindedly, his eyes searching as they walked in farther. "Luhorn!" he shouted, startling Wynona.

"Deputy Chief," Officer Luhorn said, standing at attention.

"Where's the chief?"

The officer pointed behind him. "He's interviewing eye witnesses in the offices. The rest of the team are organizing the party goers and workers."

Rascal nodded. "Thanks."

Wynona skipped a little to catch up with Rascal's fast pace, but she didn't want him to slow down. Somewhere inside was Prim, an innocent bystander who was being accused of something she didn't do.

"Skymaw," Rascal said, greeting another officer as they entered the convention area.

Wynona nearly lost her breath when she caught sight of the amount of people standing around the room. The space was huge and filled with creatures of every species, shape and size. A minotaur stood off to one side, still holding a drink in his hand as his extra loud voice echoed his displeasure. A group of elves were huddled together, looking like they would rather be anywhere but stuck in that room. On the opposite end of the spectrum, there were dwarves, sprites, fairies, older creatures and a large group of teenagers who looked like they were probably shifters, if the way they were hissing at the officers was any clue.

Officer Skymaw tilted his head toward the far corner. "He's back there," the black hole said in a low tone. "Ms. Le Doux." He tilted his head in greeting.

"Hello, Office Skymaw," Wynona said politely, hoping her voice hid her anxiety.

"Your fairy friend is with the chief. Hurry back, but watch your step."

Wynona gave the friendly officer a grateful smile. "Thank you."

He nodded solemnly and then went back to crowd control while Rascal tugged Wynona through the masses.

The hallway behind the room was nearly as crowded as the ballroom. There were more officers standing in the darkened space than out in the conference room, making it all the more intimidating.

Wynona was extra grateful she was with Rascal, as every officer nodded and acknowledged his presence.

"Right in there, sir," a small dwarf said, waving an arm toward a closed office door.

"Thanks, Snaldrog," Rascal said. He glanced at Wynona. "Here we go." Without knocking, he turned the knob and headed inside.

Wynona couldn't help but be right on his heels. She needed to see that Prim was alright, that her friend hadn't been hurt in any way, other than false accusations.

"Strongclaw," Chief Ligurio snapped as the two of them came inside.

Wynona stood with her mouth gaping open as Rascal closed the door behind them. "Prim," she breathed.

Prim sat in a chair in her fairy form, her head hanging down and her pink hair looking like a rat's nest. She didn't even look up at Wynona's entrance.

Violet stirred and poked her head out of Wynona's pocket, then immediately darted down Wynona's leg and raced across the floor to Prim.

"One of these days someone's going to step on that thing," Chief Ligurio grumbled.

Wynona pursed her lips to keep from sending him a glare. Instead she followed her companion and came to Prim's side, kneeling down on the carpet. "Prim?" Wynona asked softly, tucking several chunks of pink hair behind the fairy's pointed ears. "Prim, are you alright?"

Teary pink eyes finally came up to meet Wynona. "Wy," Prim said hoarsely.

Wynona nodded and gave a shaky smile. "Are you hurt?"

Prim slowly shook her head. "I didn't want you to find out like this." Her bottom lip shook. "I'm so sorry I blew you off. I didn't want you to know."

Wynona's heart stuttered and her own eyes filled with tears. "Oh, Prim." She wrapped her arms around the tiny body and held her friend tight. "It's going to be okay. We're going to get this figured out."

"They think I killed her!" Prim cried into Wynona's shoulder.

Wynona looked up at Rascal as he walked up behind Prim's chair. His face was stoic and resigned. "I know," Wynona said, cupping Prim's face and bringing it up so they could see each other. "But we're going to get it figured out, okay? I know you're innocent, you know you're innocent, Violet and Rascal know as well." She raised her eyebrows. "Okay?"

Prim sniffed and nodded, then smiled down at Violet, who was cuddling into Prim's neck. The mouse had always kept her distance from the fairy...until now. Apparently, Violet had a soft spot for people in distress.

"Ms. Meadows," Chief Ligurio said in a firm but still kinder than normal voice.

Wynona and Prim looked up at the vampire. There was a flicker of emotion in his red eyes, but he still looked every bit the chief of police.

"Now that Deputy Chief Strongclaw and Ms. Le Doux are here, I think we need to talk this out," the chief said directly to Prim.

She nodded and wiped at her eyes, rubbing mascara down her cheek. She straightened in her seat. "I'm ready." She narrowed her gaze, showing just a hint of her usual sass. "But I'm innocent."

CHAPTER 6

Wynona sent a thankful smile to Rascal when he grabbed a chair so she could sit next to Prim. She kept a hold of Prim's hand while the chief began the interrogation.

"Why don't you tell me in your own words what happened?" Chief Ligurio said, his face drained of all emotion.

Prim pinched her lips together before speaking. Her usual pale color was even lighter than normal and the harsh fluorescent lights of the small office did nothing to help. "I was working tonight—"

Wynona gaped. "Working? What do you mean?"

"Ms. Le Doux," Chief Ligurio scolded. "Now, I waited for you to be here, but if you're going to cause a ruckus, I'll have you escorted out."

Wynona snapped her mouth shut and nodded. She definitely didn't want to get kicked out of this. Her friend needed her. But what in the world was Prim doing working? She ran a flower business, not an entertainment one. Maybe she had provided arrangements for the party?

"For the first hour I walked around like usual, working the room," Prim continued.

Wynona had to physically bite her tongue to keep from asking more questions. Apparently, it wasn't flowers that brought Prim into this.

"But then I was due for my break," Prim said. She dropped her gaze to her hands, clutching her fingers together. "I came into the hallway and got a water bottle. After drinking it, I was going to go back out, but I had a thought." Her pink eyebrows furrowed together. "I've been working here for over a month, but have yet to be paid, despite the fact that I've asked for my paycheck multiple times." Prim scrunched up her nose. "So I thought maybe before going back out to the convention, I'd stop by her office and talk to Madam Ureo again."

Wynona held her breath. There was definitely more to this story than she understood. Prim worked for herself, and was a successful flower fairy. Why in the world was she working for this...Madam Ureo? And why would someone hire an employee then not pay them?

"Did you kill her before or after she turned you down?" Chief Ligurio pressed.

Prim's head snapped up and red flooded her cheeks. "I didn't kill her," she ground out. "When I came into the office, the lights were off, so I assumed Madam Ureo had gone home for the evening. I flipped the switch a couple of times, but nothing happened." Her body started to tremble and the defiance in Prim's voice faded as she continued her story.

"As I turned to go, I heard a sound and turned back toward the desk. Something was rolling on the ground and I walked over to pick it up."

Wynona followed Prim's pink eyes as they went to a bag with a red covered wand on the desk.

"I found the wand, but in the dark it took me a minute to realize it was covered in blood."

Chief Ligurio looked far from impressed with the story. "And the lights just happened to go on after that?" He huffed. "That's a little convenient, don't you think?"

Prim cocked her head. "I'm aware of that, Chief. But that's exactly what happened. While I was trying to figure out why the wand was rolling around, the lights came on, blinding me. After I was able to see, I saw Madam Ureo's body and put together the fact that there was a stab wound in her chest."

"Was it from the wand?" Wynona asked weakly.

The chief's eyes darted to hers. "It appears that way, but we'll have to wait for the coroner's report."

Wynona felt her stomach churn. Despite the fact that she had helped solve two murders in the last few months, she definitely wasn't immune to the horror of it all.

"Why don't you finish," Chief Ligurio said, turning his attention back to Prim.

"I think you know the rest," she muttered. "Right as I realized what was going on, there was a scream from the hallway, a million people came rushing in, they all accused me of murder, I changed and ran away, but someone still caught me." Prim tore her hand from Wynona's and folded her arms over her chest. "But that still doesn't make me the murderer."

The chief was making notes on a tablet, his eyes not on the women, but he nodded. After a moment he finished, then turned his face up. "If you were innocent, why did you run?"

Prim threw her hands in the air. "Wouldn't you freak out a little if an angry mob began to drag you out of the building? I was half afraid they were going to burn me at the stake!" She glanced guiltily toward Wynona. "No offense intended."

Wynona shrugged. Now wasn't the time to be worried about ancient history.

The chief rubbed his forehead. "I'm guessing we're going to find your fingerprints all over the wand."

"Of course you are!" Prim practically shouted.

Wynona squeezed her friend's shoulder and she could see Violet trying to calm the fairy as well. "Prim. I know this is frustrating, but let's try not to lose our cool, alright?"

Prim moaned and buried her face in her hands. "Sorry. But how was I to know that I shouldn't touch it? I couldn't even tell what it was." She looked up. "But that wand isn't mine. What would a fairy be doing with a wand anyway?"

Chief Ligurio leaned back in his seat and folded his arms over his chest. "You have a witch friend. Who's to say you didn't get it from her?"

Wynona began losing her own cool at that point. "Chief Ligurio," she said as patiently as she could manage. "If I didn't know any better, I would say you're *looking* for reasons to put Prim away."

The Chief scowled.

"Did anyone actually *see* her commit the murder?"

He reluctantly shook his head. "No. But there are too many pieces of evidence for us to ignore." He held up his hand, fingers folded, then brought one up. "She was found on the scene." He put up another long, slim finger. "She had the bloody murder weapon in hand." A third finger arose. "She had motive and opportunity." His hand fell to the desk. "Those are hard things to ignore, Ms Le Doux."

Wynona nodded. "I understand that, but don't you think the motive is a bit weak? Who would kill the very boss they were trying to get money from?"

"The same person who was being denied what they wanted," Chief Ligurio argued back. "I've seen it before."

Wynona shook her head. "Prim didn't kill anyone."

"Is this one of your famous gut feelings?" the chief pressed.

"No," Wynona snapped. "Just common sense. I know her. She wouldn't kill anyone."

Chief Ligurio leaned onto the desk and folded his hands together. "Did you know your friend is in debt?"

Wynona stilled.

"That she had to take on a second job in order to pay the mortgage on the recent addition she made to her greenhouses?"

Wynona slowly turned to look at Prim. She didn't know any of those things. Was this what Prim had been keeping from her? But why? Why would her best friend hide something like this?

Prim's bottom lip trembled. "I'm sorry, Wy. I wanted to tell you, but I was so embarrassed. You know how the retail business can be. I had a couple of bad months and suddenly I was behind."

Wynona slumped. "Prim," she whispered. "You should have said something."

"I know, but I was too embarrassed."

"Still feeling confident in your knowledge of Ms. Meadows?" Chief Ligurio interrupted.

Wynona scowled. "Yes. Just because she didn't tell me her financial situation doesn't mean she's a murderer." She shook her head pleadingly at the chief. "You have to know this."

Chief Ligurio's face softened just a little. "I'm afraid I don't. I'm not familiar with Ms. Meadows and have never had any dealings with her in order to know her character."

"But you know me and I'm vouching for her!"

"Not good enough," Chief Ligurio said, rising from his seat. "I'm sure her lawyer will appreciate having you as a character witness when the time comes, but until then, my investigation will be moving in the most plausible direction. The one that says she killed Nelara Ureo."

At his command, a couple of officers came over to bring Prim to her feet.

"Chief, you can't do this," Wynona said, standing and moving toward him. "You have no proof!"

"I have plenty of evidence," Chief Ligurio said tightly. "It's enough for me to hold her until the coroner's report comes back. Once we're sure the wand was the killing weapon, we'll be bringing up formal charges."

"I didn't do it!" Prim shouted as they moved her to the door. Her wrists were bound with old hag thread, so Wynona knew her friend couldn't change into her human form, making it difficult for her small legs to keep up with the officers.

Officer Skymaw stood in the doorway and watched as Prim was escorted out.

"You have to believe me!" Prim cried.

Wynona bit back a sob and started to race after them, but Rascal took her arm.

"Hold on," he said softly. "They're doing things by the book. We can't stop them."

"She's innocent," Wynona said hoarsely. "I have to stop them."

Rascal shook his head. "I believe you...and her, but if we want to help her, then we have to play by the rules as well. Racing around, shouting and arguing, will get us nowhere."

"I'd listen to him," Chief Ligurio drawled. "I understand your position with Ms. Meadows and truthfully, I find it difficult to believe her a murderer as well." He raised his eyebrows. "But I have to follow the evidence. And right now the evidence points to your friend."

Wynona wiped at her eyes. "I know," she said. "But I promise you she's innocent."

Chief Ligurio shrugged. "We'll see." He gathered his tablet and papers before heading to the door. "Strongclaw, they'll be collecting evidence for a while. I expect you to oversee it."

"Yes, sir," Rascal said.

Wynona looked over. "I'm guessing I need to find a ride home?"

"Unless you wanna stick around and look at the scene with me."

Wynona jumped when she heard squeaking and scratching against the floor. A purple streak darted into the room and Wynona bent down to catch her little furball. Shame trickled in Wynona's stomach. She had been so concerned about Prim she had completely forgotten Violet had been on Prim's shoulder. "You okay?" Wynona asked.

Violet chattered and huffed a couple of times.

"I know," Wynona said soothingly. "I don't like it either, but Rascal's right. We need to do this by the book." She rubbed Violet's fur. "They're collecting evidence now. I'm sure once they really look into things, they'll be able to see it wasn't her."

The words felt hollow, but Wynona truly hoped they proved true. That would absolutely be the best case scenario. She understood Chief Ligurio's stance. The circumstances were definitely not good for Prim, but Wynona believed her friend completely. Prim absolutely, no matter how desperate she was, would not kill someone.

The very idea of Prim stabbing someone with a wand was almost more than Wynona could stomach.

"I'll stay and help," Wynona told Rascal. She wanted to be there when they found evidence that Prim was innocent. And there had to be some. Wynona refused to entertain any other scenario.

"I figured." Rascal sighed and scrubbed his face. "This isn't going to be easy for any of us, but I need you to be able to set aside your personal feelings if you're going to stick around." His golden eyes flashed. "I like Prim too. But we have to be impartial."

Wynona pinched her lips together. "I can't promise I'll be completely impartial. But I can promise to try." She shook her head. "That's all I can offer."

Rascal nodded. "That'll work." He took her hand and led her out into the hall.

"Ms. Le Doux?"

Wynona tugged on Rascal's hand so she could turn to face Officer Skymaw.

The tall man rubbed the back of his neck as if slightly uncomfortable. "I know things look upsetting right now, but I promise I'll...we'll take care of Ms. Meadows."

Wynona gave him a small smile. "Thank you, Officer Skymaw. I can't tell you how much I appreciate that."

He nodded jerkily, then turned and walked away, his long legs eating the distance quickly.

Wynona turned back to Rascal, who was eyeing his leaving officer. "Rascal?"

He blinked and shook his head a little. "Let's go find whoever's running the collection."

Wynona frowned but didn't speak. There were too many things to worry about right now, but the most pressing one was finding evidence that pointed to Prim's innocence. Once that was done, then Wynona could breathe easily enough to worry about the other parts of her life. But Prim needed to come first.

CHAPTER 7

Wynona walked to the spigot, refilling the watering bucket for the umpteenth time before going back to where she had ended. It had only been twenty-four hours, but Prim's plants had already looked droopy, so Wynona had taken on the task of watering them while her friend was still being held behind bars.

"Don't worry," Wynona said softly. "She'll be out soon." Wynona had no idea if her words were true. Try as she might, she hadn't been able to find a single thing at the crime scene that pointed to someone other than Prim. Not that anything had specifically pointed to Prim either, but with all the eye witnesses, it was a hard fight to take on.

Even after the watering, the plants still looked limp, almost as if they were depressed that Prim wasn't there.

Wynona set the can on the shelf and sighed. "Me too," she whispered. She couldn't blame the foliage. They thrived when Prim was around, since plants were her gift. But take away the source of the magic and suddenly the world was a little less bright.

Wynona's phone rang and she pulled it out of her pocket. "Hello?"

"Hey, Wy, we got the coroner's report back."

Wynona let out a sigh of relief. "Wonderful. Are they letting Prim go?"

There was silence on the other side of the line.

"Rascal?'

She could practically hear Rascal pushing a hand through his messy hair. "I don't have all the details, Wy. Why don't I come get you and we can head down to the office together?"

"What does it say?" Wynona asked more forcefully.

"All I know is that the wand wasn't the reason for the death."

"Then what was?"

"I don't know more than that, hon. Let me pick you up and we'll go find out together."

"But why do you sound as if the wand finding is a bad thing?" Wynona pressed. "Chief Ligurio has a witness with her with the wand. If it didn't kill Madam Ureo, then that's a good thing, right?"

"Are you still at the greenhouse?"

"Rascal!" she scolded.

"Wy, I promise I'm not trying to be difficult, but I don't have all your answers. I know the wand wasn't the murder weapon and I know the chief didn't sound happy when he called me. Fighting isn't going to help us get there any faster. Do you want to meet me there or should I pick you up?"

She deflated. He was right, of course, but that didn't mean Wynona had to be happy about it. "Come get me, I guess."

"Be there in five."

The phone call cut off and Wynona put the device back in her pocket. She rubbed her aching forehead. The coroner's report had been her last bit of hope. The wand situation was difficult, but if it wasn't the murder weapon, then surely they had to let Prim go free. Wynona couldn't think of another scenario.

"Violet?"

There was a scratching sound and Violet darted out from behind a planter.

"Rascal's coming to pick us up," Wynona explained. "They have the coroner's report."

With a panicked squeak, Violet raced over and climbed up Wynona's pants before settling on her shoulder.

"Did you say hi to your friend?" Wynona asked, trying to ease the tension in her body as they walked outside and locked up the greenhouse.

Violet huffed and grumbled.

"Are you still fighting about that cracker?" Wynona scolded. "Vi, how are you ever going to have friends if you don't share?"

Violet stomped her feet and tugged a little on Wynona's hair.

"Ouch!" Wynona put her hand up to stop the tantrum. "I'm sorry, but it's true. If you keep being stingy with your snacks, you'll never have anyone to spend time with." She rolled her eyes when Violet went off on another tirade. "I know you have Prim, me and Rascal, but don't you want friends that are closer to your own size?"

Violet grumbled and curled into a ball, effectively shutting Wynona out.

"Your choice," Wynona said, shaking her head. She loved that she and Violet were so close. In fact, the mouse had proven to be more than a friend on many occasions and Wynona was starting to suspect the mouse had something to do with her emerging magic. It seemed the purple creature was always around when things went haywire. Though Wynona had no idea why, as of yet.

The revving of a large engine caught her attention and Wynona turned to face the massive truck headed her way. She climbed up quickly after Rascal pulled in, not giving him time to come open her door for her.

"I'm sorry I don't have better news," he said in a low tone as he pumped the steering wheel, turning the large vehicle around.

Wynona leaned her head back against the seat. "It's not your fault. I'm sorry I'm on edge."

They merged into traffic and, once settled, Rascal rested his hand on her knee. "It's totally understandable. I don't know what we're going to find, but I'm sure we'll get it all figured out." There was a pause. "Did you get the plants watered?"

Wynona nodded. "Yeah. But I feel like they won't perk up again until she comes back. They seemed to miss her."

Rascal gave Wynona a funny look. "Really? The plants miss her?"

"Haven't you ever seen them react to Prim?" Wynona asked.

Rascal shrugged and shook his head. "I've never been to her greenhouse. That's kinda your territory."

"Oh." Wynona blinked a couple of times. "Sorry."

He glanced over and winked. "No worries. I'm kinda partial to tea houses anyway."

She smiled and didn't even try to stop her blush. Rascal's senses were too keen anyway. He knew exactly what he did to her.

He squeezed her knee one more time, then put his hand back on the wheel and concentrated on navigating traffic until they pulled into the precinct.

Wynona's heart was beating painfully against her chest as they entered the building.

"Deputy Chief, Wynona," Officer Nightshade said solemnly. She tilted her head toward the back. "They've got Ms. Meadows in Chief's office."

"Thanks, Amaris." Rascal tightened his hold on Wynona's hand and led her through the hallway.

"I was wondering when you'd make it," Chief Ligurio said as Wynona and Rascal ducked inside.

"We're here now, sir," Rascal said calmly. He let go of Wynona so she could go sit next to Prim, and stood next to Officer Skymaw near the door.

Wynona took Prim's hand. "What did you find out?" she asked.

His red eyes darted her way and Wynona was sure she saw a flash of remorse before he cleared his throat. "I'm sure Deputy Chief Strongclaw let you know that the wand was not the cause of death."

It was a statement, not a question, but Wynona nodded anyway.

Prim made a face. "There was so much blood. If the wand didn't kill her, what did?"

Chief Ligurio looked at Prim and tilted his head consideringly. "She was poisoned."

Wynona's eyes widened and Prim gasped. "With what?"

"They found traces of daffodil in her system," he continued.

Wynona covered her mouth and shook her head. "Oh, no."

Prim frowned. "Daffodil? As in the flower? Why would that be such a big deal?"

"Because daffodils are poisonous to birds," Wynona whispered.

Chief Ligurio looked her way, his eyes narrowed. "And just how did you know that, Ms. Le Doux?"

She noticed he was back to using her formal name. Wynona wasn't a fan. It meant he had put distance between them once again. In the past, that would have had Wynona shrinking, but instead she sat up straight. Chief Ligurio knew her well enough. He might like to appear intimidating, but she wasn't afraid of him anymore. "Remember all those hours I spent reading books?" she responded. "Thirty years is a long time to be by yourself." She shrugged. "I know a lot of things."

He scowled, but turned back to Prim. "Do you grow daffodils, Ms. Meadows?"

Prim swallowed hard and turned to Wynona with a panicked look.

Wynona racked her brain to remember if she had watered any daffodils today. She closed her eyes and hung her head when she realized there were several plants tucked against the far window, in the newer part of the greenhouse.

"Daffodils symbolize new beginnings," Prim began to babble. "I've got a couple of weddings coming up, and I always slip a few into the bride's bouquet."

She was squeezing Wynona's hand so hard at this point that Wynona was sure her fingers were going to break off.

"But all florists have daffodils!" Prim cried as the chief made a motion. "It's not an uncommon flower! You can find them in any earth creature's garden!"

Two officers came up behind Wynona and Prim, each officer taking one of the fairy's arms.

"Primrose Talula Meadows," Chief Ligurio said, talking loudly over Prim's protests. "You are hereby charged with the murder of Madam Nelara Ureo. You have the right to remain silent..."

Wynona was frozen. The room suddenly seemed to be silent as she watched the horror unfold around her, and she was powerless to stop it. She had been sure that they would find a way to prove Prim's innocence. This wasn't right. It couldn't be!

"WY!" Prim screamed, bucking as the two men pulled her to the doorway. "Help me!"

Strong arms wrapped around Wynona from behind. Wynona hadn't been held by Rascal very often and this should have been a soothing, enjoyable time, but she could barely feel him. Instead of a pleasant buzzing against her skin, she found herself feeling burned as her skin grew hotter and hotter. Her vision filled over with a purple haze and she could barely breathe.

"Wynona!" Rascal hissed directly in her ear. "You've got to get yourself under control!"

A heavy, deep shout finally pulled Wynona from her frozen state and she sucked in a breath, her vision clearing and the heat of her skin slowly coming down to normal.

"What was that?" a deep voice bellowed.

Wynona looked over to see Officer Skymaw bent over, his back heaving with each breath, sweat dripping off his forehead. He looked up, his eyes wary as he stared at Wynona and Rascal, who was still directly behind her.

"What are you?" Officer Skymaw whispered, his voice sounding exhausted.

Wynona shook her head. "I don't know what you mean."

The policeman straightened and turned his attention to Rascal. "What are you hiding?"

Rascal put up his hands, a fiery red color spanning his palms and down his arms. "It's not what you think, Daemon."

"Then what is it?" the large man ground out. "I have *never* felt anything like that before, even when holding back the entire presidential family!"

Wynona looked back and forth between the two men. "What's going on?"

"You don't even know?" Officer Skymaw shouted.

Wynona winced and stepped back.

"What's going on in here?" Chief Ligurio demanded, his head coming back into the doorway. He had followed the officers out into the hall in order to continue to recite Prim's rights and had missed whatever was causing the current silent argument between two of his officers.

"Nothing," Rascal said tightly, his eyes glowing bright enough to light the entire room as he stared Officer Skymaw down.

To his credit, Skymaw didn't flinch at his superior's dangerous look, but held his own for a few seconds before nodding. His fathomless black eyes darted to Wynona, then he turned purposefully toward the chief. "Ms. Le Doux is worried about her friend, is all. We were trying to keep her from doing something foolish."

Chief Ligurio grumbled, then disappeared into the hallway again.

Officer Skymaw pointed a long finger at Rascal. "You have some explaining to do."

"What are you talking about?" Wynona asked desperately. She looked between the two men. "We need to focus on helping Prim, and I get the feeling this is something completely different."

Rascal ignored her. "Meet at the tea house tonight after work."

Wynona's jaw dropped. How dare he act as if she wasn't even there, and inviting people to her place? It wasn't like she particularly cared if Officer Skymaw was there, but Rascal was going too far. "Excuse me?" she asked.

Before anyone could say anything else, Chief Ligurio came back in. "You're handling this awfully well," he said warily as he went back to his chair.

Wynona fought the temptation to continue staring down the other silent officers in the room. Something had happened and she had no idea what. But if they were meeting at her tea house tonight, then she was bound to find out. "I'm just planning my next move, Chief," she said with a little more sass than usual.

"I don't think you should get involved," he warned. "I know you've been helpful in the past, but this time it's personal. You're not thinking straight when it comes to your friend. Let us do our job."

"Actually, I think you're the one not thinking straight." Wynona marched up to the desk, ignoring Rascal's groan. "My *friend* is innocent. You've accused her of something she didn't do and I plan to see that justice is served." She put her hands on the chief's desk and leaned in. "And just for the record...it's always been personal." She raised an eyebrow. There was a buzz running through her system that seemed to be giving Wynona a strength of courage she didn't normally feel and she couldn't decide if she liked it or not. "First you tried to shut down my shop, next you attempted to lock up my sister and now you're charging a person who is more family than friend of a crime they didn't commit." She took in a deep breath as Chief Ligurio narrowed his gaze. "You do your job...and I'll do mine."

With that parting shot, she spun on her heel and left the room. She didn't even care that Rascal didn't follow her. Right now she needed to cool off. He had crossed a line earlier and her emotions were near raging. The walk home would do her good.

And maybe by the time Rascal and Officer Skymaw showed up at the tea house, she'd be calm enough to keep from hexing them both.

CHAPTER 8

Wynona was still a little angrier than normal by the time Rascal and Officer Skymaw arrived at her shop that evening, but at least she didn't feel like cursing anyone.

Violet, who had been clingy all day, scampered to the door as soon as it opened, knowing immediately that one of her favorite people had arrived.

Wynona could hear Rascal's low tones as he spoke to the purple mouse, his footsteps growing louder as they came through the front entry. She paused behind a chair and waited for him to walk through the threshold, doing her best to hold back frustrated words and accusations at his high handedness earlier in the day and demanding to know what he and Officer Skymaw had been talking about behind her back.

But when Rascal shuffled in, his messy hair looking worse than usual and his face looking drawn and worried, all her righteous anger immediately deflated.

"Rascal," she breathed, rushing over to his side. She put a hand on his cheek. "I don't think I have to ask how your day was."

He closed his eyes at her touch and took a deep breath. A small smile and tired chuckle broke free. "Probably for the best," he said back. He opened his eyes, took her hand and kissed her palm.

It was then that Wynona realized his palms were an odd color. She gasped and grabbed them both, holding them out. "Did you get...burned?"

Rascal's affectionate look shifted to one of wariness. "Sort of."

She pulled him farther into the shop. "What do you mean, sort of?" Wynona demanded. "Sit." She placed him at one of the tables and immediately went to her herb collection in the cupboard. "Cal-endula," she muttered to herself as she picked through the jars. Final-ly finding what she wanted, she turned to heat up some water, but Lusgu had beat her to it. The kettle was already whistling.

"Rags are in the third drawer," the brownie janitor grumbled, pointing one of his long fingers across the kitchen.

"You're a lifesaver," Wynona gushed, knowing that Lusgu was not a fan of Rascal. She grabbed what she needed, put it and the hot wa-ter all on a tray and headed back out to the front room.

The presence of Officer Skymaw made Wynona stumble and she almost dropped everything, having not heard him arrive.

"Let me," the officer said, his voice a little too calm. His black eyes were cautious as he took the tray from her and brought it to the table.

Wynona frowned when she realized he was keeping his distance from her in a way that said he was fearful. Though she couldn't un-derstand why. "Thank you," Wynona said just as carefully. After a moment, where she still couldn't figure out his reticence, she shook her head and turned back to helping Rascal. "How long ago did you get these?" she asked, setting up to steep the tea.

Rascal eyes grew sad. "Earlier this morning."

Wynona paused. "After I left?"

He slowly shook his head.

There was something she was missing. Wynona reached for the chair behind her and sat in it. "While I was there?" she whispered.

He nodded.

Her eyes grew unfocused as she tried to recall how Rascal could have gotten burned. He had picked her up, they'd gone to the station, they'd listened to the report, Prim had been taken. Nowhere in that schedule could he have...

She gasped. "Did *I* do this?" Tears immediately pricked her eyes when he hesitated. "Oh my goodness." Wynona put her hands over her mouth. "I couldn't! How could I have done this?" Tears began to slip down her cheeks. What was wrong with her? She could barely even remember having a magical episode at all, let alone one that allowed her to burn Rascal.

"Sweetheart." He reached out to her and Wynona jumped from her chair, nearly falling as she scrambled back, unwilling to risk hurting him further.

"She honestly doesn't know." Officer Skymaw's voice was full of wonder, as if just now realizing things were completely out of her control.

"I don't know?" she asked with a bitter laugh. "I'm starting to find out I don't know anything!" She bit back a sob. "I'm so sorry," she whispered thickly to Rascal. "I didn't mean to."

Rascal was on his feet and walking toward her like she was a spooked centaur foal. "Wy, I know you didn't mean to do it. It was just an unfortunate accident."

"One that burned you!" she cried. She fisted her hands together and brought them to her chest to keep from reaching for him. It physically hurt to stay back. She really, *really*, liked Rascal, and their blossoming relationship was magical and wonderful. Everything Wynona had hoped for. But how could it continue if she could hurt him at any time without even knowing she did it?

Rascal put his reddened hands in the air. "I know this is frightening, but we're going to figure it out together." He pinned her with his gold gaze. "Did you hear that? Together. You're not alone anymore and this one little setback isn't going to stop us." He shook his head. "The only thing that will do that is if you change your mind about us."

Wynona felt herself softening. "What if you change your mind?"

Rascal winked. "That'll never happen. Where else would I find someone with a purple mouse?"

Wynona put her hands in her face and let the tears come. She was so overwhelmed with happiness and worries and relief and fear and...she couldn't even put her emotions into words. She sagged into his chest when Rascal's arms wrapped around her and she felt him kiss the top of her head.

"We'll get it figured out," he whispered in a low tone. "One step at a time."

Violet poked out from Rascal's front pocket and she whimpered against Wynona's cheek as she rested against his broad chest.

A throat cleared and Officer Skymaw sounded decidedly uncomfortable when he spoke. "This little reunion is great and all, but I think maybe we need to get some things settled."

Wynona pulled away from Rascal and wiped her eyes. "You're right. I'm sorry."

Officer Skymaw scratched his chin. "I think someone needs to catch me up on what's going on with you, Ms. Le Doux. I thought you had no magic at all."

Wynona scrunched her nose and waved a hand at the table. "Why don't we have a seat? I can treat Rascal's burns and we'll tell you what we know." She paused mid-step. "But this has to be kept between us," she explained. "If my family ever found out my magic was emerging, well...I don't think any of us would like the consequences. And it's Wynona."

Officer Skymaw studied her carefully, then nodded and sat across the table from her and Rascal. "Okay...Wynona. Feel free to call me Daemon." He folded his large hands on top of the table. "I'm ready."

While she soaked Rascal's hands and wrapped his burns, she told him her story. The disappointment at her birth, the mental abuse and loneliness of her childhood. She told him about her grandmother and how she was the only reason Wynona survived as well as escaped her horrible family. The story ended when she explained how she had been seeing signs of magic ever since escaping and had finally figured out they weren't Granny Saffron's protection, but Wynona's own magic breaking through the curse, though no one knew why.

When she had finished, their teacups were drained and Officer Skymaw was leaning back in his seat, his black eyes wide with shock. "That's quite a story."

Wynona nodded. "I know." She handed a cracker to Violet. "But it's the truth."

"So, today at the precinct...?" He trailed off, his eyes going back and forth between Wynona and Rascal.

Wynona turned to Rascal as well. She actually wasn't quite sure what had happened.

He gave her a sympathetic look. "You got upset when they took Prim out," he said softly. "And when I tried to stop you, I think your magic tried to protect you."

"Do you know how a black hole works?" Officer Skymaw interrupted.

Wynona turned to him and paused. "I have to admit, I'm not sure. I know magic is null and void around you." She tilted her head. "But then how in the world did I burn Rascal?" She was grateful when Rascal reached over to grab her hand, rubbing her knuckles in a soothing pattern and sending a silent message that he held no grudge against her.

"Magic isn't actually null and void," Officer Skymaw explained. He cleared his throat. "Magic can happen, but I have the ability to..." He made a face. "I suppose it's like I suck it into a black hole. I take it into myself, thus forcing the magic to dissipate."

"You actually suck it inside?" Wynona asked in shock. "Ooooh..." She leaned in closer. "That's what happened at my parents' house. That's why you were working so hard, but not actually moving."

He nodded and huffed out a laugh. "Yeah. Your mom is crazy powerful." His humor dropped. "But it was nothing compared to what I felt with you today."

Wynona's cheeks heated up and she leaned back. "It wasn't intentional," she said softly.

"And that makes it worse," Daemon stated. "If you had been trying, I'm not sure I would have been able to contain you."

Rascal gave her hand a squeeze. "As soon as we get the chance, we'll start to practice your control," he said.

Wynona rolled her eyes. "As soon as we get the chance." She folded her arms over her chest. "My best friend is in jail, I run a full-time business and the people around me can't seem to stop being accused of murder." She gave him a look, though it was mostly playful. "When exactly is that free time going to be?"

Rascal chuckled. "I don't know, but we'll figure it out." His eyes flashed. "Together."

"I think he's right," Daemon said. "We need to get Prim free first, then we can work on your magic."

"We?" Wynona asked.

Violet grumbled and shook her head at Daemon.

Wynona grinned. "I think you just got told off by a purple mouse."

He raised his eyebrows. "How else are you going to contain any accidents?"

Wynona paused and looked down at Violet. "He has a point."

Daemon's smile was nothing short of smug.

Rascal, however, wasn't as impressed. "I don't think we need an audience."

Wynona touched his arm. "He's right though. I don't want to risk hurting you again. I didn't even know I was using magic at the precinct today. I was too caught up in my emotions."

Rascal pushed a hand through his hair. "I understand, but I still think we'll do better if you're not worried about a bunch of onlookers."

Daemon gave his superior a look. "I already know the secret," he said in a low tone. "I promise not to spread it around. Look, Deputy Chief, you know me. You know I'm not the type to break my word."

"You're right," Rascal said, leaning forward. "I do know you. But what I don't know is why you're so interested in this situation."

Wynona felt like she was watching a tennis match, her head going back and forth between the two men. Just like at the office earlier that morning, she felt as if she wasn't understanding their conversation.

"It's not what you think," Daemon said softly, his eyes never leaving his boss.

Rascal raised a dark eyebrow and Wynona noticed some fur starting to sprout on the back of his hands. "Are you sure?" There was the slightest growl to his tone, letting her know he was truly upset.

"Rascal," she scolded. "What's going on?"

Daemon put his hands in the air. "I promise. My interest in Ms. Le Doux is purely platonic."

Wynona's jaw dropped and she turned back to Rascal. "You've got to be kidding me."

He closed his eyes and shook his head, the beast fading before he looked at Wynona. He shrugged. "Did you really think I wouldn't ask?"

Wynona groaned. "You're an idiot."

He smirked. "I know. But right now I'm your idiot, so..."

Wynona laughed lightly and shook her head. "Men."

"Back to the matter at hand..." Daemon said wryly. He made a face. "I had no idea working with the two of you was going to be like wrangling toddlers."

Wynona straightened in her seat. "Sorry. We're not usually quite so..." Her eyes darted to Rascal, who still sat looking pleased with himself. "Distracted."

"Glad to hear it," Daemon shot back. "Okay...so...Primrose...Ms. Meadows. What can you tell me about her?"

Wynona took a deep breath, her emotions still dangerously close to the surface. She did her best to hold it together...for Prim. "She's a fairy," Wynona started.

"But she has no wings," Daemon pointed out.

"Correct," Wynona responded. "She was born without them."

Daemon nodded. "And?"

"She's the premiere flower grower in Hex Haven," Wynona continued. "If you saw her with plants, you would be amazed at her abilities. They thrive in her very presence."

"Interesting," Daemon murmured. "And she's in financial trouble at the moment?"

Wynona tucked her hair behind her ear. "That's what they said. She just put an addition onto her greenhouse. I had no idea she had stretched herself so thin. Until the murder, I didn't even know she had a second job."

Daemon scratched his chin. "Why do you think she kept it from you?"

Wynona played with her teacup and shrugged. "She mentioned that she was embarrassed about it, but she had to know I wouldn't have judged her."

"Working at The Siren's Call isn't exactly known as a classy job," Rascal pointed out. "It may have had to do with the line of work rather than the fact she was working."

Wynona nodded. "True. I'm guessing she needed something that was at night though. Otherwise she wouldn't have time to take care of her plants."

"So, she got herself in a pickle, picked up a second job, got in a fight with her boss, her boss ends up dead, and the murder weapon is a flower that Prim happens to grow?" Daemon clarified.

"That about sums it up," Wynona said, folding her hands neatly on the table.

"And you believe she's innocent?" he continued.

"I *know* she's innocent."

"You have that much faith in her?" Daemon pressed.

"I do." Wynona put her chin in the air. "Anyone who knows Prim, truly knows her, would never doubt it."

Daemon tapped his long fingers on the table for several seconds before nodding his head. "Okay. I believe you. Where do we start?"

Wynona laughed. "You're determined to get involved, aren't you?"

Black eyes were deadly serious as they met Wynona's. "Twice I've seen you fight for what you believed, Ms. Le Doux."

She didn't miss the fact that he'd gone back to a more formal address after Rascal's interrogation.

"Both times your intuition and beliefs were spot on and a criminal was brought to justice. I've worked under Chief Ligurio for many years and he's the best of vampires, but that doesn't mean he doesn't make mistakes." He leaned forward. "After watching you, I'm starting to realize that when you contradict the Chief, you have a reason for doing so. If you say Prim is innocent, then I'm willing to help bring the real killer to justice."

The sincerity in the man's statement was touching and Wynona almost sighed at such a speech. She barely knew Daemon, but she could feel that he was one of the good ones. Having him on their side would only be a boost to their investigation. "Thank you," she said, just as sincerely. "And I think the first place we should start is back at the scene of the crime."

CHAPTER 9

Wynona took comfort in Violet's wiggling body in the front pocket of her pants. She hadn't planned to start this investigation by herself, but both Rascal and Daemon needed to work, and that left Wynona on her own. Her shop didn't open until a little later, so she was able to come in the morning and look around without any interference...she hoped.

The front door of the theatre had been locked, so Wynona found herself walking around the back, looking for an alternative entrance. A back door lay ahead, but when she tugged on the metal handle, it was also locked.

Wynona huffed and put her hands on her hips. "Now what?" she muttered to no one in particular.

Violet squeaked and poked her head out of the pocket.

Wynona looked down. "Think you can do something about this?" She scrunched up her nose. "I'd try a spell, but with my luck, I'd burn down the building."

Violet's face said she agreed with Wynona.

Wynona reached into her pocket, picked up the tiny purple rodent and set her on the ground.

Without a word, Violet squeezed under the door and disappeared.

Wynona waited...and waited...and soon grew worried. "Vi?" she whispered at the door. "Are you okay?" The last time Violet had opened a door for her, it had been quick and Wynona had been able to hear the mouse the whole time. But right now there was nothing. "Oh!" Wynona jumped back when the door opened, nearly smacking her in the face.

A large man in a black t-shirt and slacks gave her a weird look. "All you had to do was knock," he said in a grumbly tone.

"Uh, sorry," Wynona said, feeling slightly intimidated by his severe glare. He was still holding the door, though, so Wynona began to slip through when his hand stopped her.

"Aren't you forgetting something?"

Wynona's heart was about to burst through her ribcage. "Am I?" she stuttered.

The security guard rolled his eyes and opened his hand, showing Violet looking perfectly content in his large palm.

"Vi!" Wynona reached and picked up her friend, cuddling the creature to her chest. "Sorry about that," Wynona apologized.

The man huffed and let the door slam behind them before he stormed off into the dark recesses of the backstage area.

Wynona took a moment to catch her breath from the encounter. She had permission from the police to be there, but somehow she still felt like a criminal as she slunk around. "Obviously not a very good criminal," she grumbled to herself.

Violet chattered her agreement and Wynona scowled.

"Well, what were you up to?" Wynona demanded. "You were supposed to get us in the door."

Violet began waving her arms around and arguing.

"Yes, you did get us in, but why get a security guard? The guy looked like he wanted to rip me in half!"

Violet rolled her tiny eyes and went back to her explanation.

Wynona groaned softly. "It doesn't matter," she finally interrupted. "We're in, we're both safe and we'll count that as a win. Plus, it's probably better that they know we're here. That way we won't get in trouble later."

Violet muttered under her breath and began to smooth her fur.

Wynona slid the mouse back into her pocket and then made her way carefully down the hallway. She had to walk with her hands in front of her since most of the lights were off, which was probably because the center was only open during the evening performances. Up ahead, however, Wynona could see some dim lights, which were more than likely the offices and dressing rooms of the employees.

Using her phone flashlight, Wynona read the name on the first door.

Brell Tuall

Wynona chewed her lip, trying to place the name. If the woman had a personal office, there was a reason for it. Before she could figure it out, however, she heard shouting from inside and the door opened.

Wynona squeaked and stepped back, almost tripping over a box.

"Who are you?" a low voice growled.

She couldn't see his face, since the light was behind him, but whoever it was, he wasn't very welcoming. "Uh, hi," Wynona stammered. "I'm Wynona Le Doux." She straightened her shirt and smiled, holding out her hand.

"Le Doux?" A woman's voice came from the room and another body appeared in the doorway. "Are you related to President Le Doux?"

Wynona swallowed her desire to cringe every time someone asked her that. "Yes. He's my father."

"Oh!" The woman tapped the man on the shoulder as she looked over him. "You must be the one who opened that tea shop."

Wynona nodded. "Yes." She glanced down the hall, but it was still dark and appeared empty. "Are you Ms. Tuall?"

"Mrs.," the man grunted.

"I apologize," Wynona responded humbly. "I'd like to speak to the two of you about Madam Ureo." Light suddenly blinded her and Wynona covered her eyes, noticing that the man had flipped a switch next to the door. "Thank you," she added.

"We already spoke with the police," Mr. Tuall said, folding his arms over his chest. "What do you have to do with anything?"

Wynona had to fight hard to keep her smile on her face. This guy definitely didn't want her around here. "I'm just helping the police out," she hedged. "Sometimes I help work on cases such as this."

Mrs. Tuall pushed her husband aside. "Come in," the woman said sweetly. "We don't have anything new to share, but I've always wanted to meet the presidential family."

Wynona had to bite back another sigh. Still...if her family name helped, then she would use it. "Thank you," she said to Mrs. Tuall just before sitting on a chair covered in flowers.

Mrs. Tuall sat opposite on a couch while her husband chose to stay by the door, looking like he wanted to throw Wynona out on her ear at any given moment.

The room wasn't fancy, though it appeared that Mrs. Tuall did the best she could. The furniture was faded and the small side table was stained with a watermark. The artwork on the walls appeared cheap and mass produced, while the wallpaper was curling in the corners.

A large makeup area took up the wall behind Mrs. Tuall, with bright lights, wigs and costumes hanging haphazardly off to the side by a dressing screen. All in all, it was pretty much what Wynona would have expected in a place such as this. The Siren's Call wasn't known for being upscale, which, she guessed, was why Prim hadn't wanted Wynona to know that she was working there.

"It's not much, is it?" Mrs. Tuall asked with a slightly bitter laugh. She folded her elegant fingers in her lap. The woman was stunningly beautiful and reminded Wynona of a siren she had met during her first case helping the police. Mrs. Tuall looked around, her dislike plain on her face.

"Oh, it's fine," Wynona assured her. "You must be very important to the troupe if you have your own place."

Mr. Tuall snorted. "Haven't you ever heard of Vampiria?"

Wynona's eyes widened and she turned back to Mrs. Tuall. "You're the vampire impersonator?"

Mrs. Tuall's smile looked slightly uncomfortable, as if she didn't like being in the spotlight. "Yes." She shrugged. "It was just something I kind of fell into and discovered I was good at it." She held out her hand and her husband came to join her on the couch. "In fact, it was during one of my performances that I met Fable." She gave him an adoring look and to Wynona's surprise, Mr. Tuall returned it.

"What a wonderful love story," Wynona responded, feeling like a third wheel at the moment. "Have you worked for Madam Ureo the whole time?"

Mr. Tuall's lovesick face disappeared so quickly, Wynona had to blink. His face grew angry and ripples of tan and black fur pulsed under his skin.

Wynona made a mental note that he was some kind of shifter, more than likely a cat from the color combination. No wonder he was so grumpy. Large cat shifters were notoriously territorial and the fact that Mr. Tuall shared his wife with large crowds, when predator cats were mostly loners, had to keep him on edge at all times.

"Yes," he said tightly. "Brell's contract has been with Ureo the whole time."

"She gave me a shot when I needed a job," Mrs. Tuall explained softly, stroking her husband's arm. "She must have seen something I didn't because she gave me a ten-year contract and I'm only halfway through it at the moment."

Wynona tilted her head. "Did you want out of the contract?"

"Is there a point to this visit?" Mr. Tuall asked, jumping to his feet. "Things are in an upheaval around here and we don't really have time for all this. There's another show tonight that Brell should be resting for."

Wynona frowned. "Another show? The theatre wasn't closed down?"

Mr. Tuall laughed without humor. "Oh no. All shows and contracts are going to be honored as is," he said darkly. "Ureo's partner, Equinus Rujins, has come out of the woodwork, and made the announcement just this morning."

"I didn't realize Madam Ureo had a partner," Wynona said, not moving yet from her chair. She hoped if she just ignored his demand to leave and changed the subject, she could keep them talking. There were definitely some hard feelings in this group and Wynona wanted to pick it apart a little.

Mr. Tuall grumbled and began to pace, his strides measured and strong, just giving a further clue to his paranormal origins.

"Madam Ureo had a silent partner," Mrs. Tuall began to explain, her worried eyes straying to her husband over and over again. "Mr. Rujins is a troll and had originally been a financial backer only." Mrs. Tuall brought her warm brown eyes to Wynona. "But with Madam Ureo's death, he said he plans to keep the business running and that he will take over Madam's role now that she's gone."

Wynona tapped her knee and stilled when she felt Violet stirring in her pocket. She hoped the mouse was hearing everything. The situation had been a little too hectic for Wynona to bring Violet out, but hopefully the rodent was forming her own opinions and they could discuss thoughts later. "Any idea where I can find him?" Wynona asked.

"Two doors down the hall," Mr. Tuall said in a disgusted tone. "He doesn't have an office yet, so he's using one of the dressing rooms."

Wynona nodded her thanks. She had a feeling she wouldn't be able to find out any more at the moment, so she slapped her knees and stood. "Well, thank you for your time. I appreciate it." She walked to the door, then paused with her hand on the doorknob. "Oh, and I know the police already asked, but can you please tell me where the two of you were when Madam Ureo was killed?"

Mrs. Tuall glanced at her husband before answering. "I was in here getting ready to go out on stage." She gave a tired smile. "It takes longer than you would think to transform into a vampire."

Wynona noted the woman's warm, golden skin tone and figured that was true. Turning brown into white couldn't be an easy job. Her makeup bills were probably astronomical. "And you, Mr. Tuall?"

His eyes were narrowed and for a moment, Wynona didn't think he would answer. "I was backstage looking for Brell."

"And you didn't think to look in the dressing room?" The question was out before Wynona could think better of it. She didn't particularly want to antagonize the predator, but the story didn't make sense.

"I'm pretty sure he stopped by while I was in the bathroom," Mrs. Tuall said, pointing out the door. "It's across the hall and down a little ways. I don't have a private one."

"Ah. Gotcha." Satisfied with the answer for the moment, Wynona nodded and let herself out. Once in the hallway, she took a deep breath. Her heart was still beating faster than normal and Wynona was reminded yet again of how much she didn't really belong in the police world. She simply didn't have the stomach or nerves for confronting scary people.

But she also couldn't let Prim go to jail for something she didn't do.

Squaring her shoulders, Wynona knocked on the next door.

"Yes?" came a shout from inside.

"My name is Wynona Le Doux," Wynona said to the wooden frame. "I'd like to ask you some questions, if you have a few minutes?"

The door opened. "Le Doux? Are you related to President Le Doux?" A very handsome man stood in the doorway, his eyes an unusual shade of green. When he blinked, a second lid was slightly slower than the outside eyelid.

Gorgon, Wynona decided. The man was a snake shifter. "I am," she said with her usual practiced smile. "I have a few questions about Madam Ureo's death, if you don't mind."

"I've always wanted to meet someone from the presidential family," the man said, stepping back. "Come on in. Though I don't know what I can tell you that I haven't already told the police."

"I know," Wynona assured him, noting that the dressing room was almost an exact replica of Mrs. Tuall's. The only differences were the style of costumes hanging around. "But I'd like to ask anyway, if you don't mind."

"I don't mind at all," the man said, waving to the same flower chair as she'd sat in in the other room. He rushed over when she sat down and grabbed a watering can from the table. "Sorry. Forgot to put this away."

Wynona waited until he was on the couch before she went through the same questions she had posed for Mr. and Mrs. Tuall. She tried to relax, reminding herself that this would take time, and not be frustrated when her host was more interested in life at the presidential palace than in answering questions about the death of his boss.

CHAPTER 10

Wynona took a deep breath before knocking on Mr. Rujins's door. She had spoken with all the star impersonators and actors who were under contract to Madam Ureo and not one of them had shed any new light on the situation, though most had spent a great deal of time trying to turn the subject back to Wynona's family.

The fact that their contracts were being honored by their new manager had come up several times and now Wynona was determined to meet him.

She glanced at her cell phone, grumbling when she realized she didn't have much time left if she was going to get back to the shop in time for opening. This would have to be a quick interview.

She gave three short raps on the door and folded her hands in front of her. Violet wiggled in her pocket and Wynona glanced down. "I need you to listen, okay?"

Violet poked her nose out of the top of the pocket and made a face, but ducked down quickly when the door opened.

"What do you want?"

The gruff, gravelly tone was far from friendly and Wynona had to brace herself to keep from turning away. Her stress levels were already through the roof today, she didn't want to do this.

"Hello," Wynona said in her most pleasant voice. "I'm Wynona Le Doux. I was hoping I could ask you a few questions."

Black eyes looked her up and down. "Le Doux?"

Wynona held back her sigh. When was that going to stop being a thing? "Yes," she said, just as politely as before, though it was forced. "Le Doux."

The troll wasn't much taller than Wynona, but his craggy face said he was definitely much older. There was a sharp intelligence in his eyes that told Wynona she needed to tread carefully. He folded his arms over his thick chest. "And what's your act?"

Wynona blinked. "Excuse me?"

The troll groaned and shook his head. "I don't have time for idiots," he grumbled. "Either show me what you do or we're done."

Wynona opened her mouth, then paused, still unsure what was going on.

"You sing? Is that it?" He waved his hand through the air dismissively. "I don't need another singer. I've already got a mermaid and a siren who take care of that crowd." He started to turn around, but Wynona reached out and grabbed his arm.

"I'm not here to be hired," she said hurriedly.

The grumpy manager glared at her hand and Wynona pulled it back, but refused to back down completely.

"I'm here on behalf of the police, regarding Madam Ureo's murder. I'd like to ask you a few questions."

His eyes narrowed even farther, looking almost closed as he studied her. "I wasn't in town during that. I don't see how I can help you."

Wynona tilted her head. "I'm sure you have some helpful information, even if you weren't here. Can I have a few minutes of your time please?"

Violet stirred in Wynona's pocket, but didn't emerge, for which Wynona was grateful. The last thing she needed right now was a mouse running wild and getting squashed by an angry troll.

"You have two minutes," the manager huffed, turning to go back inside his office.

Wynona had to hurry or the door would have slammed in her face. She managed to close it quietly behind her and then stood in the middle of the tiny dressing room turned office while Mr. Rujins took his seat behind a makeshift desk.

"I haven't moved into my office yet," he grunted, settling himself in his seat. "The police still have it closed off."

Wynona nodded, though she was doubtful that his real office would have chairs for his guests. She had a feeling he didn't encourage visits. "I'm fine with standing," she said, putting her practiced smile back on.

"One minute, forty-five seconds," he said, his attention not on her.

"How long did you know Madam Ureo?" There was no point in beating around the bush. If Mr. Rujins was going to keep a timer, Wynona was going to use every second.

"We grew up together," he said with a sneer.

"And when did you become business partners?"

"When she opened this place fifteen years ago."

"What was your arrangement?"

Mr. Rujins folded his arms over his chest and leaned back in his seat. "I put in the money, she put in the work." He raised his bushy white eyebrows high. "Happy?"

"You didn't have a say in how the business was run?"

He shrugged. "I didn't want one. I don't like people."

Wynona could feel the truth in that statement.

"But my parents had a decent horde when they passed, so I was looking for a way to do something with it. Nelara had an idea, but no capital."

"So you were her...bank, so to speak?" Wynona pressed. "How were the proceeds split between you?"

Black eyes rolled to the ceiling. "You're trying to find out if I killed Nelara for the money." He leaned into the desk, black finger stubs spread wide. "I didn't."

"Because you were where?"

The gravelly laughter was a sound Wynona hadn't expected at all. She knew she was pushing hard, and she had been prepared for more anger, but not for amusement.

"Your two minutes are up," he stated with a wild grin.

Wynona didn't move, simply smiled.

The rumbling laughter came again. "I can see why the police sent you instead. You're quite tenacious." He leaned back, his harsh look softening just a touch. "Are you sure you're not interested in show business? I could easily find a use for you."

This time when his eyes traveled over her, Wynona did step back. "No, thank you." Her words were firm. "But I do want to know where you were the night Madam Ureo died."

The troll grumbled and rubbed one hand over his face. "I was at home. The same place I always am." He splayed his hands over the messy desk. "Coming in to run this piece of junk is the first time I've left my house for any substantial bit of time."

"So the theatre is enough for you to live on?" Wynona asked.

He shrugged. "It was fine. It wasn't my best investment, but the check was steady." His voice had dropped off at the end of that statement and Wynona had to wonder why.

She glanced at the desk and noticed a ledger off to the side with some red pen markings in it. The information was quickly tucked away for future reference. "Is that your job then? To invest?"

He shrugged again, his demeanor growing colder the longer the conversation went on. "People need money."

"And you provide that." It was a statement, not a question.

"When it's worth my while." His smile was full of cracked and dirty teeth and Wynona had to wonder what he did with all that money he was implying he had. Apparently, he didn't spend it on his appearance.

She felt Violet stir again. There was something decided-ly...off...about this man and Wynona was starting to feel more uncomfortable by the second. Perhaps this was one interview that Rascal or Daemon should handle. She began to back up to the door. "Thank you for your time," she said, reaching for the doorknob behind her. She was starting to feel like it would be unwise to take her eyes off the troll.

He tilted his head consideringly. "I didn't think much of it when you first arrived—after all, you're the spitting image of your mother—but why would a Le Doux be asking questions for the police?" Slowly, the troll stood up.

Wynona felt her heart begin to speed up. "I'm friends with several of the officers and have assisted in a few cases in the past." Her palm grew slick and the doorknob slipped.

His thick legs moved faster than Wynona would have thought possible, bringing him right in front of her. His breath was as bad as his teeth and Wynona turned her head to the side, trying not to breathe. "Everyone knows the president's family doesn't get their hands dirty," he muttered in a low tone. "Why are you really here?"

"Exactly why I told you," Wynona snapped, finally grasping the doorknob enough to wrench it sideways. She stepped to the side in order to throw open the door and the troll barely managed to step back before being smacked in the nose. "I'm sure Deputy Chief Strongclaw and Chief Ligurio will have more questions," Wynona threw over her shoulder as she escaped into the hallway.

Once the door had closed behind her, she sucked in a frantic breath. Violet climbed out of her pocket and up onto her shoulder, nuzzling Wynona's chin and neck.

"Thanks," Wynona whispered, petting her furry friend. Wynona bent over, hands on her knees as she allowed her heart and breathing to calm down. Purple ribbons floated through her peripheral vision and she shut her eyes, focusing only on calming down her body. The last thing she needed right now was a magic explosion. She had absolutely no control over her emerging magic and with her luck,

Wynona was positive she would burn the theatre to the ground or something equally as devastating.

Slowly, more slowly than she would have liked, Wynona felt the fear and anxiety ebb, allowing her body to calm down as well.

When she felt in control, she straightened and took one last deep breath. "Okay," she whispered to Violet. "I think I'm okay."

Violet whimpered, but settled comfortably into her usual spot.

Wynona's eyes happened to land on a wall clock, and she bit back a curse. "Shoot, Vi. I gotta get back." Spinning on her heel, Wynona raced for the back exit to the alley. She had a business to run and if she didn't hurry, she would have several angry patrons.

The security guard glared, but otherwise didn't speak as Wynona rushed past.

"Thank you!" she called out, darting into the alley and running to her Vespa. She started the engine and merged into traffic as quickly as she could manage without causing an accident.

The cool breeze felt wonderful on her hot cheeks and neck as she rode through the streets to her own business. While she drove, Wynona's mind wandered. At first she hadn't thought there would be much to tell Rascal and Daemon when they met after work tonight, but now Wynona was starting to rethink that.

Something was different about the new manager. He might have been a troll, but the feeling she had around him told Wynona he had all the instincts of a shark.

Her instincts were screaming that he was more than he appeared to be and since they had served her well in the past, she knew she would have to ask Rascal to look into his background.

Parking the Vespa in the back of her building, Wynona rushed through the kitchen door. "Lusgu!"

It took a moment, but the brownie came through the swinging kitchen door.

"I'm so sorry I'm late," Wynona gushed, quickly filling all her kettles with water. "Would you mind helping me get the water hot so that I can set the tables?"

The small creature rolled his eyes and flicked his fingers, removing the kettle from Wynona's fingers and starting an intricate dance of pots going through the water stream.

Wynona sighed in relief. "Thank you," she said sincerely. "Did Gnox and Kyoz bring the pastries?"

Lusgu huffed and tilted his head toward the back counter. "And left you with no clean silverware," he grumbled.

Wynona had to pause to take a breath. "They emptied the silverware drawer?"

Lusgu scowled. "Every last piece."

She sighed. Those imps were so much trouble, but Wynona was in need of their help. If only she could figure out a different way to get their baked goods to the shop. Maybe she needed to hire someone to bring them from the bakery instead of having them delivered by the imp twins. That would certainly save her time and money, since the two troublemakers always left a mess in their wake.

"I'm sorry," she said. "I'll have another talk with them."

Lusgu shook his head and put his focus back on the water and kettles.

Leaving her employee to do his work, she headed out to the dining area to start setting the teacups and plates. She had a few patrons who arrived at opening, right on the dot and if she wasn't ready, Wynona was going to hear about it for days.

While she adored her customers, some of them were difficult to handle on the best of days and today had been far from that.

Shoving thoughts of murders, weird managers and suspicious ledgers behind her, Wynona threw herself into what she knew best. Tea. Tonight she could talk out the other problems with Rascal and

Daemon, but until then, she had a job to do and customers to please. Hopefully, Prim could hold on just a little bit longer.

CHAPTER 11

"Sorry I'm late," Daemon said as he waltzed into the dining room, his long legs eating up the distance quickly.

Wynona gave him a tired smile as he took the seat across the table from her. It felt so good to get off her feet tonight. She felt like she had been through the wringer by the time work ended. Her head hurt, her feet ached and her nerves were still on edge from her encounter with Mr. Rujins.

A delicate shiver ran up her spine at the thought of his name. There was definitely something going on behind those black eyes and Wynona knew they needed to figure it out.

"Wy?"

She blinked and turned to Rascal, who was seated at her left.

"Can you tell us what you found out at the theatre today?" He took a large bite of a pain au chocolat, his eyes widening at the flavor.

Wynona grinned. "Those two imps are pretty amazing, aren't they?"

He swallowed and nodded. "Don't get me started, because I'll never stop." He raised his eyebrows. "Theatre?"

Wynona sighed and rubbed her sore forehead. "I can't say I discovered a lot, but I did find a few interesting tidbits."

Daemon wiped his mouth with a napkin. He had also discovered the pastries. "Such as?"

"Such as the fact that a new manager is taking over and all the current contracts are being honored, much to the dismay of a few of the actors."

Rascal frowned. "We had heard chatter about that. Good to know it's confirmed. What's the manager's name?"

"Equinis Rujins," Wynona said, the words leaving a bad taste in her mouth.

Rascal stiffened. "Say again?"

Wynona hesitated, but repeated herself. "Equinis Rujins?" She held her hand over the table so Violet could climb down her arm and settled onto the top. "He told me he had been a silent partner until Madam Ureo's death. Now he's taking over."

Rascal's face was deadly serious as he turned his body fully toward Wynona. "Tell me everything that was said and whom you got the information from."

Wynona leaned back a little. Rascal's eyes were glowing, letting her know his wolf was close to the surface and normally that happened when attraction flared between them or he was being protective, but at the moment, he felt very much like the predator and she wasn't sure she liked it.

"Deputy Chief." Daemon's voice was firm. "You're frightening her."

Rascal blinked and shook his head, the glow in his eyes dimming. When he finally stopped, he looked at Wynona and his face fell. "I'm sorry, Wy. I didn't mean to do that."

"It's okay," she said softly, still feeling slightly wary. She was fighting the urge to touch him, wanting to comfort his sad expression, but she held herself back. For a moment, he hadn't *seen* her, and that wasn't a pleasant feeling.

"No, it's not." He sighed and scrubbed his face. "I have some history with Mr. Rujins," he explained, though Wynona could have guessed that. "But that's neither here nor there." Slowly, he reached out and put his hand over hers, as if nervous that she would pull away.

Wynona relaxed under his touch and turned her hand so they could intertwine their fingers.

Rascal brought their hands up and kissed the back of hers. "I'm sorry."

"It's alright."

"Would you mind starting from the beginning and sharing everything you learned with us?"

She nodded, swallowing hard. Everything felt much more important now that she knew her instincts about Mr. Rujins were correct. And maybe this was going to be the opening they needed in order to prove Prim wasn't a murderer. If someone with a history was involved, the odds said they weren't innocent.

"I met with Brell Tuall and her husband Fable first," Wynona explained. "Brell was fairly quiet, and seemed really sweet, but her husband has a bit of a temper."

"Did you feel threatened in any way?" Daemon interrupted.

Wynona shook her head. "Not really, though he was...difficult at times. He wants Brell to move onto bigger and greater venues, but they can't break the contract they have with the theatre and Madam Ureo wasn't willing to let go of her biggest star."

Rascal scratched behind his ear. "I haven't seen her personally, but from what I understand, there's never been another impersonator like her."

"She's a siren," Wynona said wryly. "A siren acting like a vampire. Sounds like a deadly combination to me."

Daemon's cheeks were pink as he cleared his throat and stuffed another pastry in his mouth.

Wynona pinched her lips together to keep from laughing. "Have you met her, Daemon?"

He cleared his throat again and tugged at his collar. "I've seen her a few times."

"And?" Rascal pressed, looking a little too smug for his question to be purely for investigative purposes.

"And she's as good as everyone says," Daemon declared, leaning back and folding his arms over his chest. "It was at a party for the last precinct I worked at, over in Cauldron Cove. Our chief brought in a bunch of actors for All Hallow's Eve. It was only like, two years ago, so she was still on the rise to stardom, but not far off."

"Do you think Madam Ureo would go to great lengths to keep her?" Wynona asked. "Do you think she was playing fair with the contract?"

"I have no doubt that Madam Ureo kept that woman under lock and key," Daemon said with a sigh. "I don't know if the contract was fair, that's something we'd have to check. But when Mrs. Tuall began her act, she had the entire room under a spell." His cheeks turned red again. "Especially the men. It was basically like a hypnotizing act. She got a few of the officers to do stupid things like walk around imitating a gorilla or a chicken. But she was as mesmerizing as the sideshow stuff."

Wynona frowned. "After seeing how much her husband tries to protect her, I'm surprised he lets her do that kind of work. The longer we talked, the more I was certain he was some kind of big cat shifter." She turned to Rascal. "You know how territorial that type of creature can be. Why would he be okay sharing his wife with others?"

Rascal shook his head and wiped powdered sugar from his fingers. "He might not be, but the money could certainly help change his mind. Of course, it sounds like she could be making a lot more if she could get away from The Siren's Call."

"Do you think she might have had something to do with the murder?" Daemon asked, leaning in.

Wynona shook her head. "No. She was very quiet and sweet, which seems at odds with most sirens I know. They're usually pretty confident, but she and Mr. Tuall were like yin and yang. He was high strung and she was low key." Wynona tapped the tea saucer. "If anyone was willing to do something nefarious about the contract, I think it would be him."

Rascal turned to Daemon. "I'll add him to our suspect list. I want you to start looking up his background."

Daemon nodded and made a note in his phone.

"What else?" Rascal asked Wynona.

She took a soothing drink of tea. "I talked to several other actors, but nothing else seemed important. Until I arrived at Mr. Rujins's office."

Rascal scowled, but didn't interrupt.

"He told me that he and Madam Ureo had known each other since they were kids. That he had inherited his parents' hoard and was using it to invest in different businesses." Wynona shrugged. "He claimed this was the first one where he needed to actually run it, since he usually liked to be a financial backer only."

Rascal laughed bitterly. "Financial backing. That's a polite way of putting it."

"What would you call it?" Wynona asked.

"He's a loan shark," Daemon supplied. "Pure and simple."

"But the problem with a loan shark is that they don't get their hands dirty," Rascal grumbled. His napkin was in shreds at this point and he hadn't noticed, so Wynona touched his arm, bringing him back to the present. Rascal gave her a grateful smile. "Point is, Mr. Rujins has been evading the law for years. All his *clients* are too afraid to testify and he's never involved if anything becomes violent."

Wynona pinched her lips together. "I did notice that he had a ledger book open on the desk he was working at. There were some red markings on it." She shook her head. "I don't know if it was the accounting book for the theatre or something else though. I just thought it interesting. Red usually means there's a problem."

Daemon nodded. "Agreed." He set down his teacup, which looked funny against his large hand. "It's worth looking into at least."

"But carefully," Rascal said quickly. "If Rujins is involved, then this just got a lot more serious. He doesn't play for fun."

Violet whimpered and Wynona stroked her fur. "I got a weird vibe around him, so it doesn't surprise me that he's on your radar."

"What do you mean, weird vibe?" Rascal was back to being intense again.

"At first he had been really cold and hard to get talking, but after a few minutes, he became almost...predatory," Wynona explained. "I'm not sure exactly how to say it. But all my instincts were screaming that he was dangerous."

A low growl came from Rascal's throat and fur started to sprout on the back of his hands.

Wynona took his fingers between hers. "I got out of there as quickly as I could and he didn't hurt me." She shrugged one shoulder. "Just gave me the creeps."

"I don't want you going back there alone," Rascal said, his voice low and gravelly. "Please promise you'll take me with you."

Wynona smiled. "I promise."

He nodded and the fur receded. "Thank you."

Violet huffed and chattered for a moment, her remarks aimed toward Rascal. He paused and listened before nodding.

"You're right. She does need control."

Wynona rolled her eyes. "I did just fine, thank you very much," she argued.

"Uh...guys?"

Both of them looked at Daemon.

He spread his hands to the side. "I don't speak mouse. Care to translate?"

Wynona laughed softly. "Sorry. Violet was telling Rascal about how my magic surfaced when I felt threatened at the theatre. But I got it back down without blowing anything up."

"This time," Rascal admonished. "What happens when you can't get it to calm down? What happens when you don't have a black hole around to help?"

Wynona picked at the tablecloth. "I know I need to practice and get things under control, but getting Prim out of jail is my first priority at the moment."

Rascal slapped the table. "I understand that, but you aren't any help to her if you end up behind bars yourself because you hurt someone."

Wynona sighed. "I know."

Rascal massaged the back of her neck. "Hey...don't worry. We'll get this all taken care of, okay? Everything's going to be just fine."

The tears that pricked Wynona's eyes couldn't be helped. She was so spent at the moment and yet so worried. She was desperate to help her friend, but struggling with her own problems as well, and it was starting to feel overwhelming. She sniffed and dried her eyes on a napkin. "I know," she responded. "I'm sorry. I'm not sure why I'm such a watering pot."

Rascal scooted back his chair and pulled her onto his lap. "I've got ya," he said, his voice low and soothing. He pressed her head onto his shoulder. "Just relax for a few minutes, huh? It's going to be fine."

With his large arms around her and his voice rumbling through her, Wynona let out a long breath and fully relaxed into his hold. She had a fleeting thought that she could do this forever. Being close to the wolf shifter felt so good...so right.

He made her feel protected and safe, as well as delicate and precious. It was as if all was right with the world and together they could solve any problem that came their way. All of those were new feelings for Wynona, something she had never experienced while growing up. In fact, her family had gone out of their way to make sure she knew just how unwanted and worthless she was.

"Feeling better?" he whispered.

She nodded and went to sit up, but Rascal's hold tightened.

"No hurry," he said. "I've got all evening. Might as well make use of it."

The front door closed and Wynona pushed her way upright. "Sorry," she said with a grin. "I think we scared off Daemon."

Rascal chuckled, the sound lovely and deep. "If he can't handle a little PDA, then he doesn't belong on the police force."

She made a face. "What does one have to do with the other?"

Rascal shrugged and grinned. "I don't know, but it sounded good."

Wynona playfully slapped his chest. "You shouldn't tease him like that."

"And you shouldn't tease me like that," Rascal argued back.

"I'm not teasing you."

"Yes, you are. You're sitting right on my lap and you haven't kissed me yet." He shook his head and tsked his tongue. "What's a wolf to think?"

"That kissing was far from my mind when I was worried about my friend," Wynona shot back.

Rascal dropped his head back and groaned. "That wasn't fair. I have no argument for that."

Wynona laughed and pulled his head back. She leaned in and gave him a soft kiss. "Thank you for comforting me."

"Thank you for going to the theatre," he whispered, his eyes on her mouth. "I think we're onto something here with Rujins."

Wynona nodded. "I agree. He certainly sounds like a good suspect."

Rascal's warm hand cupped the side of her head and slowly started to pull her in. "But we can't do anything about it at this time of night," he said softly. "So perhaps we should do something better with our time."

Wynona melted against him as her handsome shifter kissed her. There were still plenty of things to worry about and she probably should plan her next move in helping free Prim, but right now Wynona couldn't concentrate enough to do anything but kiss Rascal back.

A scampering noise let her know even Violet was leaving the two of them alone and Wynona couldn't quite find it within herself to be upset about that. She got so little time with him and the more she got to know him, the more Wynona wanted.

So instead of worrying about everything life was throwing at her, she gave herself tonight. Tonight to let her mind and body rest, tonight to recover from the load she was carrying and tonight to enjoy the attentions of the man she was dating. Tomorrow would come soon enough and by then...she'd be ready.

CHAPTER 12

The next morning brought grey skies that matched Wynona's mood. Rascal had gotten a call last night right before he went home that the search warrant had come through and they would be meeting at Prim's greenhouse in the morning.

An unspoken invitation had been extended at the door and Wynona had nodded in assurance that she would be there. There was a small part of her that had debated rushing over in the middle of the night to hide any daffodils that might be in the building. But even for her best friend, Wynona couldn't quite bring herself to do such a thing.

"She's innocent," she reminded herself as she started her scooter. "The truth will out." The words were far from reassuring and Wynona's stomach churned as she made the drive over.

Violet held onto the side of her basket peering over the edge as they drove, her purple fur blowing in the breeze.

The sight normally made Wynona smile, but not today. She had a sinking feeling that nothing good would come from the search. Prim was innocent, but Wynona knew it wouldn't look that way, and she had yet to figure out how to find the real killer.

Several police cars were already parked in the back of the greenhouse when Wynona arrived. The addition that Prim had recently added made the place look massive and Wynona knew it felt just as big inside. She was so proud of her friend for wanting to expand, but devastated the mortgage was what had led to this fiasco in the first place.

A tall, dark head started walking her way and Wynona hooked her helmet onto the scooter handles.

"Good morning," Rascal said with a sad smile.

Wynona gave him one back. "Have you gone in yet?"

He shook his head. "No. Chief isn't here." As if his words were a premonition, one last squad car pulled up behind Wynona.

"I should have known," Chief Ligurio grumbled as he stepped out from behind the wheel. He shook his head. "Stay out of our way, Le Doux. You're not thinking straight in this case."

Wynona gave a curt nod, but refused to say anything more. She knew why he wanted her to stand back, but she couldn't promise she wouldn't interfere. Someone was setting Prim up and Wynona was going to figure out who. Being here today would let Wynona know exactly what evidence the DA would be using, and hopefully give Wynona some ideas on what to do next in her evidence search.

They crowded around the back door and Chief Ligurio took a key from his pocket, glancing at Wynona. "Ms. Meadows has voluntarily agreed to let us search."

Rascal's hand went to Wynona's back, his warmth giving her strength.

She was grateful the police wouldn't have to jimmy the door in order to get in. "Do you mind if I water the plants while we're here?"

Chief Ligurio hesitated, then nodded. "Let us search first, then you can do what you need to."

"Thank you," Wynona said softly. She walked beside Rascal as they went inside, the wet heat slapping her in the face. Her emotions fell even farther when she looked around the wide space. The plants had been watered only a couple days before, but there wasn't a piece of greenery in the house that was still standing. Every single leaf, flower and piece of foliage was wilted and limp, hanging out of their pots. Wynona's hands went to her mouth. "Poor Prim."

Rascal whistled low under his breath. "I'm guessing this isn't how it usually looks."

Her head shook slowly. "It's normally a wonderland. They must miss her."

"The idea of plants missing people is still weird." Rascal scratched behind his ear.

Violet emerged from Wynona's pocket and chattered.

"Huh." He pursed his lips. "I hadn't thought of that."

"What did she say?" Wynona asked.

Rascal raised his eyebrows. "You didn't understand her?"

She made a face. "I'm getting better at it, but sometimes it's still difficult."

He nodded. "She just said that plants are more sentient then we give them credit for. Even humans say that they respond to music, so why not an earth fairy?"

Wynona lifted Violet out of her pocket and set her on her shoulder. "Makes sense. Prim once told me that flowers are excellent sources of information."

"Maybe I need to hire Prim for my investigations unit," Rascal teased. "After she gets exonerated, of course."

"Of course." Wynona walked in farther and picked up a watering can. The police were milling around, checking all the tables, plants and bookshelves. Every shovel and bag of soil was inspected and Wynona found herself wanting to tell them to leave it all alone, but she held her tongue.

Chief Ligurio was right. She was too close to this case.

"Chief!"

All the heads turned toward the call. Wynona looked worriedly at Rascal, who tilted his head toward the officer and took Wynona's hand to lead her there.

The officer held a pot with a half dead flower inside. The bright yellow color was fading, but there was no mistaking what flower it was.

"There are another dozen pots over there." The officer shifted his body to aim toward the far table.

Chief Ligurio looked at Wynona. "You know what this means."

She bit the inside of her cheek to keep from crying. "Yes."

"We'll have to put this in the evidence file."

Wynona wrung her hands together. "Can't you wait just a little longer? Give me more time!"

"Chief!" Another officer rushed up, a book waving through the air. He passed it through the crowd of people to his boss.

The vampire turned it over and read the title. "Plants and Their Poisons."

Wynona's eyes widened.

Chief Ligurio sighed. "I think we've found all we need, crew. Let's go back."

"But she's innocent!" Wynona cried. Purple sparkles began to flash in her periphery and Wynona knew she was dangerously close to losing it. She had felt it from the moment she woke up this morning that this would not be a good trip. That she would come away from the greenhouse farther from their goal than ever.

"Wy," Rascal warned.

"Ms. Le Doux." Officer Skymaw said, calmly stepping up next to her. "Good to see you today."

Wynona slumped against Rascal's shoulder. She could physically feel the magic draining from her system as Daemon helped her keep it under control. "You too, Officer Skymaw," she said, keeping it formal since they were in front of a crowd.

"Let's go," Chief Ligurio said in a loud tone. He hesitated as the officers all started to leave. "I truly am sorry, Wynona. I know this isn't what you wanted to have happen."

"She's innocent," Wynona said in as calm a tone as she could manage. "And I'll prove it."

The chief's face was full of pity, but he nodded and turned to leave.

Rascal and Daemon waited until everyone was gone before turning to Wynona. "We need to get this figured out now," Rascal stated bluntly. "Another slip-up like that and the chief will know everything."

Wynona rubbed her aching forehead. "I know. I'm sorry." She looked up at Rascal with tear-filled eyes. "He's right though. I'm too close to this. I felt like this was a bad idea all morning, and there was nothing I could do to stop it."

"You're still positive that she's innocent?"

Wynona spun to look at Daemon, shocked he would even ask. "Yes!"

He rubbed the back of his neck and nodded. "Okay. But the Deputy Chief is right. Your magic needs to be under control or this whole thing is going to blow up in our faces."

Violet whimpered.

"I know," Wynona responded to them both. "But what do I do? I've read about magic, I've seen it done, but I've never actually channeled it myself." Her knuckles began to ache from her tight hold. "It's not like I had magic and then lost it, I've never experienced it at all."

Daemon made a face. "I don't use magic, I absorb it. So I'm not sure I'm much help." He turned to Rascal.

Rascal raised his hands. "I don't really have magic, other than being able to shift."

"That's closer than what I do," Daemon argued.

"Okay, just stop." Wynona shook her head and put her hands on her hips. "If little kids can do this, I should be able to...right?"

Rascal looked warily at Daemon, before nodding. "Absolutely."

She gave him a mock glare. "Thanks for the confidence."

His grin was completely unrepentant.

"Okay." Wynona rubbed her hands together. "Let's start with something small."

"Bring me that hand shovel." Rascal pointed to the small instrument on a table about three feet away.

"Good idea." She glanced at Daemon. "You ready to interfere if I lose it?"

He shrugged. "Sure."

"Okay." Wynona took a deep breath. This should be easy. She was a full grown adult, picking up an object was child's play. She stared at the shovel.

It didn't move.

Wynona's eyebrows pulled together and her stare turned into more of a glare. "Come on," she whispered, shouting in her mind for the shovel to move.

There wasn't the slightest rustle.

"Usually your magic comes out when you're emotional," Rascal said, coughing over the last word.

"If you suggest kissing her as a way to make the shovel move, I'm out of here," Daemon said wryly.

Rascal laughed. "I hadn't thought of that, but it's a good idea."

Wynona rolled her eyes. "Rascal. This is serious." She swung an arm toward the table. "My sister could move that thing without thinking about it. Why can't I?"

"DUCK!"

A very large body crashed into Wynona and took her to the ground. A loud crash sounded just as she hit the floor, but it didn't come from Wynona. "Oof!" The air rushed from her lungs and for a few precious seconds, Wynona couldn't breathe at all.

"Sorry, sorry, I'm so sorry," Rascal gushed, immediately getting up on his knees and hovering over her. "Where did I hurt you? Did I break anything?"

Wynona shook her head. Her ribs were slightly sore, but it was the fact that she couldn't suck in oxygen that was the real problem. She could feel her face getting red.

"Wy! Breathe!" Rascal put his hands on either side of her face and Wynona's lungs released.

She sucked in a massive gulp of air and choked as it tried to settle in her tight chest. "I'm okay," she wheezed. She took a few more breaths as Rascal continued to panic over her. "I'm okay."

Slowly, he stood up and helped her to her feet. After making sure she was steady, Rascal promptly pulled her into his chest. "I changed my mind. No more magic. We got along just fine without it before. We can keep on that way."

Wynona was thoroughly enjoying his embrace, but she wasn't quite sure what had set him off. "Rascal," she crooned, rubbing his back. "I don't understand what happened." She pushed back and searched his face. "Why did you tackle me?"

A throat cleared and Wynona looked over to see Daemon tilting his head toward the wall. Looking over, Wynona gasped. Several pots were broken, with dirt lying everywhere and a table full of tools mixed into the mess. Her hand shook as it came up to cover her mouth. "Did I do that?" she asked, her voice hoarse.

Rascal nodded.

"Are you sure?" She turned to Daemon this time and he looked just as worried as Rascal.

"You cleared the whole table."

Wynona looked over to see the officer was correct. She had not only moved the shovel, but she had brought every item on the table straight toward them, and apparently at a fast enough speed to break through thick ceramic and terra cotta.

She looked back at Rascal. "Thank you."

He pulled her back under his chin, not saying anything with words, but his body language spoke volumes.

"Violet!" Wynona jerked back, her hand automatically going to her shoulder. "What happened to Violet?"

Rascal looked stricken. "I was so worried about getting you out of the way of the tools that I didn't even stop to think..." He hand went through his hair, making it stand on end. "Vi?" he called, starting to walk around the space. "Vi, are you okay?"

Wynona dropped onto all fours and started searching the area. "Violet? Please answer me!"

Even Daemon began walking around, though he didn't call out the mouse's name.

Several heart stopping seconds went by before squeaking could be heard coming from a plant several feet away.

Wynona paused to listen.

Soon a pink nose, followed by a purple head emerged, sending a shock of relief through Wynona's system.

"Violet," she breathed, scrambling over and picking up the mouse, cuddling the creature to her chest. "Are you alright?"

Violet grumbled, but nodded her affirmation. When Rascal came over, however, Violet pushed away from Wynona and stood on her hind legs. Her paws went to her hips and she gave a scolding that lasted a full two minutes.

Rascal squatted down and held out his hand, waiting patiently while Violet grudgingly came over. "I'm sorry, Vi. I didn't mean it." His eyes darted to Wynona, then back. "I was trying to keep her safe."

Wynona tried to keep up with their conversation, but it moved too quickly and her head felt fuzzy and drained.

"I promise." Rascal handed the mouse back and helped Wynona to her feet.

"Everything okay now?" Daemon asked.

"We came to an understanding," Rascal explained, then blew out a breath. "But I definitely think we're going to need more practice and a greenhouse with tons of breakable objects isn't the place to do it."

Wynona nodded wearily. She was going to have to brew herself a cup of matcha when she got back. All she wanted was a nap, but she still had a full day of work ahead. "Truer words have never been spoken," she muttered.

"So what do we do next?" Daemon asked as they all headed outside, locking the door behind them.

"I think we need to go back to the theatre," Wynona offered. "That'll give you both a chance to speak with Mr. Rujins, and I never got much of a chance to poke around the theatre itself. There has to be something there that we missed."

"It's a plan." Rascal helped her strap on her helmet and got her seated on her Vespa. "You sure you're okay to drive?"

Wynona smiled. "Yeah. I'm just tired, but the drive will help me clear my head." She turned over the engine. "Seven?"

Rascal tweaked her nose. "On the dot." He stepped back to give her room to go, and winked.

Wynona smiled, made sure Violet was settled in her basket and then pressed the gas. It was going to be a long day.

CHAPTER 13

Rascal and Daemon were waiting for her when Wynona pulled up to the theatre that night. Her body was bouncing on adrenaline and green tea while her mind was screaming for rest. All day she smiled and served tea and treats while inside she was mourning for her friend.

Chief Ligurio was creating an evidence file against Prim. That meant that the time to clear the fairy's name was now or never. The DA would also be gathering evidence and if Wynona didn't have a break through soon, she was going to have to watch Prim be convicted of murder.

"Hi," she said breathlessly, as she rushed to meet the men. "Thanks for waiting for me."

"Where's Violet?" Daemon asked, a small frown on his face.

Wynona couldn't stop the small laugh. "She grows on you, doesn't she?"

He rubbed the back of his neck. "She's pretty spunky for something smaller than a cookie."

The enjoyment of his bashfulness helped Wynona relax just a touch, but she forced herself to not lose focus. "I asked her to stay behind tonight. I can't seem to get rid of the feeling that we're missing something." She spread her hands to the side. "But I'm not sure where. So Violet's job was to search through my books to see what I'm forgetting."

Daemon's eyebrows shot up. "She can read?"

"As well as I can," Wynona responded. "I'll admit I have no idea how she learned, but that mouse is pretty amazing." She glanced at Rascal, who looked ready to laugh. "What?"

He leaned into her ear. "I think you'll find that Violet can do anything you can do."

Wynona frowned and leaned back. "What?"

He shook his head. "We'll talk about it later." Rascal looked over at his officer. "We're off the clock, but I've found that staying professional helps people be more forthcoming in what they know."

Daemon nodded. "Makes sense." He took a deep breath. "This place gives me the creeps."

Rascal chuckled. "Scared, Skymaw?"

He shook his head. "No. Just have never understood why people want to pretend to be something else."

"Not all of us like who we are," Wynona said before she could think about the words.

Rascal jerked his head toward her and his eyes flashed a brilliant gold. "Maybe we need to talk about more than just Violet," he mused, his tone slightly growly as if his wolf was close to the surface.

She took his hand and gave him a sad smile. "Sorry. I shouldn't have said that."

Rascal tugged her over and left a sweet kiss on her cheek. "I wouldn't change you for anything."

"Aaaaand, that's our cue to go inside," Daemon said dryly, obviously done with the show of affection.

Rascal's smirk was entirely too conceited, but Wynona let it slide. She wasn't about to get between two males intent on driving each other crazy.

The noise coming from inside the theatre was loud, even in the parking lot. It was obvious they had a performance going tonight and Wynona wasn't thrilled with the idea of squeezing her way through the crowd, but she was willing to do just about anything in order to help prove Prim's innocence.

"There's a door around back," Wynona announced, leading the men that way. "It's probably better than forcing our way through the front."

"True enough," Rascal mumbled. He knocked hard on the metal door. It took a few moments, but eventually the same security guard Wynona met the other day pushed it open.

"Can I help you?" he growled

Rascal held out his wallet with his badge in it. "Deputy Chief Strongclaw," he said in his serious tone, not the least bit put off by the man's grumpiness. "We need to look around the area."

The security guard folded his arms over his chest, letting the door rest against his hip. "The police already looked," he said snidely, then tilted his head toward Wynona. "And your little play thing snooped around on her own. Maybe she should just tell you what she saw."

Wynona's eyes almost bugged out of her head. The man hadn't treated her like this at all when she'd been here by herself. What in the world would cause him to be so stubborn and rude tonight?

"Last chance," Rascal said congenially, though even an idiot could hear the steel in his tone.

Wynona held her breath when the security guard glared. She was not interested in viewing a fight tonight.

"Two predators," Daemon whispered in her ear.

Wynona jerked a little, not knowing he was so close. She glanced over her shoulder and Officer Skymaw gave her a look. When Wynona came back to the two men, she could see exactly what he'd been talking about. She wasn't sure what kind of shifter the security guard was, but he was extra bulky, several pounds heavier than Rascal.

Rascal's eyes glowed. "Stand down," he growled.

The security guard's lip started to curl before he pulled himself back under control. He shook his head hard as if clearing something, then stepped backward on stiff legs. "Sorry, Deputy Chief," he grunted. "It's been a long week."

Rascal nodded curtly and led Wynona inside. Daemon followed behind.

A shiver ran down Wynona's spine as they walked into the darkened interior of the theatre.

Rascal squeezed her hand. "You okay?"

She nodded, warily watching the security guard as he disappeared down the hallway. "Do you have to do that kind of thing often?"

Rascal turned to look at the other shifter, then shrugged. "Sometimes." He faced Wynona, his eyes still glowing slightly from the encounter. "When two apex predators meet up, it doesn't always go smoothly."

"Do you know what he is?"

Rascal grinned. "A grizzly."

Wynona gasped. "You can't be serious."

His eyebrows shot up. "Why wouldn't I be serious? What did you think he was?"

She rubbed her forehead. "I guess that explains his size," she muttered.

Rascal chuckled and squeezed her hand again. "Come on. Let's look around."

"Do you want to split up?" Daemon asked as they maneuvered their way down the narrow hallway.

Rascal hesitated, then shook his head. "No. I think we're better...and safer...together."

Daemon nodded. "Alright. Where to first?"

"That's Mrs. Tuall's dressing room," Wynona pointed out.

"Good a place as any," Rascal responded. He led the way and knocked on the door. When no one answered, Wynona realized Brell was probably performing.

"We should check the stage," she said, pointing farther down the hall.

Rascal nodded his understanding. "Let's hit a few more doors on the way."

The next ten minutes were spent trying dressing room doors, but no one seemed to be in.

"Are they all performing?" Wynona asked in exasperation. "I thought Mrs. Tuall did her thing alone."

"She does," Daemon supplied. When Wynona and Rascal looked his way, he scratched his chin as if uncomfortable. "I mean...she sings during her act, and it's a solo thing. But if this is anything like the one I saw before, there are other characters mingling with the crowd in their costumes."

Wynona rubbed her forehead. "This is so weird. If they're interested in vampires, why don't they just hire a vampire?"

"It's just like celebrity impersonators in the human world," Rascal stated as he led them down the hall. "The real thing isn't always available. And even here we get groups that are obsessed with certain supernaturals." He smirked. "Did you know there are shifter fan clubs?"

"You've got to be kidding," Wynona said, her jaw dropping. "That can't really be a thing."

He nodded. "With Mrs. Tuall doing the vampire thing, I'm guessing they get fangirls as well."

Wynona pinched her lips. She definitely did *not* like the idea of Rascal having a fan club. Their relationship was still new, but she liked him...a lot...and Wynona wasn't sure she was up to competing with a bunch of other women who wanted his attention.

"Don't worry," Rascal whispered low in her ear. "I've never been one to enjoy the limelight."

She huffed, but smiled. Somehow he just always seemed to know what she needed to hear.

Sultry singing could be heard as they got closer to the stage area and Wynona's eyes widened. Now she understood. Even without seeing Mrs. Tuall in all her glory, the sound of her voice was mesmerizing.

It felt as if her voice were a living, tangible thing, floating through the air and wrapping around Wynona's head. She found her footsteps speeding up, as if she couldn't wait to see the siren in action.

"Wynona," Rascal said, tugging her back. "We need to be quiet." He put a finger to his lips and Wynona paused.

She hadn't realized she wasn't being quiet, but as she'd sped up, her footsteps had become clearly audible, and that probably wasn't proper manners backstage during a performance.

She grimaced. "Sorry," she whispered. She shook her head. "Something's a little...off."

He nodded and they stepped up behind the front curtain. Wynona glanced over her shoulder for Daemon, but he was nowhere to be found. She tugged on Rascal's sleeve.

"Where's Daemon?" she mouthed.

Rascal rolled his eyes and pointed across the stage. Brell stood in the middle, dressed in a slinky, black sequined dress that hugged every perfect curve. Her hips swung from side to side and her red lips were curled up at the corners as she sang, while a flash of her fake extra long canines happened every few seconds. They were impressively realistic looking. Wynona had to give the costume credit.

The audience was amazingly quiet, completely enthralled by the siren's song. Hundreds of eyes were glued to the stage. Even as other actors obviously meandered through them, the patrons paid no attention to anyone but Brell.

But it wasn't until Wynona looked past Brell that she spotted Daemon. He was standing at the edge of the curtain line on the other side of the stage. His black eyes were wide and fixated and his hands were clenched into fists. He appeared to be straining, but Wynona couldn't see anything that was holding him back. "Why's he so mad?" she whispered.

"He's stopping his own magic," Rascal said softly in her ear. "He can't disrupt her performance, so he's having to keep from sucking hers in."

Wynona nodded. It didn't look like a very pleasant job. Her eyes roamed the crowd again. "You know, I've wondered why no one heard Madam Ureo during the fight," Wynona mused. "Even though the poison is what killed her, there was enough blood with the wand that she had to have been alive when she was stabbed."

Rascal's eyes glowed slightly as he looked at her. "You're right. And there's no way the madam would have been quiet when that was thrust into her chest. In fact, harpies aren't known for being quiet at all. She more than likely made quite a racket."

Wynona nodded, then thrust her chin at the crowd. "Yeah, but watching them all now, it makes more sense. Her siren song has them all completely bewitched. They wouldn't have heard a thing."

Rascal rubbed his chin. "Good point."

"What are you doing here?"

The voice was, unfortunately, familiar as Wynona turned around. "Hello, Mr. Truall," she said as pleasantly as she could. Her eyes went to the hunched, older creature behind Fable. "And Mr. Rujins." Wynona found herself more grateful than ever that she hadn't come alone tonight. Neither of these men were pleasant as individuals, so to have to deal with them all at the same time? No, thank you.

"Ms. Le Doux," Fable snapped. His eyes darted to Rascal. "And who are you?"

Wynona could feel Rascal puffing out his chest from behind her and she knew he would be putting on his policeman face. "Deputy Chief Strongclaw." His eyes drifted, then narrowed at the manager. "Rujins."

A crooked smile, revealing those dirty, cracked teeth spread across the troll's face. "Hugo...how nice to see you again."

"I wish the feeling was mutual," Rascal said in a dark tone.

Mr. Rujins chuckled, but the sound was like rocks grinding together and Wynona had to fight a wince. "Still poking your nose into other people's business, I see."

Rascal's smile was anything but pleasant. His teeth were sharper than normal and gleamed in the low backstage lights. "It's my job," he said with careful enunciation. "Perhaps if you were on the correct side of the law, you might find that I wasn't bothering you so much."

"Uh, uh, uh," Mr. Rujins said in a provoking way. "I was acquitted, remember?"

Rascal had no response for that, but Wynona felt like she was starting to get a clearer picture of the situation. The history between these two wasn't pretty. But right now was not the right time for grandstanding. "Mr. Rujins," she said, stepping between the men. "Would you please be kind enough to open Madam Ureo's office? I'd like to have a look around."

Those yellow eyes narrowed while Mr. Tuall scoffed. "Why would he need to do that? You're not a police officer."

"No, but I am," Rascal said with that same dark smile. "And she's with me."

Mr. Rujins spread his hands wide. "I have nothing to hide, Deputy Chief. I'm more than happy to open the office." He turned and began shuffling away. Wynona eyed Mr. Tuall, who looked less than pleased with the outcome, and did her best to keep her distance as she walked past him. Rascal's massive presence behind her helped her feel safer about poking around. She should have brought him in the first place.

"I'd like to get this place cleaned as soon as possible," Mr. Rujins said, pushing open the door and stuffing the keys back in his pocket. "As soon as you officers give me the clear, of course."

"Thank you," Wynona murmured as she stepped inside.

"I'd like to see your accounting books," Rascal said, stopping in the doorway to speak to their guide.

Wynona turned to see what Mr. Rujins would say. She knew something was up with the books, but would he admit it?

Mr. Rujins's smile tightened, but he didn't so much as flinch. "I'm afraid you're going to need a warrant for those," he said. He tilted his head. "I'm already letting you poke around without complaint, though we both know you're not here in your official capacity. If you want to dig deeper, I suggest you go through the proper channels." He glanced toward Wynona. "Ms. Le Doux." Then without another word, the troll was gone.

Rascal growled low, but stepped inside and closed the door.

"We're not going to get the warrant, are we?"

Rascal pushed a hand through his hair. "It won't be easy, since they think they already have their killer." His eyes were bright when he looked up at Wynona. "But we'll give it a try."

CHAPTER 14

"Do you know if the office is untouched?" Wynona asked as soon as they were alone. The office was fairly bare and it made her wonder if the police had taken most of the room in for evidence.

"Other than the office chair, it should be untouched," Rascal confirmed. "Nothing else had blood on it," he explained.

Wynona nodded and felt a small shiver race up her spine. She might have a weird curiosity that helped her solve crimes, but that didn't mean she enjoyed blood and gore. Slowly, she began to wander through the office. "Nothing really looks out of place," she murmured. "I'm guessing that means there was no struggle."

Rascal nodded. "I think you're right," he said with a huff. "Which means Madam Ureo more than likely took down the daffodil unknowingly." He pushed a hand through his hair. "But how? Could it have been in a tea?"

Wynona nodded. "Sure. You can make almost anything into a tea. But I can't imagine that daffodil tea would taste good." She wrinkled her nose. "In fact, it would have been fairly bitter." She put her hands on her hips. "Which means it was probably mixed with something else." Wynona racked her brain for everything she knew about tea. "I don't remember daffodils specifically," she muttered, "but if it was by itself, I can't imagine anyone drinking enough to kill them, and if it was mixed with something else, it would have been hard to have enough in there and still hide the taste."

Rascal growled low. "So what does that mean? The daffodil couldn't have killed her?"

Wynona shook her head. "No, it could have. I don't doubt the coroner's right, I'm just unsure as to how the killer could have gotten enough in Madam Ureo to do the job." She waved her arms around. "If it had been forced down the harpy's throat, I think this place would have been a massive mess."

"I agree," Rascal grumbled. He sighed, his chest rising and falling with the motion. "What do you think of Mr. Tuall?" he asked as he started reading titles on the bookcase.

Wynona wandered around to the backside of the desk. She could see the imprints on the carpet from the office chair that had obviously been there a long time. "I think he's very protective," Wynona responded.

"Protective enough to kill?"

She shrugged. "I'm not sure. The only motive I can think of would be to kill in order to break the contract." Wynona glanced up at Rascal, who was looking at her. "And obviously that didn't work. If Mr. Tuall was guilty, I can't see him being chummy with Mr. Rujins. Plus, it seems to me there would be better ways of getting out of something like that."

Rascal nodded. "Agreed, but I'm not ready to take him off my list." Rascal went back to the shelves. "He might be getting chummy simply so he can get close enough to kill again. Or because he's hoping to convince Mr. Rujins to let them go, even though Madam Ureo refused to."

"True," Wynona said distractedly. Her eyes were stuck on Madam Ureo's desk. Maybe there was something there, a schedule or planner that would help them know who might have been in the harpy's office at the time of the murder. The desk itself was a mess. Papers were strewn everywhere in a haphazard fashion, leading Wynona to believe that Madam Ureo wasn't the most organized of individuals. Which also made it less likely the woman would have kept a planner.

She picked through the papers carefully, trying to keep an eye out for anything that might help them in the case. "Ah-ha."

"What?" Rascal came her way.

"Her planner," Wynona said, pulling the leatherbound book out of the disarray. "With as messy as she is, I thought for sure she wouldn't have one, but here it is!" Wynona beamed at Rascal, who smiled back at her.

"Are you going to read it, or just gloat about your victory?" he teased.

Wynona made a face at him, then opened the book, flipping until she found the date of the woman's death. "Huh."

Rascal walked around and looked over her shoulder.

"There's nothing here." Wynona's shoulders slumped. "Drat. I was sure we'd find something helpful."

"Probably why the team left it," Rascal pointed out. He took the book and flipped through a few more pages. "In fact, she really has very little in here. For a manager of a large acting troupe, the madam didn't meet with a lot of people."

"Or at least her meetings weren't planned in advance." Wynona tapped her bottom lip. "If we could get our hands on those financial records, we might be able to see something more."

Rascal nodded. "Agreed. I'll try, but like I said, Chief thinks he's got his man...uh, woman."

A small smile cracked Wynona's worried face. "I suppose you could play it that the records might be evidence against Prim."

Rascal stilled. "Are you willing to risk that? What if they *do* show something against Prim? Just like the greenhouse?"

Wynona waved a hand in the air. "We were expecting the greenhouse. Prim said herself that she had daffodils." Wynona scrunched her nose. "Although, I wasn't expecting the book." She chewed her lip. "While I know Prim is innocent, the book and the plant combined certainly don't look very good."

Rascal grunted his agreement. He dropped the planner back on the desk. "I've got nothing," he said.

Wynona took a deep breath. "We can't give up yet. There *has* to be something here." She dropped to her knees. "Any chance there could be a hidden drawer or something?"

Rascal squatted down beside her. "There's always a chance. But if there was one, I'm guessing it contained all the finances which you said are now in Rujins's office."

Wynona scrunched her neck and ducked under the desk. "Why don't you call Chief Ligurio and see if you can convince him to get working on that warrant?" She paused. "The judge is back in town, right?"

Rascal nodded and grabbed his cell phone out of his back pocket. "Yes, and I'll see what I can do." He stood and walked away, the sound of ringing coming from the tiny speaker.

Wynona tuned out his chatting with the chief as she inspected the desk. She brushed her fingers over every nook and cranny, but she couldn't find anything that appeared like a secret button or even a broken piece of wood. The desk appeared to be in excellent shape. "Unlike the rest of the theatre," Wynona muttered to herself.

"What was that?" Rascal asked, coming back around to her.

Wynona stood and brushed herself off. "Nothing. Just complaining to myself. What did the chief say?"

"He'll think about it." Rascal frowned. "I'll bring it up again tomorrow. I think I interrupted his dinner and he wasn't exactly happy with me."

Wynona made a face. "Sorry."

"It happens." Rascal sighed and looked around the room once more. "Anything else you want to check out before we leave?"

"There you are," Daemon gushed as he rushed into the room. He closed the door behind him. His face flushed and he was sweating heavily.

"Daemon." Wynona gasped. "What in the world happened to you?"

He wiped his forehead on the back of his hand. "That woman is going to be the death of me," he said in a hoarse tone.

Wynona looked at Rascal, who appeared just as lost as her. "What woman?"

"The vampire, siren..." Daemon shook his head. "Whatever the heck she is."

"Mrs. Tuall?" Wynona asked in shock.

"The very one."

Wynona walked around the desk and slowly approached. "What did she do to you?"

Daemon swallowed hard and wiped his face again. "Never mind. It doesn't matter."

"It absolutely does matter," Wynona said sternly. "You look like you're about to be sick." A light bulb went off in her head. "Is this about you having to keep from taking in her magic?"

Daemon frowned. "What?"

"Rascal said it's hard for you to keep your own magic at bay," Wynona explained. "That you have to stop yours in order to let hers keep going?"

"Oh, that." Daemon gave her a couple of jerky nods. "Yeah, that's not always pleasant."

When he didn't say more, Wynona opened her mouth to ask another question, but Rascal grabbed her hand. She looked over at him and he shook his head. She gave him a pleading look and Rascal shook his head again. Finally, Wynona huffed and let the subject drop. It was clear that Daemon didn't want to talk about it, but Wynona was worried for him and she still didn't understand what had happened in the first place. "Well..." She clapped her hands together. "I don't know about you, but I think maybe we should head back to the tea shop and I'll make you two something to ease the stress."

"Good idea," Rascal said quickly. With his hand on her lower back, Rascal ushered Wynona into the hall and then out to the street. The bear shifter security guard didn't appear as they left and Wynona was grateful to miss another predator to predator encounter.

"Meet you at the tea shop," Rascal said, leaving a quick kiss on her cheek.

Wynona smiled at the gesture, loving how affectionate the wolf shifter was. Her smile lasted the whole way back to the shop, where Violet was waiting impatiently for them all to arrive. "What are you doing here?" Wynona asked. "I thought you were at the house?"

Violet shook her head.

"Did you find anything?"

Another shake of her head.

Wynona deflated. "Neither did we."

Violet's response was almost exactly the same at Wynona's.

Wynona bent down and held out her hand, then stood when Violet jumped up. She headed to the kitchen to start a kettle. "We're missing something, Vi. I can feel it."

Violet chittered thoughtfully.

"I don't know," Wynona responded. "I didn't see anything at Madam Ureo's office at all." She snorted. "I even got down on the ground and searched for a hidden drawer."

Violet responded in an excited tone.

"No. I didn't see anything. Not so much as a splinter out of place." Wynona set the kettle down and then hurried back out to the front room when she heard the men entering. "Have a seat," she said. "I'm heating up the water." Wynona waited until they were sitting. "Any requests?"

"I'll let you choose," Rascal said with a wink.

Wynona smiled at him. "Alright. Daemon?"

He waved her off as if he didn't want any, but Wynona could see better. The feeling of concentration she always got when trying to read a person's tea needs was stronger than ever. Instead of agreeing, she narrowed her eyes and stared. "Valerian root, lemon balm and passionflower," she murmured. Her eyes automatically went to Rascal. "St. John's wort, rosemary and gotu kola." Spinning on her heel, Wynona marched back into the kitchen and fixed the infusers she needed. These men needed to rest and a boost of morale and she was going to help any way she could.

"Thanks," Rascal said with a tired smile as he took the teacup from her.

"Daemon." Wynona held out the other cup. "I know you said you didn't want any, but I really think this will help."

He gave her a crooked grin and nodded. "Thanks." He set the cup in front of him and took a whiff. "Whoa. That's strong."

"It should be," Wynona said, sitting next to Rascal. "But I promise it'll help."

Daemon gave her a look. "Is this part of your witch magic?"

Wynona started to say no, then paused. "Actually...I don't know. I've always been able to look at people and know just what tea would help them best, but I had always thought it was because Granny taught me so extensively about teas and herbs." Wynona shrugged. "Grandma Saffron was an earth witch. Her specialty was in reading tea leaves."

"And did you inherit that ability?"

Her mind went back to the few times she had read the dregs in a teacup. Each time had been a frightening experience and one Wynona wasn't eager to repeat. Reading the leaves would be fine, but the onslaught of uncontrollable magic was worrisome. "I might have," Wynona said slowly. "I'm not sure what I inherited since I haven't been able to really figure out my magical abilities, or even why they're suddenly appearing. My family said my curse was for life, so I'm brand new to everything."

Daemon nodded then took a sip. He swallowed and his eyes fluttered closed before popping back open. "I can taste it," he said hoarsely.

"What? The lemon balm? Did I use too much?"

Daemon shook his head. "No. The magic."

Wynona stilled, only taking a deep breath when Rascal's large warm hand landed on her back. "You can *taste* the magic?"

Daemon nodded. "It comes with being a black hole," he explained. "Just as I can tell when it's being used so I know when to absorb it, I can taste it in foods and drinks." He took another sip and swished it around before swallowing. "Yours tastes like...sweet lavender."

Rascal grinned. "Since it's purple, that makes sense."

Daemon made a considering face. "Maybe...but the point is...it's sweet, which is good and lavender is relaxing. Your magic is strong, but so far hasn't been used for anything nefarious."

"That's quite a gift," Wynona said softly, completely shocked at what she was hearing.

"Are you saying if she did use it for something...self serving, the taste would change?" Rascal clarified.

Daemon nodded. "Yeah." He took another long drink. "But anyway..." He brushed away the subject. "This is really good and I already feel better." His black eyes shone. "Thank you."

"You're welcome," Wynona responded automatically. She fell back in her seat, feeling completely drained. How was she going to handle all this? Her best friend framed for murder, her magic seeping out more and more each day and now new revelations that maybe she had always had just a little bit of magic along the way. What in the world was wrong with her? And how had her family missed it?

There was no one nearby to give her answers and Wynona certainly wasn't about to ask her parents or sister. No...she would do what she had always done. Dig in her heels, research through books and keep moving forward. Right now...it was the only plan she had. She just prayed it was enough.

CHAPTER 15

The next morning, Wynona was anything but refreshed. Time seemed to be slipping through her fingers and if she didn't get some answers soon, Prim would pay the price. The official charges had already been put down and they were simply waiting to gather more evidence before the case went to court. Wynona refused to let that happen, but everywhere she turned, she only gathered more questions rather than answers.

"Wynona!"

Spinning on her heel, Wynona was shocked to see Akina Kimono, the A-list actress, waltzing through the front door of the shop. "Akina. What a nice surprise." Wynona went through some welcome air kisses from the movie star cat shifter. She had been one of Wynona's first celebrity guests and her support had gone a long way in helping keep Saffron's Tea House in the front page of the news. Normally, however, with as big of a star as Akina was, she set up a reservation and Wynona was able to prepare for a visit. She couldn't imagine why the actress would risk the ghost reporters crashing her visit.

Akina waved away the concern. "I found myself at odds this afternoon and wanted to come say hi." Her beautifully slanted eyes sparkled with mischief and it put Wynona on her guard.

"Oh?" She glanced around, grateful her private dining room wasn't taken. "Come in and we'll get you settled." Wynona ushered her guest to the private area. "Would you like a pot of your usual?"

Akina purred as she sank elegantly into a cushy seat in the corner of the small dining room. "That sounds marvelous."

Wynona nodded. "I'll only be a moment." She hurried to the kitchen and began grabbing the needed ingredients. She had created a tea for Akina several months ago that had a bit of catnip in it and it had been a big hit. Wynona put a kettle on the stove and filled three infusers. Next she put together a tray of pastries and built a lovely display for her guest.

Lusgu shuffled past, the broom sweeping in his wake. "Soon," he muttered as he began washing dishes. "It'll happen soon."

Wynona paused and frowned. "What will happen soon?"

Lusgu looked her way and narrowed his eyes. "Soon." Without another word, he went back to the dishes and Wynona was left to wonder what he was talking about.

She knew from experience that he wouldn't say any more, despite the fact that she was his boss. Truly, Wynona had very little control over the brownie, but she was always grateful he was around. Somehow, he always seemed to know exactly what was going on even though he wasn't involved in any of her investigations.

"Okay..." Wynona said on a sigh. Shaking her head, she finished the tray and walked it down the hall to Akina's room. "I brought some pastries just in case you found yourself hungry," Wynona said as she entered the room. She set the tray down and filled the teacup with water and one of the infusers. Straightening, she wiped her hands on her skirt. "Anything else I can do for you?"

"Sit," Akina demanded, waving her manicured hand.

Wynona opened her mouth to protest, but Akina's raised eyebrows let Wynona know her guest was serious. "I only have a couple minutes," Wynona stated, sitting primly on the edge of her chair. "I'll need to see to my other guests soon."

"Of course," Akina said in that low purr she was so well known for. "But I wanted to speak to you."

Wynona raised her eyebrows in expectation.

"I hear you've been visiting The Siren's Call Theatre."

Wynona stilled. "Yes," she said carefully.

Akina tilted her head. "Have you met Brell?"

Wynona leaned back in her seat, trying to act nonchalant. "Yes."

"Has she come to the tea shop?"

Wynona slowly shook her head. "No."

Akina nodded curtly and took a languid sip of her tea. She tilted her head back and closed her eyes as if savoring every drop. "I would hate to think that you and I are not going to be able to continue our...relationship."

Wynona frowned. "I'm afraid I'm lost." What in the world was Akina talking about? And what did anything have to do with Brell?

"Brell and I are..." Akina tapped her perfectly red bottom lip. "How does the media say it...frenemies?"

Wynona's eyebrows shot up.

"She and I *never* frequent the same places." One slender shoulder shrugged. "So if she were to take an interest in your little tea house..." Akina's chin was tilted down as her dark eyes looked up through thick lashes.

Wynona wanted to roll her eyes. She hated dealing with egos. But the last thing she needed at the moment was a turf war over her tea house. Getting Prim out of prison was enough work. So instead of making a snarky remark, she put up both her hands in a placating manner. "Akina, I've only met Brell because I was doing some investigating at the theatre. You probably heard that Madam Ureo was killed."

Akina snorted delicately and took another sip of tea.

Wynona ignored the sound and moved on. "My best friend is stuck in the middle and I've been searching for clues."

That got Akina's attention. "What friend? What clues?" Her ears twitched with curiosity.

"I'm sorry, I can't say more," Wynona stated firmly. She wasn't about to gossip about the case. Wynona hated when information was leaked around the media and there was no way Akina wouldn't take advantage of any juicy tidbit she could get. In fact, Wynona had probably already said too much.

She slapped her knees. "Okay. Now that that's settled, I need to check on my other—" Wynona's phone began to ring in her back pocket. She paused, then pulled it out. "Excuse me," she said, slipping into the hallway. "Rascal?"

"Wy, we've got a bad situation here."

"What happened?" she asked anxiously, instantly worried that something had happened to Prim.

"Brell Tuall is in the hospital," Rascal stated bluntly.

"What?" Wynona glanced over her shoulder through the open door. What were the odds that something would happen to the actress at the same time Wynona was getting the third degree about their relationship.

Akina appeared to have her focus on the food and tea, but the tiny smirk on her lips let Wynona know the cat shifter wasn't upset at the news.

"I can't say anything more over the phone," Rascal said hurriedly. "Just meet us there if you can."

Wynona chewed her lip, trying to figure out how to leave in the middle of the afternoon. With Prim gone, Wynona had no back up. "I'll see what I can do," she whispered.

"See you soon." Then he was gone.

Wynona stuffed the phone back in her pocket and rubbed her aching forehead. How was she going to get out of here?

Scuttling feet told her Violet was on her way and Wynona opened her eyes to see her tiny friend running toward her.

Bending over, Wynona picked up the mouse and tucked her onto her shoulder. "What am I gonna do, Violet?"

Violet chattered and pointed frantically at the kitchen.

"Lusgu?" Wynona whispered incredulously. "You can't be serious."

Violet chittered again.

Wynona sighed and looked toward the kitchen door. "Why do I have the feeling that if I leave him in charge, I won't have a business to come back to?"

Violet snorted and argued back.

"So you'll help him?" Wynona raised her eyebrows. "Do you really think he'll listen to you?"

Violet put her hands on her hips and her squeaky voice got angrier.

"Okay, fine." Wynona took in a deep breath. "If you say you two can handle it, then I really think I need to go to the hospital and see what this is all about."

Violet's voice turned smug as she continued talking while Wynona walked to the kitchen.

Trepidation still soared through her, but at this point, Wynona felt like she had no choice. This was just a sacrifice she would have to make in order to try and save Prim, and odds were something that involved a member of the theatre involved the case. "Lusgu?"

His answering grunt was heard before his waist high body shuffled around the counter corner.

Wynona looked at Violet, who twitched her nose, seeming to wait expectantly. "I've got an emergency and need to run to the hospital. Violet told me she felt like the two of you could handle the shop...?" This sounded dumber and dumber the more Wynona spoke. Lusgu had no table manners and would definitely *not* be a good host to her patrons. "You know what? Nevermind. I'll just—" She pointed over her shoulder, but Violet pulled on a chunk of hair. "Ow!"

Squeaking wildly, Violet ran down Wynona's arm and scurried up Lusgu's, sitting on his shoulder.

"Saffron would have gone," Lusgu grunted, scratching beneath his fedora. The hat was the only pristine piece of him and it had been that way since the day he'd arrived at the tea house. Muddy feet, filthy clothes, suspenders that had definitely seen better days and a brand new fedora. It all made for a very interesting package.

"Saffron..." Wynona's mouth gaped open. "You know Saffron?"

Lusgu turned around and flicked his fingers, firing up the stove to warm a couple of waiting kettles.

Snapping her mouth shut, Wynona grabbed her jacket. This wasn't over, but right now she had more pressing matters. She paused in the doorway. "Thank you," she said sincerely. "I truly appreciate you."

Lusgu barely glanced her way, but he did glance and in that moment, Wynona was positive she saw a light tint of pink touch his long, pointed ears.

Smiling softly to herself, Wynona dashed out the back door and hopped on her Vespa. She couldn't get to the hospital quick enough.

Hex Haven General was as busy as ever and it took a few minutes to find a parking spot. Luckily, the scooter required very little space and Wynona hurried inside as soon as she got things locked up. "Ms. Brell Tuall?" Wynona asked breathlessly as she reached the front desk.

"You and every other yahoo in the joint," the secretary snapped. "No paparazzi allowed."

"I'm not paparazzi, I'm with the police," Wynona explained, but the woman simply gave her a look. "Look, if you'll just call Deputy Chief Strongclaw, he'll vouch for me."

By this point, the woman was completely ignoring her, so Wynona pulled out her own phone. It only took one ring for Rascal to pick up.

"I'm stuck at the front desk. Can you come get me?"

"Be right there."

Wynona tapped her foot, waiting impatiently for Rascal to come. The secretary gave her a couple of dirty looks, but Wynona just smiled politely in return. If the scowl on the other woman's face was any indication, kindness might actually kill her.

"Wy!"

Wynona looked up and waved. "Excuse me," she said to the gaping employee, who was looking back and forth between Rascal and Wynona. She hurried over. "Sorry, she thought I was paparazzi."

Rascal huffed. "If only their security was this tight when we actually needed it to be," he muttered, taking Wynona's elbow. "This way." He maneuvered them through the hallways and up a set of stairs. "Quicker than the elevator," he explained. Until they finally arrived at a door with two police officers standing guard outside.

Shouting could be heard within and Wynona turned to Rascal with wide eyes.

Rascal looked to the ceiling, then back down. "Fable doesn't seem to think we're doing our job."

"Ah." Wynona followed Rascal inside.

"This should never have happened!" Fable shouted as he stood next to his wife, who looked paler than she did in her vampire make-up. "You *knew* someone was running around poisoning people and you didn't do anything about it!"

"We had no reason to believe that your wife was a target," Chief Ligurio said in a tight, but controlled voice. "This situation puts a whole new spin on the case and we'll be sure to follow up accordingly."

"What's going on?" Wynona whispered to Rascal. However, in a room full of supernaturals, many of them with extra strong hearing abilities, she might as well have shouted, as every head turned to look her way. Wynona shrunk back a little. "Sorry," she said softly. "I'm just trying to catch up on the situation."

Chief Ligurio growled and shook his head.

"What's she doing here?" Fable snapped.

"She helps us out from time to time," Chief Ligurio said nonchalantly, though he didn't explain the situation. The words sparked yet another argument from Fable and soon the two were shouting again.

Rascal leaned down, his voice almost inaudible. "Brell was brought in unresponsive earlier today. As best the doctors can tell, she was poisoned."

Wynona's eyes widened. "Poisoned," she mouthed. "With what?"

Rascal pinched his lips together and scratched behind his ear. "They think it was crushed azalea."

Wynona thought about it for a moment. "Azalea is toxic to fish," she mused.

Rascal nodded. "And sirens are related to mermaids."

"Oh man..." Wynona shook her head. "How did this happen?"

"That's what we're trying to figure out, but Fable hasn't exactly been cooperative."

"I can see that." Wynona straightened. "Wait a second. Does this mean Prim is off the hook?" she whispered. "She couldn't have poisoned Brell while in prison."

"I'm not sure yet," Rascal admitted, still speaking in a low tone. "Chief Ligurio wants to look for an accomplice."

Wynona huffed. "Crud."

"It gets worse."

She looked up.

"I don't see Fable poisoning his wife to get her out of a contract...do you?"

The realization that they were losing their only suspects hit Wynona hard in the gut. "Or Mr. Rujins," she lamented. "He wouldn't kill his star after working so hard to make sure her contract was still intact."

"Exactly."

"So, in other words, Prim, with the help of someone else, is still the best bet Chief Ligurio has."

"I'm afraid so," Rascal responded.

"But there's no motive!"

"Jealousy."

The word brought Rascal and Wynona out of their little chat.

Chief Ligurio was glaring at them and standing very close. "Been around since the dawn of time."

"Not Prim," Wynona stated fiercely. "That's not who she is."

Chief Ligurio sighed and rubbed his temple. "I hope you're right, Ms. Le Doux." His red eyes flared. "For your sake and your friend's."

CHAPTER 16

Wynona waited until Chief Ligurio and several of the officers had left before approaching the bed. Her eyes darted between the pale Brell and her angry husband. "May I speak to her for a moment?" Wynona asked meekly. She didn't want to upset anyone, but she needed to know what was going on. Especially *how* Brell had been poisoned.

Akina's visit was weighing heavily on Wynona's mind. It just seemed a little too coincidental that the star had come asking about Brell right before she ended up in the hospital.

Fable huffed and threw up his hands. "Why not? Nobody else seems to care that she almost died earlier today."

"I promise to be brief," Wynona said with a grateful nod. She touched Brell's cold hand. "Brell? Brell?" She shook the hand slightly and Brell's eyes cracked open. Wynona smiled in what she hoped was a soothing manner. "Hello, Brell. Remember me?"

Brell's eyes closed again and she shifted in the bed. "You're the president's daughter."

Wynona held in her sigh. "That's right. I spoke to you and your husband the other night. Right after Madam Ureo's passing?"

Fable growled and Wynona tried not to wince. That might not have been the best thing to bring up under the current circumstances.

Rascal obviously didn't like the way Fable was sounding, since he stepped up next to Wynona and scowled at Brell's husband. His warm hand on Wynona's lower back gave her a much needed boost and she was grateful, once again, for his support.

"I need to ask you a few questions," Wynona continued.

Brell nodded. She turned her head toward Fable. "Help me sit up?" she said in a silky tone.

Wynona blinked. The words floated around her head and she had to fight the impulse to follow through even though they hadn't been directed at her.

Fable quickly jumped to do his wife's bidding, raising the bed and fluffing her pillows. His adoration was evident in every movement he made and once more, Wynona felt certain that he wouldn't have done this. Either that, or he was the paranormal world's best actor.

"Better?" he asked, his usually sharp tone soft and questioning.

"Thank you, my love," Brell whispered, putting her hand to his cheek.

Fable sighed at the contact and pressed his own over the top of hers for a second.

Rascal's throat-clearing threw them both out of their private world and Brell turned to Wynona. Her voice was much stronger this time when she spoke. "How can I help you, Ms. Le Doux?"

"Can you tell me what happened before you got sick?"

Brell took a deep breath. "The police have all this information," she said.

"I know, but I like to hear things for myself," Wynona said with a small smile. She didn't want to admit that Chief Ligurio might not mind her tagging along, but he certainly didn't share a lot of information with her.

Brell picked at the blanket covering her legs. Even with her messy hair and smudged makeup, she was stunning. Did sirens ever look like they just rolled out of bed? The question probably deserved further investigation, but Wynona tamped down her jealousy and tried to pay attention.

"I was sitting in my dressing room," Brell said offhandedly. "A vase of flowers had been brought in, though I never did see who sent them." She shrugged at Wynona's frown. "Fans send flowers all the time. It's not an uncommon occurrence."

Fable huffed, but otherwise let her continue.

Wynona could only imagine the jealousy he was feeling at that moment. He didn't seem to enjoy her having fans at all. But then why let her continue to perform? Was it simply because she was famous? Was it because she made better money than he would have at another job? Was it because she liked it and refused to quit?

"What kind of flowers were they?" Rascal asked, leading Wynona into further questioning.

She sent him a grateful smile. Rascal probably already knew the answer, but he was helping her out.

"Some kind of lily, I think," Brell said, her bottom lip poking out as she concentrated. "They were dark red with orange streaks." She shrugged. "They were pretty, that's all I know."

Wynona nodded, making a mental note to check on it. "Great. What next?"

"I opened the card and a poof of dust flew into my face." Brell's eyes filled with tears and she suddenly looked very fragile in her bed. Crocodile tears slowly dripped down her white cheeks and she sniffled delicately. When Fable held out a box of tissues, she gave him a watery smile and lifted one from the opening before coming back to Wynona. "I inhaled in surprise and within a few seconds, I began to choke." Brell dabbed at her cheeks, taking a few shuddering breaths to bring herself under control. "I didn't see a card in the envelope before I dropped it, but after that I was too caught up in trying to breathe to pay any attention to the gift."

Wynona frowned and looked toward Rascal. She wanted to speak to him, but they couldn't say anything with their current company. Why the flowers? Madam Ureo hadn't had so much as a tiny plant in her office, let alone something as lavish as a vase of flowers.

Wynona turned back to Fable. "Who dropped the flowers off?"

"Ringer," he said.

"Ringer?" Wynona had no idea who that was.

"The security guard," Fable explained sharply. "Ringer Doom. He always brings back the deliveries. It keeps the crowds from using that to get into Brell's dressing room."

"Ringer Doom? Really?" Wynona said under her breath.

"He used to be on the wrestling circuit," Brell explained. "He actually joined the theatre only a couple of days after I did." A small smile graced her lips. "He's always so sweet. He always checks in to make sure I have what I need."

Wynona filed that bit of information away. Could Mr. Doom be in love with Brell? Could he be involved with some of the problems? But why kill Madam Ureo? And would someone who was in love with a celebrity hurt the celebrity? "He sounds like a good friend," Wynona said.

Brell's smile was bright. "He is."

"So what happened after you inhaled the dust?"

Brell's hand shook as it went to her throat. "I couldn't breathe," she said softly. "It made my eyes water and my throat close up." She exhaled shakily. "I remember collapsing to the floor and Fable rushing to my side."

Fable took his wife's hand, patting it gently between his own.

"Next thing I knew, I was in the hospital." Her eyes were wide with wonder as she looked at Wynona. Her bottom lip began to tremble. "Do you think it was the same person who killed Nelara?"

Wynona hesitated. She had no idea what to say, and instead turned to Rascal, fielding the question his way.

"We're not sure," Rascal said with authority. "But we're looking into the possibility."

Brell squeezed her husband's hand, her face growing more pale.

"But we have officers outside your door," Rascal assured her. "And we'll be doing some more investigating at the theatre."

"Thank you," Brell whispered.

Rascal nodded.

Wynona wanted to ask more questions, but Brell had closed her eyes and turned her head to the side, obviously done with the interrogation. "Thank you for your time," Wynona said softly, then with a quick glance at Rascal, she headed toward the door.

Once they were out in the hall, she and Rascal stepped off to the side, getting out of the line of traffic. "What do you think?"

"Of?" Rascal asked.

"Everything," Wynona said with a bitter laugh. She threw her hands in the air. "I feel like we're just going in circles."

Rascal scratched his head. "The only thing that seems consistent is how much the evidence points to Prim."

"Rascal!"

He put his hands in the air. "I didn't say she did it, but it just seems like everything just keeps coming back to her." He scrunched his nose. "Which is actually suspicious in and of itself. Prim is way too smart to leave behind so much evidence."

"And don't forget she was in jail for this one," Wynona reminded him. "I know Chief Ligurio says she might have an accomplice, but it just doesn't make sense. Prim is *not* jealous of Brell. Her career is with her flowers. She has no desire to take over being an actress."

Rascal nodded and sighed. "Agreed, but we have nothing else to go on at this point in time. The only people you and I had are blown out of the water with this new development."

"What about the security guard?"

Rascal narrowed his gaze. "What about him?"

"He brought Brell the flowers. Maybe they were from him to begin with?" Wynona raised her eyebrows. "She did say he had been there since she was and that he paid special attention to her. And Fable didn't seem very happy when Brell talked about him."

Rascal put his hands on his hips. "I suppose he's worth looking into, but what would be his motive? Why hurt someone if you were secretly in love with them?"

Wynona shook her head. "I don't know. That's where I get stuck. He definitely had plenty of opportunity for both murders. It's the motive that doesn't make sense."

Rascal pushed his hand through his hair. "So what do you want to do now?"

Wynona blew out a long breath. "I'm not sure," she said. "First of all, I think I need to get back to the tea shop. Can you and Daemon come over after work again? Hopefully we can let some of this information settle, and then we can make a plan?"

Rascal nodded. "Sure. Time is actually on our side a little now. With the new poisoning, the DA will have to slow down as we make sure there isn't another party involved."

Wynona nodded. "I guess that's one good thing to come from this mess."

"Take it where you can," Rascal advised. "You've seen by now that sometimes good points in a case are hard to come by."

"True." Wynona took in a deep breath. "Okay, I better get back before Lusgu runs off my entire clientele."

Rascal froze. "You left Lu in charge?"

Wynona made a face. "Yeah." When Rascal's jaw dropped, she held up her hands to the side. "Violet talked me into it."

"You let a mouse talk you into letting Lusgu, a cranky old brownie with a cleaning fetish, run your tea shop?"

"It sounds terrible when you say it like that." She pouted.

Rascal laughed and pulled her into his chest, kissing the top of her head. "Oh, Wy. One of these days we're going to help you stand up for yourself."

"Don't give me that," she said, poking Rascal in the stomach. "Violet can be very persuasive when she wants to be." Wynona leaned her head back to look him in the eye. "And she practically scolded me out of the shop. What else was I to do?"

Rascal shook his head. "Absolutely nothing. I have complete confidence in Vi. She'll see that Lu behaves."

"I hope you're right," Wynona muttered.

"Alright. Hurry back and I'll see you tonight." He gave her a quick peck, leaving Wynona flushed and slightly out of breath, then turned around to talk to one of the officers.

Wynona had to work to keep the smile from her face as she left the hospital. This wasn't the time for being giddy, but she couldn't quite bring herself to not enjoy Rascal's kiss, no matter how quick it was.

She straddled her Vespa and snapped on her helmet, then carefully pulled into traffic. The longer she drove, the more somber she became. Someone had tried to kill Brell Truall. Very likely, it was the same person who had killed Madam Ureo. But why had one poisoning worked, but not the other? They were still unsure how Madam Ureo had ingested the poison administered to her. Could they have missed some kind of delivery? Maybe Mr. Doom would have an idea. If he brought in all the gifts, then surely he would remember if something was given to the manager.

The tea shop was in perfect working order when Wynona arrived, much to her shock and delight, though the dining room was empty. "Everyone's gone?" she asked Violet, who was still sitting on Lusgu's shoulder.

Violet muttered and rolled her eyes while Lusgu grimaced.

"I'm not a waiter," he grumbled, brushing Violet from her perch and disappearing into the corner.

Violet ran up Wynona's leg and continued talking.

"Is he going to be okay?" Wynona asked softly, pointing to the place Lusgu called home.

Violet nodded and huffed.

"Well, thank you for keeping everything in line, even if it meant the patrons left."

Violet preened.

"And since we have a little time on our hands..." Wynona grabbed a pen and paper. "I think you and I need to make a list of what we know, and what we need to know. Rascal and Daemon will be here tonight and hopefully by then we can figure out a plan for going forward."

CHAPTER 17

"Wy?" Rascal called as he came through the front door of the shop.

"In my office!" Wynona called. She pounded away at her keyboard, trying to quickly finish up the books before she ran out of time.

Despite the fact that Lusgu had run off all her patrons that afternoon, many more had continued to trickle in throughout the day and Wynona had turned the closed sign almost a half hour late.

There were times when she was overwhelmed with gratitude over her success, but every once in a while, it had a hindrance...such as when she was trying to help get her best friend out of prison.

A deep chuckle came from the doorway and Wynona glanced up. Rascal was leaning with his shoulder against the doorframe, looking all too delicious in his uniform and signature smirk. "Busy day?" he asked.

Wynona blew out a breath and tried to tame her hair, though it was more than likely a lost cause. "You could say that," she admitted.

Rascal nodded and walked into the room, coming around the desk to leave a soft kiss on her cheek. Pressing one arm on the desk and the other on the back of her chair, he looked at her screen. "Ah, the best part of being a business owner."

Wynona huffed a laugh. "If you say so."

He looked around the room. "Although, I see everything survived having Lusgu in charge."

An indignant squeak reminded both Wynona and Rascal that Violet was present. The purple mouse scampered up the desk and stood in the middle, facing Rascal down.

He gave the tiny creature his best smile and held out his hand. "And how could I have forgotten one of my best girls?" His smile widened when Violet warily stepped onto his palm. "You're the whole reason this place is still standing, huh?" he cooed.

Wynona bit her cheek to keep from smiling at the mouse, who was now putty in Rascal's hand. Literally.

Violet had curled up and let loose a girly sigh, making herself comfortable in the warm palm.

Rascal's golden gaze met Wynona's and he winked.

"At least I'm not the only one who can't resist you," she muttered.

Rascal chuckled, that same deep sound Wynona adored. He gave her another cheek kiss. "I'll remember that."

"Wynona? Deputy Chief?"

Wynona slapped the arms of her chair. "Guess we better get down to business."

Rascal straightened and strode purposefully out of the room. "Coming!"

Wynona followed him down the hall and into the main dining area. "Have a seat, gentleman. I ordered pizza from the Weeping Widow." She glanced at the wall clock. "Should be here in about ten minutes."

Daemon groaned as he sat down. "I'm starting to think that I'll be dead by the time we get this case figured out," he said, rubbing his forehead.

"I think we've had enough death lately, don't you?" Wynona offered. She headed to her antique teacup display to pull some down for a drink. Pizza and tea were probably an odd combination, but right now they needed every advantage, and tea always made Wynona feel better. "Does everyone want a cup?" she asked, glancing over her shoulder.

"Always," Rascal replied quickly.

Wynona smiled at him, then looked at Daemon.

Daemon's nose was scrunched. "Tea with pizza?"

"According to you, it's *magic* tea with pizza." Wynona raised her eyebrows. "Do you want the extra boost or not?"

"I guess I do," Daemon said with a shrug. "But can it be something to give me energy?"

"At this time of night?" Wynona asked. "Or would you rather have something that helps you rest?"

Daemon thought about it for a moment. "You're right. Better make it a good night's sleep."

"On it." Wynona looked at her cups and silently debated which ones to pick. Concentrating, three of the cups just seemed...right and she reached for those. She nearly dropped one when Rascal spoke right into her ear.

"Why did you pick those?"

Wynona took a second to catch her breath. "What do you mean?"

Rascal tilted his head and narrowed his gaze. "You paused and debated. I want to know what made you choose those cups."

Wynona shrugged. "They just felt like the right ones."

Rascal looked back at their sleepy companion. "Did she use magic, Dae?"

Daemon nodded. "Yeah. It was small, but something happened."

Wynona's jaw dropped. "Are you serious? I didn't even know I did it. Why would I need magic to pick out a teacup?"

Rascal shook his head. "I'm not sure." He spoke over his shoulder. "Hey, Dae. Come over here, would ya?"

Daemon sighed, but rose from his seat and walked to the large cabinet.

"What do you see?" Rascal pressed.

Daemon stared, his black eyes flaring as he took in all the cups. "Where did you get them?" he asked.

Wynona fingered the one in her hands. "Most of them were my grandmother's. A few others I've picked up at Garem Goblin's antique shop."

"Huh." Daemon pressed a finger against one. "They all have magic. It's small, but they have magic."

"But how? They're not a magical object," Wynona argued.

Daemon shook his head. He took the cup she held out of her hand and looked it over. "It must be residual from whatever was served in it."

"So...my cups *and* my tea blends have magic in them?"

"I guess so." Daemon handed it back. "It must go along with your gift. You're probably drawn to cups that contain magic that will help your tea accomplish its purpose."

"Every day I seem to find that something more in my life is a complete lie," Wynona murmured. Her heart was hammering in her throat and she was struggling to keep her breathing calm. It seemed like every time she turned around, she was discovering something that threw everything she thought she knew on its head. "How am I going to keep going like this?" she asked no one in particular. "I can't just use magic on my customers without knowing it. What happens when the magic goes wrong? Like it did with the shovel at the greenhouse?"

Rascal squeezed her neck gently. "Breathe, Wy. It's gonna be okay."

Wynona allowed Rascal to pull her into his chest. Her hands were shaking and she felt as if she might hyperventilate.

"Come on, sweetheart," he said, rubbing her back. "Breathe for me."

She sucked in a gasping breath and collapsed against him. "I'm going to hurt someone," she whispered hoarsely. "If I don't get this all figured out, I'm going to hurt someone."

Rascal sighed. "One thing at a time, huh? Let's get Prim out of prison and then we'll get this all figured out."

Wynona nodded, slowly at first, then stronger. Forcing down her panic, she straightened. "You're right. Prim is the most immediate need right now."

Rascal tucked some hair behind her ear. "Why don't you sit and relax and we'll work to get this figured out."

The front door rang and Wynona shook her head. "You guys grab the pizza and if you're still okay with me making tea, I'd like to do so." At their nods, she started to walk toward the kitchen. "It's prepaid, but if someone wouldn't mind leaving a tip?"

"On it," Rascal said. His face was serious and he didn't look like he was happy with Wynona's decision, but she pushed on anyway.

Staying busy would help her feel better much more than sitting down and stewing in her struggles. Life seemed to be full of drama at the moment and Wynona was heartily sick of it. It had taken her thirty years to break free from her family's problems and the hope had been to find peace and contentment. She never could have guessed how wrong that would be.

A tea kettle whistled just as Wynona walked into the kitchen and she gave Lusgu's back a grateful look. "Thank you," she said, knowing it was his foresight that had it ready for her.

Instead of speaking, Lusgu grunted and used his magic to hang up the pots he'd been cleaning.

Taking the kettle, her tinctures and a filled tray, Wynona took it all back out to the dining room. The men had very sweetly waited for her and Wynona couldn't help but smile as they both shifted in their seats, obviously starving but trying to be gentlemen.

"Go ahead," she said with a small laugh. "Eat up."

Those must have been the magic words since both men dug in with gusto. It was a full fifteen minutes before they slowed down enough to speak.

"So have we taken Fable off the suspect list?" Daemon asked, wiping his mouth on a napkin.

Wynona looked at Rascal, but his mouth was full. "I think so," she responded. "For a man who seems to be so enthralled with his wife, I don't understand how he could nearly kill her." She took a calming sip of her lavender infused blend. "It seems to me that if he was truly wanting to get her out of her contract, he would have gone after Mr. Rujins, not his wife."

Daemon nodded. "Agreed."

Wynona turned to ask Rascal a question. "Is Chief Ligurio still stuck on Prim having an accomplice?"

He nodded and finished chewing. "Yes, though his list of suspects is fairly empty." He raised his eyebrows at her.

Wynona rolled her eyes. "Except me," she confirmed and Rascal nodded. "But I have an alibi, so he won't accuse me of anything."

Rascal tapped the end of his nose.

Wynona sighed and held her cup up again. "You'd think I'd be used to this by now. It seems like every time someone dies, Chief Ligurio, Deverel, is determined to pin it on me or someone in my family." She drained the last of her tea and set the cup down. It rattled slightly, drawing Wynona's attention, and as soon as her eyes landed on the dregs in the bottom of the cup, she found herself frozen.

Once again, her heart began to panic and her breathing grew shallow. The rest of the room faded away and the cup began to spin on its saucer. Wynona sat, unable to move as the cup rose into the air and continued spinning in the middle of a purple fireworks show. The lights continued for a few seconds before the cup slowly came to a stop and hovered in the air.

Wynona had been through this a couple times before and with a trembling hand, she reached out and took the cup, looking inside for the message she was supposed to receive.

"The snake," she whispered, recognizing the symbol at once. Knowing something deceitful was in her path wasn't exactly the sign Wynona would have hoped for, but it was the symbol off to the right that bothered her the most. "The skull."

"Wynona!"

She blinked at the shocking voice. The purple lights disappeared and the room came back into her vision.

"Wy, are you alright?" Rascal had taken hold of her shoulders and was squeezing them tightly.

Wynona nodded, feeling suddenly drained. "Yeah. Sorry. Whenever the tea leaves have a message for me, they tend to be a little...dramatic."

Violet grumbled and climbed down from Wynona's shoulder, collapsing on the table.

"Where did you come from?" Wynona asked. Violet had been sleeping in Rascal's front pocket when they'd started dinner.

"As soon as you froze, she jumped out of my pocket and anchored herself to your shoulder." Rascal pushed a hand through his hair. "Every time you have a magical encounter I think I lose ten years off my life."

"I'm sorry," Wynona said softly. She really wasn't trying to hurt or worry anyone, but she had no control over what was happening to her. And until life calmed down enough for her to have more than five minutes to herself, Wynona didn't see that changing.

"It's not your fault." Rascal took her hand and pressed it between his two warm ones. "I know you're not doing this on purpose."

A choking sound had Wynona looking over at Daemon, who was deathly pale. "Daemon! Do you need to lie down?"

Daemon shook his head and closed his eyes as he breathed deeply. When he opened his eyes again, they were almost solid black and Wynona jerked away from the fathomless stare. "You have some of the strongest magic I've ever felt," he said hoarsely. "And I don't think you're fully released yet."

Wynona shook her head. "So this is only going to get worse?" She hung her head. It was moments like this that made her think life might have been better if she'd stayed at the castle. A flash of memories reminding her what she used to go through at the hands of her family brought Wynona back to her senses. "Okay." She put her palms on the table. "Like Rascal said earlier, we're just going to have to handle this one step at a time. Prim first. Then my magic."

"What caused this episode?" Rascal asked.

"The tea leaves needed to be read," Wynona explained. "I saw two symbols. The snake, meaning that something in our path is deceiving."

Daemon snorted. "It didn't happen to mention what?"

Wynona gave him a sarcastic smile. "I wish."

"Go on," Rascal urged, sending a glare Daemon's way.

"The other was the skull," Wynona said, her voice a little softer.

"Meaning?"

"Exactly what you would think. Danger."

Rascal blew out a breath. "Right." He took in a fortifying breath. "So now what?"

"Now I clean up this mess and you two get some sleep," Wynona remarked. "I know we were planning on hashing out the hospital today, but honestly, I don't know that there's much to say. Brell was almost killed. We don't think her husband or her manager would have done it. Prim obviously couldn't have either. And now we're back to ground zero."

"Other than Mr. Doom," Rascal reminded her.

"Right," Wynona agreed. "Other than Mr. Doom." She pinched her lips together. "So do we go back and talk to him?"

"Maybe." Rascal scratched his chin. "I'll see what Chief's plans are. He might be planning on that anyway."

Wynona nodded and began to put the dishes back on the tray.

"Let me help." Daemon jumped to his feet.

"I've got it," Wynona said. "You're my guest."

"A guest which you've fed multiple times and I think we're good enough friends for me to help out at this point, don't you?"

Wynona smiled. "Thank you."

Rascal picked up the plate of leftover pastries Wynona had brought out. "I've got these!"

"Of course you do," Wynona hollered at him, laughing softly.

Rascal paused in the kitchen doorway. "Vi mentioned you made a list of stuff for the case. You want to make me a copy of it?"

"Sure." Wynona looked at Daemon. "Can you take this in the kitchen? Lusgu will probably insist on doing the dishes."

"No problem."

"Thanks." Wynona took off across the room and down the hall. She pushed into her office and went to pick up the paper, which was sitting on the edge of her desk. She groaned when she saw how her normally neat stacks of paper were strewn together, more than likely from the windy firework display only a few minutes before.

Wynona started to reach out to fix it, when she paused. She tilted her head. The mess reminded her of something. But what was it? Her mind churned and she stared harder. It was right... Wynona's eyes shot open and she gasped. "Rascal!" she shouted, rushing out of her office.

He poked his head out of the kitchen.

"We need to go back to the club," Wynona said breathlessly. "I think I figured something out."

He blinked. "Okay." Rascal ducked back into the kitchen, then reemerged with Daemon in tow. "Let's go."

CHAPTER 18

"What are you doing here?" Mr. Doom growled. He had opened the back door at their knock, though he was anything but pleased to see them.

"Police business," Rascal said, stepping in front of Wynona.

Wynona didn't argue the point, grateful that Rascal was willing to stand between her and danger. She wasn't exactly feeling up to dealing with a grouchy bear at the moment. Violet stirred in her pocket and Wynona put her hand gently over the top.

"Please move aside, sir," Daemon said from Rascal's side. "Madam Ureo's office is still a crime scene until the police release it. As such, we are entitled to come search it at any time."

Mr. Doom's growl was low but strong. The edge of his lip curled up and he shook his head. A dark shadow passed over his face, but the man shook himself...hard. "Fine," he ground out. "But you're not allowed in Mrs. Truall's dressing room."

Wynona could feel Rascal stiffen and she put her hand on his back. He relaxed, if barely. "We understand," Rascal said, his voice harsher than usual, letting Wynona know his wolf was close to the surface.

Mr. Doom nodded and stepped back, opening the door wider to allow them through.

"Thank you," Wynona said softly as she walked past.

To her surprise, Violet poked her nose out of her pocket and squeaked.

Mr. Doom's face immediately relaxed and a small grin actually tugged at his lip. "Go on," he said, his eyes still on Wynona's pocket.

Wynona nearly stumbled, she was so shocked by the large man's softness toward her little friend.

"Just keep moving," Rascal said in an aside.

Wynona cleared her throat and put her focus back where it belonged. They reached Madam Ureo's office fairly quickly and all slipped inside. Music could be heard drifting down the hallway, evidence that a show was going on tonight, though who was headlining with Brell still in the hospital was anyone's guess.

Rascal opened the office door and flipped on the light, then waited for Wynona and Daemon to enter before pressing the door closed. "Okay, Miss Vague. What did you figure out?"

Wynona walked over to the desk and pointed out the haphazard papers. "I had assumed before that Madam Ureo was simply messy," she said, her eyes scanning the desktop. "But when I went to my own office tonight and saw how the papers were scattered because of my unexpected magic show, I realized this pattern couldn't have been from someone working."

"So you think they were deliberately messed up?" Daemon asked, walking up to where Wynona stood.

Wynona nodded. "Yes. I think whoever killed her was looking for something and messed up the papers in their search."

"The question is...did they find it?" Rascal asked, coming up on Wynona's other side.

"I'm guessing we won't know until we find the hidden compartment," Wynona muttered.

"You think there's a compartment? Not just a file folder or something?"

She nodded. "Yes. Madam Ureo doesn't sound to me like she was someone who trusted easily nor was she stupid. If she could keep one of the paranormal world's biggest stars under an iron clad contract, she knew how to hide a file she didn't want anyone to know about."

"Plausible," Rascal murmured, his eyes focused on the desk. He began sifting through papers.

"I wish I knew what we were looking for," Wynona complained as she dropped to her knees and began searching under the desk again. She ran her fingers along the wood, careful to watch for any anomaly, but nothing was forthcoming.

"If we knew what we were looking for, we wouldn't have to look," Daemon said. He was also on the ground, but he was searching the front of the desk.

"Nothing in the tea leaves about secret compartments, huh?" Rascal teased.

Wynona stuck her tongue out at him. "You try reading them next time."

He chuckled. "I'll leave the witchy tricks up to you. I've always been a little too...wild, for such rules."

Wynona rolled her eyes, but grinned while Daemon groaned.

"If you two get started, I'm out of here," he shouted from the other side of the desk.

"Sorry!" Wynona called out. She stood up and brushed off her pants. "If there's something under there, I can't find it."

"Switch me," Rascal said, dropping down.

Wynona shifted over and began gathering the papers, glancing at them only in passing as she moved them out of her way. Before they could dig much further, the door burst open.

"Deputy Chief Strongclaw. Why am I not surprised?" Mr. Rujins's gravelly voice drawled from the doorway.

Wynona looked over and held back a wince. He really was a frightening sort of man, much worse than Mr. Doom's large bulk. It was the eyes. Mr. Rujins had a gleam in his eyes that looked like someone who would feed you to the ogres if he thought it would save himself.

Rascal rose to his feet and puffed out his chest. "Mr. Rujins. Can we help you?"

"My guard informed me that you were here digging around." The old man tilted his head and narrowed his eyes menacingly. "I seem to recall asking for a warrant the next time you showed your face."

"This is still a crime scene," Rascal said with a harsh smile. "I don't need a warrant to look around in here."

Mr. Rujins's smile was more of a sneer. "When does the department plan to release this space? We have a business to run, after all. How am I supposed to do that if I don't have access to all of the company's paperwork?"

Wynona tried to hold in her surprise. She had assumed that Mr. Rujins had all the financial records and contracts in his possession, but if his angry statement was to be believed, he was missing some. And she had a feeling what he was missing was exactly what she needed to see.

Her eyes went back to the desk rather than continuing to watch the men stand off with each other. There had to be something there. There just had to be. Mr. Rujins wouldn't be so upset with their presence otherwise. Her mind began to wander as she looked... Just who had searched the desk to begin with? It had been messy when she'd first come into the crime scene. Had it been messed up during the murder? Or had someone searched the desk afterward?

She jerked her head up at the arguing men. "Just when was it you got in town, Mr. Rujins?"

The fighting stopped and those creepy eyes turned her way. "What was that?"

"You told me you didn't live here," Wynona said.

He nodded, his eyes growing more narrow by the moment.

"I'd like to know when you arrived." She stuck her chin in the air, determined not to show any weakness. Years of abuse from her family had taught Wynona that perceived weakness meant being taken advantage of. Even if she didn't feel confident or brave, faking it was the only way to go.

"I came when I was informed of Nelara's death."

"And that was?" Daemon inserted, using his height to appear more intimidating.

Mr. Rujins snarled, the sound just as gravelly as his voice. "I believe it was two days after her death."

"You weren't in town before then?" Wynona was disappointed with his response. She'd been sure they would find he had been there earlier.

"No," Mr. Rujins snapped. "Now what is this all about?" He folded his thin arms over his thick chest. "Have I suddenly become a suspect in this murder?"

"I didn't say that," Wynona responded softly. "But I also don't believe you're telling us the truth." Her eyes went back to the desk.

"That's quite an accusation," Mr. Rujins argued, stepping farther into the room.

Rascal used his long legs to move around and keep himself between Wynona and the irate manager. "I find it best to listen when she talks," he said with a sharp-toothed smile.

"You would," Mr. Rujins huffed. "She has you whipped just like the dog you are."

What Wynona wouldn't give for some kind of magical sight at the moment. Why, oh why, couldn't she use her magic when she needed it. Her eyes bugged open. "Daemon!"

He spun from where he was standing next to Rascal, helping create a united front.

Wynona leaned across the desk. "Do you see anything magical?" she whispered. It was more than likely futile to try and be quiet. Several paranormal creatures had obnoxiously good hearing, but Wynona wasn't sure about trolls, so she was hedging her bets.

Daemon smirked and shook his head. "Well, I feel like an idiot. How did I never think of this before?"

Wynona waved at the desk. "Don't worry about it. Let's just see what we can find before Rascal and Mr. Rujins kill each other."

Daemon nodded and stared at the desk, his eyes almost completely black as he let them rove over the entire thing. He hesitated at one point and Wynona couldn't help but press on it.

"What is it?"

Daemon tilted his head. "I thought I saw something, but now it's gone."

Wynona went back to the area. "Here?"

He nodded. "It was faint."

Rascal and Mr. Rujins's voices were getting louder and Wynona felt herself begin to panic. The law might be on their side, but she definitely wasn't looking for a fight. They needed to get this settled.

"Come on this side," Wynona instructed. "Try it from a different angle."

Daemon followed her instructions and came over to stand next to her. "There it is again," he murmured.

Wynona cleared all the papers from the area. Slowly, she brushed her fingers along the top of the desk. The only thing she could see was the grain of the wood. But there had to be more than that. Harpies didn't have extra special powers. Madam Ureo would have needed to have a point of reference if she had a secret compartment.

The voices grew angrier and Daemon grimaced. "Sorry, Wynona. But I need to help."

"Go," she responded. "I'll work on this."

He nodded and quickly disappeared from her peripheral view.

"What would a bird see?" Wynona murmured to herself. Closing her eyes, Wynona wanted to smack herself. Birds had excellent vision. They absolutely could *see* something that Wynona couldn't. She was definitely going to need something to help her have better vision.

Violet finally emerged from Wynona's pocket and leapt onto the table.

"It's about time you showed up," Wynona muttered.

Violet huffed indignantly, then glanced at the men who were still facing off. Luckily, no blood had been shed as of yet. Coming back to Wynona, Violet got her friend's attention.

"Do you see something?" Wynona asked.

Violet twitched her nose and rubbed her hands.

"I'll have your badge for this," Mr. Rujins shouted. "Mark my words!"

"You are completely welcome to complain to Chief Ligurio if you feel you have been mistreated in any way," Rascal said back, in a maddeningly calm tone, but the dark edge to it told Wynona he was close to losing control to his wolf.

"And if you think you'll keep using that little witch as an excuse, then you'd better be prepared to—"

"Violet!" Wynona shouted, as Rascal shimmered and turned into the predator he was. "We need it now!"

Violet squeaked and used her tail to follow the pattern of the wood grain.

"Deputy Chief!" Daemon shouted, throwing himself on top of the snarling animal.

"What are you doing?" Wynona screeched to Violet. She had no idea what the tail was supposed to do.

Violet rolled her eyes and pointed at her tail again.

"Someone is going to get ki..." Wynona trailed off as her eyes adjusted to what the tail was portraying. The lines of the wood looked like... "A bird! Oh my gosh, Violet, you're amazing!"

She brushed the mouse aside and traced her finger over the hidden design. It made sense now... Only a person with eagle eyes...or harpy eyes, Wynona corrected herself, could have found such a thing.

As she followed the lines, a popping sound, followed by a rush, of air came from her right. Wynona glanced over her shoulder and a door in the back of the bookcase had popped open.

"What did she just do?" Mr. Rujins shouted, starting to rush forward, but his progress was halted by a giant wolf. "She has no right to do that!" the troll screamed.

"What's in there?" Daemon grunted as he continued to hold onto Rascal.

Wynona rushed over and lifted out the stack of papers. She could see some piles of money in the back, but she wasn't worried about those. She held several file folders, one of which had Brell Truall's name on it. Another was a stack of ledgers. In her quick glance, Wynona had no way of knowing if there was something wrong with them, but there certainly had to be a reason they were locked in a secret safe. "I've got it," Wynona called out. She bent over to pick Violet off the ground. "Such a clever girl," Wynona cooed as she put the mouse in her pocket.

When she straightened, Rascal had turned human again and he was physically restraining Mr. Rujins.

"She can't have those!" the old troll was screaming, over and over.

"I think we need to have a little talk down at the station," Rascal ground out. "Let's go."

Daemon looked at Wynona. "Can you carry those okay?"

She nodded, hugging the evidence to her chest.

"I'm going to help the Deputy Chief."

"Okay. I'll follow."

Daemon gave a curt nod, then followed his boss, and all four of them worked their way down the hall and toward the back entrance. Between the shouts, growls and threats, Wynona knew it was going to be a long drive to the precinct.

CHAPTER 19

"What's the meaning of this?" Chief Ligurio shouted as he burst into the interrogation room. His hair was messy, as if he'd been sleeping and Wynona had to pinch her lips together to keep from laughing.

She had never seen the chief anything but pristine, so seeing him unkempt was a new experience and actually brought down his level of intimidation to something more manageable.

His red eyes landed on Wynona and Chief Ligurio pointed a finger at her. "If this isn't a complete break in the case, you're through."

Wynona nodded, her hands folded meekly in her lap. "I understand, but I really think you want to hear what we found."

The chief huffed and stormed to his usual spot at the desk in the middle. Mr. Rujins was sitting in the chair on the other side and he looked ready to tear the next person who spoke to him into tiny pieces. "Mr. Rujins," Chief Ligurio snapped. "How are you mixed up in all this?"

The manager leaned back, though the sneer never left his face. "Your man...or should I say, dog..."

The pleasure on Mr. Rujins face was so obnoxious Wynona wanted to smack him and she didn't resort to violence very often.

Violet crawled out of her pocket and scrambled up Wynona's neck, nuzzling into the crook there.

Wynona reached up and scratched the tiny creature's ears. "Thanks."

"...weaseled his way into my theatre tonight and then dragged me out against my will," Mr. Rujins continued.

Chief Ligurio looked over his shoulder. "Rascal?"

Rascal stepped forward and dumped the whole pile of folders onto the desk. "We were in the office, which is clearly marked as a crime scene, and Mr. Rujins tried to stop us from taking these from a hidden safe we found in the bookcase."

Wynona couldn't see Chief Ligurio's face, but the way Mr. Rujins's face grew slightly pale told her all she needed to know.

"How did you find the safe?" Chief asked Rascal.

Rascal's still glowing eyes darted to Wynona and back.

The Chief grunted, but didn't turn around. "Have you looked through them?"

"Only a little."

Chief Ligurio's head came up. "And you believe Mr. Rujins is involved in something found in these papers?"

Rascal shrugged. "All I know is that he didn't want them gone and grew violent when they were discovered."

"They're my papers," Mr. Rujins argued, straightening his tie and sitting upright again. "You have no right to take them."

"I have the right to take anything from a crime scene," Chief Ligurios said easily as he thumbed through one of the folders. "Tell me, Mr. Rujins. What do you expect us to find that you want so desperately to hide?"

"I'm not hiding anything," the troll argued. "But a man has a right to privacy of his business and I have no doubt that if Nelara kept those locked up, they contain confidential information that shouldn't be shown to every slimy creature to crawl through this building."

Wynona's jaw went slack. She couldn't believe how belligerent Mr. Rujins was being.

"I want my lawyer," he continued.

"We haven't charged you with anything..." Chief Ligurio's head came up a little. "Yet. Why would you want a lawyer?"

"I have the right to call an attorney and I intend to stop you from keeping those documents," Mr. Rujins growled.

Chief Ligurio shrugged. "Luhorn, take him out to the lobby and let him make a phone call."

Wynona watched as one of the attending officers led the troll out by his arm. The room grew very quiet after he was gone.

Chief Ligurio spun in his chair. "While I want to hear exactly how you found these, I'm more interested in us using the time we have." He handed a file to Rascal and held one out to Wynona. "The law is on our side, but it's still good to be prepared. Sometimes the right connection can take precedence over the rules."

Wynona stood and hurried over to take the offering. "This one is a section of the financial records." Wynona scrunched her nose. "Are you sure you want me looking at this? I'm not going to be very fast."

Chief Ligurio snorted and switched her. "Rascal, get Grimcrest in here."

Rascal headed to the door and stuck his head out, calling to someone in the hall.

Wynona gave him a questioning look.

Rascal grinned. "She's a griffin. Numbers are her specialty."

"Ah." Wynona nodded. "I'm guessing that comes from having ancestors who used to hoard gold."

"Used to?" Rascal tapped the end of her nose and leaned his hip against the desk before going back to his own folder.

Wynona opened her file and realized that she now held Brell Truall's contract. It instantly caught her attention and she began to read in earnest. When Violet squeaked in frustration, Wynona opened it wide and held it so they could both look at the contents.

"Yeah, Chief?" A woman with long metallic silver hair poked her head in the room.

"I have some ledgers for you to look at," Chief Ligurio said, holding out the papers.

The woman appeared to be in her mid-forties, but when her eyes flashed silver with delight, she looked much younger. A strong, athletic body came through the doorway and took what was offered. "Looking for anything in particular?"

Chief Ligurio shrugged. "Anything abnormal. You know the drill."

She nodded, her eyes never leaving the page.

Wynona watched in fascination as Officer Grimcrest's eyes flashed down the page, absorbing everything so quickly it was like she never read a single line before turning it over.

Page after page was discarded while the whole action was punctuated with grunts that Wynona couldn't interpret. The woman either appeared to be enjoying her delicious helping of integers or she was getting ready to cough up a hairball.

A deep chuckle drew Wynona's attention and she realized Rascal had been watching her stare at the newcomer. Wynona shrugged. "Sorry," she mouthed.

He shook his head and glanced at his fellow officer before shrugging. He had seen it all before and was used to it. But he obviously found Wynona's reaction funny.

The woman handed the papers back to the chief. "Page three, line sixteen. Page seven line twenty-one, page eleven line two."

The chief highlighted the areas, then looked up.

"Whoever kept these was skimming off the top," Officer Grimcrest explained. "Those are the biggest places, but they're scattered approximately every nine lines or so. And best I can tell, several people are benefitting."

"Good heavens," Wynona breathed.

"Thank you, Officer Grimcrest," Chief Ligurio responded. "You're free to go."

The officer nodded at her boss, then at Rascal, and finally smiled at Wynona before exiting the room.

"Whoa," Wynona breathed.

Chief Ligurio rolled his eyes before marking some more things on the records. "So we now have evidence Madam Ureo was cheating the company, and apparently not alone. I wonder if Equinus suspected."

"I think he must have," Rascal responded. "When Wynona spoke to him right after he arrived, she saw more ledgers on his desk all marked in red."

"But did he know for sure?" Wynona inserted, stepping closer to the desk. "I wonder if the marks were his own concerns and his reaction to us finding these papers was because he had searched for them himself without success."

Rascal and the chief looked at each other as if communicating without speaking. Grudgingly, Chief Ligurio turned her way. "The idea holds merit."

Violet chittered her displeasure at his lackluster response, but Wynona shushed her.

"Should we bring him back in?" Rascal asked, setting down his file.

Chief Ligurio pursed his lips, then nodded. "Might as well. We have him here. Perhaps he'll cooperate enough to answer some questions while he waits for his lawyer."

Rascal sent a message down the hall and within a couple minutes, Mr. Rujins came storming back in, his attitude obviously just as difficult as before.

"Decide to hand over the papers?" Mr. Rujins asked with a sharp grin.

Chief Ligurio leaned onto his desk, his long pale fingers folded together. "We'd like you to explain some of the discrepancies we found on your business's records."

Mr. Rujins stiffened. "Excuse me?"

"Were you aware that Nelara was keeping a little more than her fair share?" Rascal asked nonchalantly.

Mr. Rujins narrowed his eyes and his lip curled up. "I *knew* she was up to something."

"You did, didn't you?" Rascal pressed. He leaned across the desk. "Is that why you killed her?"

Wynona's eyes widened. She hadn't expected Rascal to jump in so quickly. While it was definitely a motive for murder, they still had a lot of questions to ask before convicting anyone.

Mr. Rujins gave a barking laugh that turned into a heavy cough. "You'd like that, wouldn't you, dog?" He leaned forward, meeting Rascal face to face. "How's that sister of yours doing? She ever make it in the art world?"

Rascal's growl was harsh, causing Violet to squeak and duck into Wynona's pocket. Chief Ligurio put up his hand and gave his second in command a look.

A little piece of the Rascal puzzle cleared itself in Wynona's mind. She had gathered there was history between the two men, now she knew a little more. She just hoped Rascal's sister was alright after whatever she went through at Mr. Rujins's hands.

Mr. Rujins's look was completely confident. "I didn't kill anyone," he stated. "But I did suspect her of stealing money."

"And?" Chief Ligurio asked.

"And what?"

"What did you plan to do about it?" the chief asked.

Mr. Rujins shrugged. "I would have taken the evidence to the proper authorities, of course."

Rascal stomped away, his growl lingering in the air.

"That would have been very chivalrous of you," Chief Ligurio drawled.

"I seek to help the public," Mr. Rujins added.

Wynona held back her eyeroll. This man was getting worse all the time. How anyone was willing to let him become a partner in their business was beyond her. The creep factor in the room was almost thick enough to choke on.

A heated presence came to her back and Wynona knew that Rascal was standing there. Careful to remain unseen, she reached back and took his hand. The touch did exactly what she hoped it would and she felt him let out a breath and relax slightly. When she went to pull back, her job done, Rascal gripped tighter.

Heat raced up her neck and cheeks, but Wynona did her best to remain nonchalant. She didn't need to draw attention to their little show of affection.

"We'll be looking deeper into your alibi," Chief Ligurio said succinctly. "Now that we've established a credible motive, I'm willing to entertain the thought that maybe our current suspect is innocent."

Wynona managed to stop herself from leaning over to kiss the cold cheek of the chief, but she was unable to keep her smile from her face. Finally, *finally*, she was starting to create some doubt in Chief Ligurio's mind about Prim being involved. It wasn't a full reconciliation, but it was a start, one that Wynona was very grateful for.

"You won't find anything," Mr. Rujins's snapped, his relaxed tone gone. "I wasn't in town."

"Then you have nothing to worry about." Chief Ligurio gave a head jerk to the officer who had been escorting Mr. Rujins, but the troll slapped a hand on the desk.

"I want to know what else you found in that safe."

Chief Ligurio's eyes flared. "What business is it of yours?"

"It's my livelihood," Mr. Rujins argued. "I have every right to know what was in there." His beady eyes flitted to the folder still being held in Wynona's free hand before focusing back on the chief.

She had almost forgotten that she held Brell's contract in her hand and from the argument going on across the desk right now,

Wynona was certain there was something in there she needed to see. Dropping Rascal's hand, she quickly opened the folder and began to skim.

"She has no right to read that!" Mr. Rujins shouted, rising out of his seat.

Rascal's growl grew and even Chief Ligurio finally stood up. "She is cooperating with the police in a volunteer capacity and has been given leeway in this case," he said, glaring down at the troll. "Now sit down or I will have you removed."

Wynona tuned them out and continued searching for what could have made the troll so upset.

...in the case of death, the performer Brell Truall *will hereby be released from her contract forthwith...*

Wynona gasped. "Rascal," she breathed, pointing to the spot.

"That's mine!" The officer behind Mr. Rujins, grabbed his shoulder and began dragging him from the room at the command of Chief Ligurio.

Rascal snatched the file from Wynona's hands. "Here it is, Chief," he said, handing the paper to his boss. "This is what he was trying to hide."

"Mrs. Truall doesn't have to stay at the theatre," Chief Ligurio said with a beleaguered sigh. He pinched the bridge of his nose. "When I said I wanted a break in the case, Ms. Le Doux, I wasn't looking for you to give me multiple new suspects."

"We still need to find out if the Trualls even knew about this clause," Wynona murmured. "I still struggle to see Mr. Truall poisoning his wife."

Chief Lirugio groaned. "I need sleep." His eyes were brighter than normal when he looked at Wynona. "We'll follow up with all this tomorrow. Until then, stay out of fights with trolls."

Wynona gave him a sheepish smile. "I'll do my best."

The vampire shook his head and stood up, quickly leaving the room.

"It's late," Rascal stated, his voice still a bit gruff. "Let's get you home."

"You'll let me know what you find tomorrow?"

He nodded. "You know I will." Swinging his arm around her shoulder, Rascal kissed her temple. "Thanks for your help tonight."

"Thanks for believing me," she whispered back.

Rascal grinned and winked. "Always."

A girly sigh sat on her lips the whole way home, but Wynona managed to stay poised until she was in her house, then she let out a little squeal of victory and sweetness before she and Violet dropped off to bed.

CHAPTER 20

Wynona couldn't get away from work fast enough the next day. She knew Rascal and Chief Ligurio wouldn't be at work first thing after their late night, but Wynona had been too keyed up to sleep in very long. Then she'd been forced to work all day, as if she hadn't just discovered evidence that might help her friend get out of jail and point the finger at someone else.

Now she was speeding down the street toward the police station, hoping they had figured out the connection between the embezzlement and Madam Ureo's death. There was no way two big crimes like that weren't connected. The question wasn't if, but how?

Was Madam Ureo killed because she had been taking money? Or did one of her partners grow greedy and kill her so they could take a larger share? Was Mr. Rujins telling the truth that he was innocent of the murder? Was he lying about when he arrived in town?

So many questions...

Wynona parked her Vespa, locked up her helmet and hurried inside. She had left Violet back at the shop tonight. The tiny creature had been tired after the long day yesterday and had opted to go to bed early rather than tag along. Apparently, she didn't think this meeting was going to be as important as previous ones.

"Hey, Wynona!" Officer Nightshade said with a toothy smile as Wynona walked into the lobby.

"Hello, Amaris," Wynona replied. She pointed down the hall and raised her eyebrows.

"I think he's waiting for you." Amaris winked.

Wynona shook her head, but couldn't hide the flood of color in her cheeks and she knew Amaris's vampire sight took it all in. The snickering behind Wynona as she walked was a dead giveaway.

Throwing back her shoulders, Wynona knocked on Rascal's door, then pushed it open and poked her head in. The space was empty. "Probably with the chief." Closing the door once more, Wynona moved a little farther down the hall and knocked again. This time, however, she didn't dare open it on her own. Her knock was quickly answered.

"Wy!" Rascal exclaimed. "Come on in."

He opened the door farther and Wynona stepped inside. "Hello, Chief Ligurio."

He grunted. "Ms. Le Doux."

Wynona looked back and forth between the two men. "Did you two find anything this afternoon?"

Rascal's smile fell and he scratched behind his ear. "We're figuring some things out, but..."

"What? What's wrong?"

"We think your Ms. Meadows might have been one of the partners in the embezzling," Chief Ligurio said bluntly.

Wynona gawked. "You can't be serious."

He nodded. "I am." He turned the papers in front of him around and pressed them to the end of the desk. "Take a look."

Wynona walked over, her knees slightly shaky. There was no way Prim would be involved in this kind of thing. She studied the papers, lines and highlighted areas. Very little of it made sense to her. "I don't know what I'm reading," she finally admitted.

Rascal came up beside her and put his finger on the papers. "These are the numbers that Officer Grimcrest pointed out."

Wynona nodded. "I can see that. Those numbers don't match up with the math, so that's where Madam Ureo took a share, right?"

Rascal nodded. "Right. But if you look over here..."

Wynona's lips moved slightly as she read through the notes. "Those are Madam Ureo's partners?" Wynona asked hoarsely.

Rascal nodded.

"And you're sure that's Prim?" Off to the side of the ledger were notes written in the same handwriting as the ledger itself. It gave initials and amounts. It was easy to assume those were partners in the illegal venture. But the one that stuck out the most were the initials P.M. The amounts written by those initials were smaller than any of the others, but were there just the same. "Prim said she hadn't been paid, that's why she was trying to speak to Madam Ureo again. Is it possible this is someone else? How could Prim be a partner if she wasn't getting paid?"

"It's possible," Rascal hurried to assure her.

"But not likely." Chief Ligurio spun a pen between his fingers.

"There have to be hundreds of creatures with those initials," Wynona argued.

"Maybe. But how many of them are already mixed up in this mess?" the chief retorted.

Wynona shook her head. "You can't just assume. You have to find out for sure."

"That goes both ways, Ms. Le Doux." Chief Ligurio leaned forward onto the desk. "You can't assume she's innocent."

"I know her," Wynona said fiercely. "I'm not assuming anything."

The vampire shrugged. "We'll see." He tilted his head consideringly and narrowed his red eyes. "I have to say, Ms. Le Doux. You might want to reconsider who you spend your time with. You seem to spend an inordinate amount of time trying to prove the innocence of those you call friends and family."

"Believe me, I know," Wynona grumbled. At one point, she would have blamed that on Chief Ligurio. From the first moment he had accused her of murder several months ago, he had seemed intent on taking revenge on her family by putting one of them in jail.

When Wynona had turned out innocent, the next one accused had been Wynona's sister, Celia.

That case had opened up a coffin of skeletons that led to the discovery of Chief Ligurio and Celia's past relationship. Wynona was pretty sure there were still feelings there, but neither party involved seemed willing to find closure.

"Have you identified anyone else on the list?" Wynona asked, looking between the two men.

"Not yet," Rascal said. "We actually were just about to have Prim brought up so we could talk to her about it."

Wynona pressed her lips together. "If it's alright with you, I'd like to be here when you talk to her."

"She's been indispensable during some of our other interviews, Chief. We could use her ideas," Rascal added.

Chief Ligurio paused, but ultimately nodded. "As long as you don't try to lead the conversation, I'll let you stay."

"Thank you." Wynona looked around, then smiled when Rascal pointed out a chair. She reached out and gave his hand a squeeze. Now wasn't a time for a peck on the cheek, but she'd be sure to thank him later.

The room was awkwardly quiet for several minutes while they waited for Prim to arrive and Wynona couldn't keep her foot still. It bounced until she was shaking her chair. When Chief Ligurio glared her way, Wynona forced herself to stop and smile serenely.

Rascal choked on a laugh and covered it with a cough, but no one misunderstood the original intent. His sparkling golden eyes met Wynona's and he winked at her.

Wynona rolled her own eyes and tried to lean back in her seat, but she was too wound up. She hadn't seen Prim for several days and was anxious to know she was okay.

The door finally opened and a very subdued fairy was escorted in. The orange jumpsuit clashed horribly with her bright pink hair, which had been pulled back into a tight bun, very unlike Prim's normally bouncy curls.

Her change in style wasn't the reason Wynona found herself concerned, however. It was the utter look of defeat on her friend's face. If Prim had been born with wings, they would have been dragging on the floor.

"Prim," Wynona breathed, her eyes filling with tears.

Prim looked up, her pink eyes widening in surprise. "Nona?"

Wynona stood and walked over with her arms out. Surely the chief wouldn't care if she held Prim for just a moment. When she was closer, Wynona dropped to her knees to be on the same level as the fairy and Prim fell into her friend's hold with a broken sob.

"It's going to be okay," Wynona whispered, squeezing tightly. "We're working on getting you out of here." She didn't bother to mention that their latest evidence hadn't been as helpful as Wynona had planned. Right now Prim needed hope...badly. And as her best friend, Wynona had every intention of giving it.

"My plants," Prim whispered thickly. "I can feel them dying."

Wynona had no words of comfort. She had been to visit the greenhouse several times, but no matter how much she watered them, the plants were still folding over and turning yellow. They needed Prim's magic. "I know. But when this is all over, we'll fill that greenhouse to the brim and you'll never have to leave it again."

Prim leaned back and wiped her makeup-less face. "If I don't get out of here soon, the bank will repossess it all and then it won't matter that I was innocent."

Wynona shook her head. "I won't let that happen." She grabbed Prim's shoulder. "No matter what. I'll take out a loan on the shop if I have to, but this isn't the end. You have to believe that."

Prim nodded, though it was slow. "I know. Thank you for everything you're doing." She looked up at Rascal. "You too, ya crazy wolf."

Rascal cracked a grin, but it wasn't as playful as usual.

Chief Ligurio cleared his throat and Wynona knew she had pushed the boundaries long enough. She stood and helped walk Prim to her seat, getting her settled before going back to the edge of the room so she was out of the way.

"Ms. Meadows," Chief Ligurio began. "In a search of Madam Ureo's office, a safe was discovered that held papers about the business." He pushed them forward so Prim could read them. "As you can see, they're the financial ledgers." His long white finger began pointing to spots. "These are where we discovered that Madam Ureo was skimming money off the profits."

"What!" Prim screeched. "She was making *extra* money and she still couldn't pay me?"

Chief Ligurio raised an unimpressed eyebrow and waited for Prim to quiet down again. "Off to the side are a list of...investors or partners, if you will."

"So there was more than one?" Prim growled, the sound almost humorous in her high fairy voice. "How deep does the conspiracy go?"

"That's what we'd like to ask you," the vampire stated.

Prim stiffened. "What?"

Once again, Chief Ligurio pointed at the paper. "One of the investors is a P.M."

Prim swallowed audibly. "And you think that's me, don't you?"

Chief Ligurio nodded slowly. "It would seem plausible."

Prim slapped the top of the desk. "It's not! I had nothing to do with this."

"Did Madam Ureo ever mention anything about her little operation?"

"No!" Prim said fiercely. "I don't know how to prove it to you other than to say, check my bank statements. There is absolutely no extra money there. None. Not a single penny. If I was dealing in something like this, I can guarantee you that there would be more in my account than the measly few hundred bucks there are."

Chief Ligurio took a deep breath. "We'll be doing just that." He pulled the papers back and studied them. "Can you offer us anything else? Anything Madam Ureo might have said or hinted at? Any meetings she refused to allow others into? Any people she kept hidden?"

"If she kept people hidden, how would I have seen them?" Prim asked snidely.

"Prim," Wynona scolded. Prim was a master of gossip. The question hadn't been unreasonable at all, but Prim was quite obviously not herself at the moment. "Just answer the question."

Prim grimaced but her tight muscles slumped a little. "Not that I was aware of. I didn't actually have a lot of interaction with her," Prim admitted. "She hired me, after making sure I knew how worthless I was. I worked for a couple of weeks, but never got paid." Prim wrung her hands together. "When I asked about it, I was brushed off. But after a few more weeks went by, I decided to try again. The whole purpose in taking the job was to help pay the mortgage. I couldn't do that if I never got a paycheck."

"What exactly did she say when you asked about it?" Rascal folded his arms over his chest.

"The first time she said it would be coming and that I was a nuisance," Prim grumbled. "But the second time, she told me there wasn't enough to pay a wingless fairy. She made sure I knew I was low on the priority of the few funds she had to work with."

Scowling on Prim's behalf, Wynona looked up at Rascal. "Sure didn't look like they were doing badly the other night," she offered. "There were plenty of people in that crowd."

Rascal nodded. "Indeed." He turned to his boss. "What do the books say?"

Chief Ligurio was staring at Prim, as if trying to figure her out. "None of the numbers, despite the skimming, would indicate the profits were low. In fact, with Mrs. Truall's help, they're one of the most successful clubs in the area."

Prim pinched her lips and slapped a fist against her thigh. "I *knew* she was lying. That's why I went back again! But..."

The end of the sentence wasn't necessary. They all knew exactly what Prim had found.

"Do you have anything else to offer?" Chief Ligurio asked.

Prim shook her head sadly. "No. I'm sorry."

Wynona's heart clenched. She knew they were going to take Prim away now and she wasn't ready. "I'll come visit soon," Wynona whispered, her throat thick with tears as Prim was gently guided from her seat.

"Just get the real killer," Prim said, shaking her head. "I love you, but I want out of here permanently, not for a fifteen-minute chat."

Wynona nodded. "I will."

The door closed and the room fell silent.

"Deputy Chief Strongclaw," Chief Ligurio snapped. "Find out how many other employees were lacking a paycheck." He huffed. "If Ms. Meadows is telling the truth, then I doubt she's the only one with that story."

Wynona smiled. Now they were getting somewhere. Chief Ligurio wouldn't pursue this if he didn't think it had merit. "Thank you," she said sincerely.

He waved her off. "I want this case over with. It's been on my desk for far too long."

Jumping out of her seat, Wynona rushed over to Rascal. "We can still go tonight," she said eagerly.

He grinned and shook his head. "Do you ever sleep?"

Wynona shrugged. "That's what matcha is for."

Laughing, Rascal took her hand. "I'll check in soon, Chief."

"See that you do," came the rough reply.

Wynona could hardly keep herself from running. When she had arrived at the precinct, she had thought once more that everything was lost, but now the hope had been restored. Someone had to know something about the money and Wynona was going to find them. No matter what it took.

CHAPTER 21

"Hello, Mr. Doom," Rascal said with a tight smile.

Once again, Wynona and Rascal found themselves outside The Siren's Call, knocking on the back door for entrance. They probably should start going through the front, but the back way was much less intrusive and wouldn't involve passing through the performance hall.

"Deputy Chief," Mr. Doom said just as snarkily. "Back so soon?"

"We'd like to question the employees," Rascal stated.

"It's a performance night," the security guard growled.

"I understand, but we have reason to believe some of them hold evidence that is pertinent to the case at hand." Rascal's voice was calm, but firm. He wasn't about to let the man in front of him keep them from getting inside.

Wynona was so grateful for his interference. She didn't handle confrontation well and would have struggled with getting past the extra large shifter. Though, Violet had seemed to soften him. Perhaps Wynona needed to start being more careful about bringing her on these missions.

"Mrs. Truall only just got back from the hospital," Mr. Doom argued. "She shouldn't be bothered."

Rascal began to stiffen and Wynona knew it was time to step in and try a gentler approach. "We promise not to disturb her," she said with a gentle smile. "If I need to speak to her, I'll be sure to keep it brief and as non-stressful as possible."

Mr. Doom's eyes narrowed.

"An innocent woman has been put in jail and a killer roams free," Wynona said softly. "We need to solve this and it might include

Mrs. Truall. I understand you wish to protect her, but Madam Ureo's death needs to be answered for."

"If you already have someone in custody, why are you still looking?" he ground out.

"Because she's innocent."

"How do you know?"

Wynona bit back a sigh. How many times was she going to have to defend her confidence in her best friend? At least one more time, apparently. "Because the woman in jail is my best friend. I know her. I know she's not a murderer. And if you had gotten to know her during her few weeks here, you would know the same thing."

He huffed and pushed a hand through his thick hair. "Fine," he grumbled. "I don't like it, but you're right. The real killer needs to be found." Pulling the door open farther, he let Wynona and Rascal enter.

"Thank you," Wynona whispered, touching his forearm in gratitude. She paused. "Mr. Doom?"

His eyebrows rose.

"When was the last time you were paid for working here?"

Those eyebrows slashed down angrily. "What kind of question is that? Are you saying I look poor?"

"No, no," Wynona hurried to respond. "We're simply checking on a lead. It would seem that Madam Ureo didn't pay everyone on time. I was trying to see if you were in that number."

His anger dissipated rather quickly this time. "I get paid when I get paid," he said with a shrug.

"I don't understand." Wynona tilted her head.

"My contract says it should be every two weeks, but sometimes it's three or four before the deposits come through," Mr. Doom remarked. His attention was focused on something down the hall. "Madam Ureo always told me the profits fluctuated too much for the pay to be consistent."

"Thank you for your help," Wynona said. This time her smile was more genuine. The bear wasn't a bad guy...just protective. Turning to Rascal, they headed toward the first dressing room.

"Do you want to split up?" Wynona asked. "We can cover more people that way."

Rascal shook his head. "No way am I leaving you by yourself in this place. Besides, with a performance going, there might not be that many people to talk to anyway."

Wynona nodded her agreement. "Okay." She looked down the hall. "Shall we start at the beginning then?" She waved at the door directly in front of them.

Rascal stepped forward without a word and knocked. No one answered. This happened on the next three doors they tried as well. Everyone seemed to be out with the audience.

They hesitated outside Mrs. Truall's door, Wynona feeling uncomfortable with bothering the siren. "I don't have any specific questions for her," Wynona admitted to Rascal. "Perhaps we should wait until we do."

He nodded. "Sounds fair." He pushed a hand through his hair. "But what now? If we can't speak to any employees, we can't figure out if they've been paid."

Wynona pinched her lips and shook her head. "I'm not sure. Maybe we should try the office again." She started to walk down the hall.

"We already found all the paperwork," Rascal whispered behind her. "What could be left to find?"

"Maybe she kept records of when she paid people?"

Rascal snorted. "If they were visible, the evidence team would already have them."

Wynona sighed and grabbed the doorknob. "I get it, but there has to be something we're still missing. All of the evidence still aims toward Prim. The killer had to have slipped up somewhere." She pushed the door open.

"Well, I doubt it's in here," Rascal huffed. "We've been through this room enough times for us to know it by heart."

Wynona gave him an indulgent smile. "So pouty."

Rascal growled playfully. "Don't test me," he warned, his eyes sparkling.

Wynona laughed. "Come on, big bad wolf. We've got work to do."

Rascal grumbled, but followed along.

The next half hour was spent pouring over everything they had already seen more than once. If there was something new in the room, Wynona couldn't find it. Finally, she folded her arms in a huff and leaned her hips against the edge of the desk. "What am I missing?"

Rascal growled low and slumped against the wall. "If I knew, you wouldn't have to ask the question."

Wynona pinched her lips and slowly walked around the room. She just knew there was something here. Her eyes went over the papers still strewn over the desk. The wall safe was still hanging open. The desk held no chair as it had been taken in for evidence. A small bookcase and a coffee stand were the only other pieces of furniture in the room.

Wynona paused. "Did the coroner say for sure that the daffodil was ingested?"

Rascal hummed. "Uh...yeah. Pretty sure."

"It wasn't like injected or something?" Wynona's eyes never left the coffee station.

"No. At least, not that they mentioned. If evidence of a needle had been seen, I would think they'd mention that." He stood and walked over to her. "What're you thinking?"

"I don't know yet." Wynona narrowed her eyes at the coffee maker and mugs, then slowly walked over. "I wonder how much of this she drank," she mused.

Rascal scratched the back of his head. "No idea." He frowned. "Do you think coffee would be strong enough to mask the daffodil?"

Wynona pursed her lips and tipped her head from side to side. "Possibly. But it's hard to know for sure." She lifted the coffee maker lid. "It's full." She looked over her shoulder at Rascal. "Almost like she prepared but then didn't actually start it."

Rascal shrugged. "She was killed in the evening. Maybe she had it prepped for the next day. Not everyone drinks caffeine at night."

"True..." Wynona shook her head. "But something is still off." She picked up the mug sitting next to the maker. The sides of it were stained a dark color. "I'm guessing she drank a lot," Wynona said wryly, showing the discolored cup to Rascal.

"Looks like it. But what does that prove?"

"Nothing yet." Wynona set it down and paused. "Did she only have one mug?"

"What?"

She pointed to a spot on the shelf. Two round circles without dust were evident. "It looks like she had more than one mug." Wynona looked at Rascal. "But where's the second one?"

He frowned. "Good question." He searched around the display. "It doesn't look like it's around here."

Wynona spun and headed back to the desk.

"Find something?"

She shook her head. "Not yet. But that mug has to be somewhere, right? It wouldn't have just disappeared." She paused. "Did the evidence team take it?"

"Just a sec and I'll check." Rascal turned toward the door and made a phone call.

While he was busy, Wynona walked around to the back of the desk and began a search. Drinking the daffodil would be the most likely scenario, especially if an injection wasn't involved, although how a creature would get the harpy to drink poison was still in question.

"No mug was taken in," Rascal stated, coming to Wynona's side. "Find anything else?"

She shook her head. "No...but I'm guessing if we find that mug, we'll find something useful."

"I'd bet you're right." He leaned on the desk and looked over it. "It could be that's how she ingested the daffodil."

"Right. But we still don't know if she knew what she was drinking."

"Finding the mug won't tell us that, but at least we could dust it for prints if nothing else," Rascal said.

"If we had the mug, your team could probably figure out what substance had been in there."

"And how would that help us?"

"If it was a tea," Wynona explained, "then Madam Ureo more than likely took it willingly. Because there would have been no way to hide the flavor."

Rascal ran a hand through his hair. "I can't imagine anyone drinking poison willinging."

"Me either, but we live in a world with magic." Wynona turned to look at him. "Could she have somehow been spelled to drink it?"

He nodded slowly. "It's possible."

Wynona gasped and grabbed Rascal's arm. "Has Daemon looked at the body?"

"Not that I know of."

"Can he see if there was a spell used? Does a trace of it stick around if a body has expired?"

Rascal stilled. "I don't think anyone has ever asked him that before." He leaned forward and kissed her cheek. "Wy, you're a genius."

She flushed under his praise. "If I was a genius, I would be able to figure out who was framing Prim and know where the missing mug was."

Rascal chuckled as he made another phone call. "Strongclaw here. Find me Officer Skymaw." He winked at Wynona. "Considering he's been on the force for three years and we've never asked him that question, you're closer to a genius than the rest of us."

Wynona grinned. "I promise not to tell Chief Ligurio you said that."

"Good idea." Rascal's eyes left her. "Daemon? I need you to do me a favor." He paused to listen. "Right. Can you go down to the morgue? I want you to look at Ureo's body and tell me if you can see any traces of magic. Something that might have been the lingering pieces of a spell." Rascal's eyes were unfocused as he listened. "Uh-huh. Okay...perfect. Thanks." He quit the call and put the phone in his pocket. "He's headed out now. He was only doing paperwork, so the timing is good."

"Great," Wynona breathed. "The sooner we get this figured out the better. What else did he say?"

Rascal took her hand and began leading her out of the room. "He said he'd never tried that before, but he'd see what he could do." He opened the office door. Voices could be heard down the hall, letting them know the actors were coming back from their performance.

"If magic lingers in teacups, hopefully it also lingers in bodies." Wynona couldn't stop a small shudder.

"It might linger better on inanimate objects though," Rascal pointed out. "A living, breathing organism might not be a good host after the fact."

She sighed. "Good point. But if the remnants of a spell can be found, that's a point in Prim's favor. She doesn't have magic that could cast a spell."

"Good point." Rascal tilted his head toward the voices. "While Daemon is heading out, should we interview a few more actors? See if anyone is missing any paychecks?"

"Perfect." Wynona squeezed his hand. "It'll help pass the time until he gets back to us."

"Right." Rascal led them down the hallway. "Here we go."

CHAPTER 22

An hour later, Wynona and Rascal were back at the station, waiting for Chief Ligurio to finish a phone call.

Wynona's leg bounced as they sat in the hallway. "Do you think the names will mean anything?"

Rascal took a long breath. "I'm not sure. But I hope so. For Prim's sake."

Wynona nodded. "I know. I can't believe how many people were being short changed at the theatre and absolutely no one had reported it to the police."

Rascal cleared his throat. "You do realize that there might have been a reason for that, right?"

Wynona stilled. "What do you mean?'

"I mean..." He blew out a breath and didn't look her in the eye. "They might have stayed away from the police because the missing paychecks had to do with the embezzling. Each and every one of them could have been in on it."

"But why would they do that?" Wynona argued. "The gorgon said he was bumming food from family in order to survive. If they were embezzling, wouldn't they be living better than that?"

"We don't actually know that he was telling the truth," Rascal pointed out.

Wynona huffed. "Maybe not, but it seems a weird thing to lie about. No one likes to admit they're broke."

"But there had to be a reason they didn't come to us," Rascal said gently. "I know Madam Ureo was a hard nose, but having a dozen people in her employment that were all too scared to bring in the law seems a little...unbelievable."

Wynona scowled and folded her arms over her chest. "I still don't think they were involved. I mean...any of them could have been the killers, I suppose, though their alibis all sounded solid. But I don't think any of them were willing participants in the embezzling. They wouldn't be living on pennies if they had illegal money coming in."

"We don't actually even know if they were involved in the embezzling," Rascal pointed out. "We need to compare the lists."

"Well, if the chief would ever get off the phone..." Wynona grumbled.

Rascal chuckled and stood up, pulling her with him, just as the door opened. "You're cute when you're pouting," he whispered.

Wynona glared, but it only made Rascal laugh harder.

Chief Ligurio was sitting behind his desk, sipping a hot mug. "What did you find?" he asked without preamble. Apparently, they were well past pleasantries by this time of night.

Rascal set the list of names on his boss's desk. "These are all the employees we spoke to that said they haven't had steady paychecks, and some claimed they've never had any at all."

Chief Ligurio's red eyes snapped to Rascal. "Why didn't they report it?"

Rascal shrugged. "No one would say and at this point we can only guess."

The chief growled and went back to the paper. His frown grew before he opened a file and pulled out the ledgers.

Wynona found herself edging closer to the desk as everyone's eyes went down the two lists. "They all fit," she said breathlessly, her heart pounding in her chest.

Two growls filled the room and Wynona couldn't tell which one belonged to which predator. With a curse, the chief slapped his hand down on the desk. "Just what kind of racket was she running?"

Rascal shook his head. "I don't think anyone knows for sure." He pointed to the ledgers. "Unless they were in on it."

"Alibis," Chief Ligurio snapped.

Rascal glanced at Wynona before answering his boss. "Every person we spoke to was accounted for the night of the murder. Most of them were surrounded by patrons out in the theatre."

Chief Ligurio threw himself back in his chair and scrubbed his hands down his face. "So we're still hanging onto only one subject."

"What?" Wynona shouted. "You can't be serious!"

Red eyes glared at her. "Do any of the others have time frames when they were off the floor?"

Wynona slumped. "Not that we're aware of."

"Then the only person who had motive *and* time was Ms. Meadows," he argued.

"What about Mr. Rujins?" Wynona asked in despair. "He hasn't proven his whereabouts yet."

"You're right," Chief Ligurio conceded. "And he's due in any minute with his lawyer." The chief grumbled under his breath and pushed a hand through his pristine hair, causing it to fall across his forehead in a boyish manner.

Until this case, Wynona had never seen the vampire so rattled. He always looked cool and in charge, but this time around he was on edge and less than pristine. The stress of the case was obviously getting to him the same way it was draining Wynona.

A knock on the door interrupted their meeting before anything more could be said.

"Enter."

"Chief?" Officer Nightshade poked her head in. "They're here." She gave Wynona a sympathetic smile before ducking out and allowing Mr. Rujins and his lawyer to enter.

"Chief Ligurio," the lawyer said in an official tone. "This is rather late for an interview."

Chief Ligurio stood and nodded. "I understand, but evidence is coming to light, which has us reexamining your client's whereabouts at the time of the murder." He waved to a couple of chairs. "Please sit and let's see if we can settle this."

Rascal walked over to Wynona and ushered her to the corner. She folded her arms over her chest, frustrated, but obedient. She had been so sure she was going to make headway tonight and instead it all seemed to be falling apart.

Somehow the murder, the embezzling and the attempted murder were all connected, but none of the dots made sense. And each time Wynona thought she'd found a clue to prove Prim's innocence, it all seemed to implode, leaving Prim still locked away in jail. Wynona felt like the worst best friend ever. Why was it that when it counted most, she couldn't put two and two together in order to save the person who was more family than friend?

"What was it you needed?" the lawyer asked silkily after adjusting himself in the chair. He crossed one leg over the other and stared across the desk as if he were bored.

Wynona tried to figure out what kind of paranormal he was, but the man appeared human, meaning he could be a dozen and one different things. She would have to wait until he showed his hand.

Chief Ligurio had sat back down and now leaned his elbows on to his desk, folding his hands together. "Where was your client the night Madam Ureo was murdered?"

Mr. Rujins rolled his yellow eyes and shook his head. "Did your dog over there not take notes? We've been through this already."

Wynona felt her anger on Rascal's behalf rise. She didn't like bullies and each time she met Mr. Rujins, he proved to be worse and worse. She looked sideways to see Rascal standing stoically at her side. At least he was handling the abuse better than she was.

The lawyer put a hand on Mr. Rujins arm, as if in warning. "While my client needs to curb his tongue, he's correct. This is something we've been over multiple times."

"Maybe so, but we have recently established that he was lying."

Wynona held back a gasp. Was the chief telling the truth? Or trying to bluff a different answer out of Mr. Rujins? No one had said anything to Wynona about proving the troll's alibi was false.

Mr. Rujins's face darkened, but he stayed quiet, allowing his lawyer to do the talking.

"Where did you hear such a thing?" the lawyer said with a laugh. "We've told you the truth. In fact, my client has been more than cooperative, despite the fact that you have kept his office under police control for far more time than it should have been."

Chief Ligurio didn't so much as flinch at the volley. "We have an eye witness that saw Mr. Rujins in the vicinity of the theatre the night of the murder." The vampire tilted his head to the side. "And before you claim they were mistaken, let me just say that the witness is a paranormal with keener than normal eyesight and Mr. Rujins's looks aren't easily mistaken for another."

The troll huffed and squirmed while his lawyer looked his way. "So I was in town. There's no crime in that."

"There is if you killed Madam Ureo," Chief Ligurio argued back. "And lying to the police makes it look like you were absolutely involved."

The lawyer leaned over and whispered in his client's ears and Wynona wished she had the ability to hear. From the curl of Rascal's lip, he had heard everything.

Mr. Rujins straightened in his seat. "I came into town to confront Nelara about skimming the money." He shrugged. "When I found a show going, I decided it was better to wait until there wasn't an audience, so I went to dinner."

"Where?" the chief demanded.

"Basilisk Buffet," Mr. Rujins grunted.

Wynona held back the eye roll. It just seemed to fit that he would eat at a place known for being cheap and almost inedible. She had an inkling that the price, not the taste, was what drove someone like Mr. Rujins.

Chief Ligurio glanced at Rascal, who nodded subtly, then walked across the room and stepped out the door.

"Care to tell me why your client lied?" Chief Ligurio addressed the lawyer again, pulling attention away from Rascal's departure.

Wynona was positive that they were checking on the alibi. Part of her hoped it came back another lie, that they could pin the murder on the creepy troll, but something about the situation just didn't ring true to her. If his partner was cheating him out of money, Wynona had no doubt that Mr. Rujins had the temper to kill Madam Ureo. But why almost kill Brell? The new manager had been fierce in trying to keep the contract out of other people's hands, more than likely in order to keep them from knowing that Madam Ureo's death broke the bargain.

If he was willing to hold onto the siren by breaking the law, why would he then hurt her by spiking the flowers?

"I'm sure it's easy to see why being in the vicinity of the theatre would look bad," the lawyer said smoothly. "My client is innocent. Can you blame him for wanting to avoid the scrutiny of the entire police force? Especially given your dealings together in the past?"

Chief Ligurio's right eyebrow rose in an unimpressed fashion. "So breaking the law is a good excuse? If he didn't do anything wrong, then we would have moved on. The fact that he hid his activities means we're more likely to believe he's guilty."

"I'm sure my client has learned his lesson," the lawyer said with a tight smile.

Wynona glanced at the troll, who was staring daggers at the police chief. He definitely didn't appear as someone who had learned a lesson. Instead, he looked angry he had been caught.

The door opened and Rascal stepped back in. From behind Mr. Rujins's back, the shifter gave a single nod to his boss, then looked to Wynona with sympathy.

Her shoulders fell. The alibi was solid. Someone had seen Mr. Rujins at the restaurant, meaning he couldn't have killed Madam Ureo.

Her hopes for a break in the case deflated. Why was this proving so hard? Wynona could feel herself slipping into despair. It was one step forward and two steps back. The weight of Prim's conviction was squeezing Wynona and she felt as if she couldn't breathe. There had to be something they could do! There just had to be!

"Thank you for coming in on such short notice," Chief Ligurio said to Mr. Rujins and his lawyer. "If we have any further questions, we'll let you know."

"Perhaps we could wait until the sun is up next time?" the lawyer said with a sarcastic smile. He stood and waited for Mr. Rujins, who was smiling smugly as they walked out.

Wynona's hands clenched into fists. Her emotions were all over the place and she felt tears of frustration and anger prick the back of her eyes.

Rascal practically lunged across the room and cupped her cheek. "Breathe, sweetheart. Just breathe."

When purple sparkles began to infiltrate her vision, Wynona knew why Rascal was so worried and that she needed to obey. Closing her eyes, she counted. Four beats in, seven beats out. Four beats in, seven beats out.

The warmth of Rascal's thumb rubbing across her cheekbone helped her locked muscles slowly relax and eventually Wynona was able to come back to herself.

She opened her eyes and gave Rascal a grateful smile. "Thanks," she whispered.

He nodded, then turned.

Oh man... Wynona had completely forgotten about the chief. What had he seen? Would he ask if she had magic? She definitely wasn't ready for this to become public knowledge yet.

Chief Ligurio was staring at her, but to Wynona's surprise, Daemon was standing next to his boss. "Dae-Officer Skymaw. I didn't see you come in."

He smiled at her, but it was strained. "I came in while you were upset."

"If you can't control yourself, Ms. Le Doux, perhaps you need to step down from helping," Chief Ligurio said. His voice was strong, but for the first time ever, Wynona heard a hint of softness in the tone. He felt bad for her.

"I'm fine, thank you," she responded, forcing a smile. She would have to thank Daemon later as well. He was more than likely the only reason Chief Ligurio wasn't asking about purple sparkles and ribbons.

The chief narrowed his eyes, then shook his head and turned back to Officer Skymaw. "You said you had news?"

Daemon nodded and he, along with Rascal, explained what the officer had been doing for the past little while.

Chief Ligurio glanced at Wynona. "I'll admit I've never thought to use his skills that way." He looked back at his employee. "And?"

Wynona held back the smile at the chief's praise. She knew that was all she was going to get. But she'd take it.

Daemon cleared his throat and looked uncomfortable. "I'm almost positive a spell was used."

"Almost positive?" Wynona asked before snapping her mouth shut when Chief Ligurio glared.

Daemon nodded. "I was sure I was seeing traces of magic, but it kept disappearing, then reappearing. Almost like a wisp of air." He shook his head. "I'm not sure how else to describe it. But I'm fairly certain it was a leftover spell."

Wynona frowned and looked at Rascal, who shrugged. "Is it possible she was spelled to drink the poison?"

Chief Ligurio pinched his lips together. "Sounds likely. There hasn't been any other evidence to suggest something else and I doubt the old harpy would poison herself willingly."

Wynona nodded, then yawned. "Sorry," she said, covering her mouth.

"Come on," Rascal ordered. He put his hand on her back and began pushing her toward the door. "Let's let the new things we learned ruminate. After a good night's sleep, maybe it'll all make more sense."

Wynona nodded, then paused at the doorway. "Prim doesn't have magic," she reminded the chief.

He gave her a look. "I understand that, Ms. Le Doux, but we both know there are ways around that."

Wynona's heart sank even further. Those words were true, but still...the spell had to be a key to finding the real killer. Her brain, however, was too worn to figure it out tonight.

"Goodnight, Ms. Le Doux," the chief said forcefully. "We'll pick this back up tomorrow."

Knowing she had no further argument, Wynona nodded and let Rascal lead her out into the hall. Somehow, someway, she needed to find the connection between the pieces. Hopefully a good night's sleep and a perfectly brewed cup of tea would help her see exactly what she needed in order to free her friend. There really was no other option.

CHAPTER 23

Wynona scrubbed her hands over her face. "I don't *know*, Violet. None of it makes any sense."

Violet yawned and scratched her belly. She made a few sounds, but Wynona's head was pounding so hard at this point that she couldn't really understand what her mouse friend was saying.

"Let's go over this again," Wynona said, forcing herself to sit up.

Violet groaned.

"We have to figure this out!" Wynona snapped, then paused and pinched the bridge of her nose. "I'm sorry. I shouldn't have spoken like that."

Violet stood up on her hind legs and chittered softly.

Wynona sighed and fell back in her seat. "You're right. I need to go to bed, but every time I close my eyes, all I can see is Prim in that orange jumpsuit." Wynona looked away and shook her head. "I have to get her out of there." Her eyes came back to Violet. "I feel like we've unearthed too many things for us to not have figured this out."

She looked down at the scattered papers on her dining table. "Just one more time...okay?"

Violet grumbled but pulled herself closer and turned her ears toward Wynona.

"Madam Ureo was killed by daffodil extract."

Violet huffed.

"It appears she ingested it and with the evidence of a spell, we're assuming she drank it against her will while under the influence of magic."

Violet nodded.

"Mrs. Tuall was also poisoned."

Violet jerked forward as her eyes closed, but she caught herself and straightened up.

Wynona couldn't even find the situation funny. She was too far gone in her anxiety to think falling asleep while standing up was cute. "Hers was through flowers from a fan, though no one, not even Mr. Doom, knows who the fan was."

Violet rolled her eyes and splayed her hands.

"I know." Wynona chewed on the end of a pencil. "But Mr. Doom said that the person was wearing a hat and sunglasses, and the flowers weren't from any of the shops. At least not one that we can find in Hex Haven." Wynona had a sudden thought. "Oh my gosh, I'm so glad they couldn't trace the flowers back to Prim." Her eyes widened. "Can you imagine what Chief Ligurio would have said if they were able to add that to the list?"

Violet shook her head.

"Seriously. That would be terrible." Wynona went back to the papers. "A mug is missing from Madam Ureo's room. We're guessing it contained the tea or drink or whatever it was." She set that paper down. "The madam was cheating her employees out of paychecks, but everyone except for Prim was on the floor the whole time, making it impossible for them to have killed their boss." Wynona sighed. "If only Prim's break had been at another time."

Violet whimpered.

"I know," Wynona said softly. At this time of night her eyes were gritty and her throat was sore. But she couldn't sleep. The thoughts and worries swirling through her mind were too much for Wynona to handle. She had to get it all down on paper and once that was done, she found herself unable to walk away from trying to piece it all together. Nothing had been standing out to her though. None of it went together. They had a murder, a money scheme, a suspicious new manager, an attempted murder, an angry and protective husband, a missing mug, a broken contract and...Prim.

How in the paranormal world did all of this come together?

"We keep assuming that Madam Ureo was killed because of the embezzling..." Wynona chewed her bottom lip. "What if that wasn't the case?"

Violet's nose twitched.

"What if she was killed because of the contract?"

Violet sneezed and rubbed her face.

Wynona slumped. "I know...that doesn't quite work either, does it? Brell being attacked kind of takes that out of the running." Her pencil's eraser was practically gone by this point. "But if someone was upset about the embezzling, was it a person being cheated or a person who wanted more?"

Violet shrugged.

Wynona threw her head back and groaned loudly. "I CAN'T GET THIS TO MAKE SENSE!" she shouted at the ceiling.

Violet chattered loudly and stomped across the table. Within seconds, the mouse had scurried down the table and disappeared into the corner, where a small hole in the wall had become her home.

Wynona didn't even bother calling her back. She couldn't blame Violet for stalking off. Wynona wanted to leave as well, but she couldn't. Leaving meant giving up on Prim and Wynona wouldn't do it. She couldn't.

"But I also can't keep going like this." Rubbing her eyes, Wynona stood up and headed to her bedroom. She was positive she wouldn't be able to sleep, but she also couldn't stay up at the table. Maybe lying still with her eyes closed would be enough to help her get through work the next day.

Wynona kicked off her shoes and fell face first into the mattress. A couple of rogue tears dripped onto the covers and Wynona let them soak in. She was too tired to have a full crying session, but she couldn't quite keep all the emotions contained either.

Moaning, she rolled herself onto her back and resituated herself better on the bed. The room was dark and it seemed to be a symbol for Wynona's life at the moment. Darkness. She felt as if there was darkness in her mind. Something tangible that was keeping her from finding the answers she needed.

There was no question that Prim was innocent, but why didn't any of the evidence back up that fact?

In fact, it was almost too neat. The evidence was so Prim focused that in Wynona's mind, that was suspicious in and of itself. Prim was a perfectly intelligent, if slightly impulsive, adult. If she ever decided she wanted to commit a crime, she would not have left a trail that led directly back to her.

Wynona closed her eyes, but her view barely changed. The stinging behind her lids grew as moisture tried to help hydrate her dry and overused orbs. "Hang on, Prim," Wynona whispered to the dark. "I'm working on it." She took in a shuddering breath. "And I won't give up."

Wynona could feel despair trying to swallow her whole, but she forced her body to relax and her breathing to even out. Even tea could only do so much to help her. She would need to stay healthy or her ability to prove Prim's innocence would only diminish.

Minutes ticked by as Wynona fought the weight of her responsibility. She took a moment to wiggle herself under the covers and try to get as comfortable as possible. But when her mind went to whether or not Prim had a comfortable bed, Wynona knew sleep would be long in coming.

Blowing out a long breath, she kept her eyes shut and continued the mental fight for her sanity. No matter how bleak things looked, Wynona couldn't give up. Prim was counting on her.

By the time the morning sun peeked through the curtains, Wynona had no idea if she had slept at all. She had been so in and out of sleep that she was unsure how much she had actually rested.

Sitting up, she slapped her cheeks slightly, trying to wake herself up. The crushing worry hadn't relented all night and when Wynona stood up, her knees actually shook.

She pushed her hair back and headed to the bathroom. "One of these days I'll magic myself some energy," she grumbled, though she had never heard of anyone being able to do that. Magic could help her *look* well rested, but as for actually giving her a boost? It would only ever be a fantasy.

Her shower was scalding and Wynona scrubbed her skin almost raw, but nothing seemed to help her free her shoulders from her anxiety.

"There's nothing for it," she finally said to her pale, puffy-eyed reflection. "Only solving the case is going to help."

Wynona didn't even bother putting on makeup. What little energy she had today was going to have to be used for other things. This morning she would go back to the theatre. She just knew she was missing something. It had to be there.

And then hopefully, she could survive work long enough not to kill her business before she was able to get a good night's rest.

A pervasive sense of doom followed her as she ate breakfast and packed what she needed for work. Even Violet was barely functioning as they slogged their way out to the scooter.

"Okay, Violet," Wynona said as she strapped on her helmet. "I can't keep doing this. Something has to give." She looked her purple friend in the eyes. "This is the day. We're solving this now. Got it?"

Violet nodded firmly.

"Glad we're on the same page." Wynona started the scooter and the two of them took off. She was grateful for the cool wind on her face helping her stay awake. She wasn't sure her brain was awake enough to actually process anything she found at the theatre, but Wynona couldn't stay home for the morning. Doing something poorly was better than doing nothing at all.

CHAPTER 24

Wynona knew she looked less than her best as she knocked on Mrs. Truall's door, but it was not the time to worry about appearances.

The door jerked open. "What do you want?" Mr. Truall growled.

Wynona had to forcefully stop herself from stepping back as an automatic reaction to the predator. "I'm here following up a couple of leads," she hedged. "Do you mind if I speak to your wife?"

"We're busy," he snapped.

"But the show isn't until—"

"Fable?" Mrs. Truall's soft voice whispered on the wind. "Who is it?"

"That nosy president's daughter," Fable grumbled over his shoulder.

Wynona pinched her lips together. Why were people so mean? Perpetual rudeness was a pet peeve of Wynona's. Her family was constantly treating those around them as less than themselves and Wynona had spent thirty years being told she was worthless.

At her escape, Wynona had promised herself that she would *never* become like them. So even though Mr. Truall was pushing her buttons, Wynona forced herself to smile and not reflect his own attitude back.

"Mrs. Truall?" Wynona appealed into the room. "I'd like to ask you a few questions, if you don't mind."

Mr. Truall glared at her, but Wynona kept her smile in place.

"I don't mind at all," Mrs. Truall said pleasantly as she peeked around her husband's tall body. "Please...come in." She gently pushed on her husband's arm and he grudgingly stepped aside.

Mrs. Truall smiled up at him and Wynona was once again caught off guard by how apparent his infatuation was. The softening was instantaneous as he looked at his wife, but the second his gaze went back to Wynona, it turned dark.

"Have a seat," Mrs. Truall said, indicating the same flowered chair Wynona had sat in before.

"Thank you," Wynona said politely. "I'll do my best not to take up much of your time..." She trailed off as she registered the chaos of the room. "Are you leaving on a vacation, Mrs. Truall?"

"Brell, please," Brell said with a soft smile. She grabbed her husband's hand, looking adoringly at him before coming back to Wynona. "We're moving on," she declared.

Wynona raised her eyebrows. "Moving on? I thought you had a contract."

Mr. Truall growled. "The police made sure we received a copy when it was recovered from Madam Ureo's safe," he said tightly. "It states that at her death, the contract is null and void. A new manager would need a new contract." His hands clenched and unclenched.

Brell tsked her tongue and came to sit on the couch across from Wynona. "Madam Ureo had kept that a secret from us." Brell lifted a mug off a coaster and took a sip before putting it back.

Wynona tilted her head to the side. She had known the contract details, having been the one to find the papers, but she hadn't realized the Trualls were acting on it. Wynona had assumed Mr. Rujins would fight it. "You didn't know that tidbit when you signed it?"

Brell rolled her eyes and laughed in an unamused tone. "I was young and naive back then," she said. Her cheeks blushed becomingly. "I was so eager for a job that I didn't pay attention to the fine print." She shook her head. "But now I know better. Next time I sign on the dotted line, I'll know exactly what I'm signing."

"Which is exactly what we're doing tomorrow," Fable said, coming to sit next to his wife on the couch. He took her hand, pressing it between his own. "Brell has been offered a movie contract." His dark eyes were less harsh as they met Wynona's this time. "We're meeting with our lawyer tomorrow to go over the details."

"Sounds like an excellent plan," Wynona praised. "And congratulations."

"Thank you," Brell said breathlessly. "It's all happening so fast! I've only been out of the hospital a couple of days and we spoke to Mr. Rujins only yesterday, and now I've got a job offer!" She was beaming like the noon day sun. "It's all a dream come true, but hard to believe it's actually happening."

"Wow..." Wynona nodded slowly. "What did Mr. Rujins say when you broke it with him? I can't imagine he was pleased to have his star leaving."

Fable was immediately on his feet, pacing the room and snarling quietly under his breath.

Brell watched him, but didn't act surprised or worried. "He wasn't very happy, that's for sure. But he really had no legal leg to stand on." She picked up her mug and leaned back on the couch in a relaxed manner. "In fact, keeping us on the same contract would have actually been against the law. If we had found out about the contract much later, we would have had grounds to sue."

"Which is exactly why Mr. Rujins wanted to hide it all from us," Fable grumbled.

Brell pulled the mug away from her mouth. "Oh, I'm so sorry. How rude of me." She raised her eyebrows. "Ms. Le Doux, would you like some tea?"

"Wynona," Wynona corrected with a smile. "And tea sounds lovely."

"Fable, would you be a dear and get her a mug?" Brell asked her still-standing husband.

He nodded curtly and walked to the corner of the room where a drink station, almost exactly like the one in Madam Ureo's old office, stood. Apparently, when they created the room in the theatre, all the side rooms had all been built identically. "Chamomile or blood orange?" he asked.

"The orange sounds wonderful," Wynona said.

Fable grunted, but fixed the drink, poured himself some coffee and brought them over, handing Wynona a steaming mug.

"Thank you," she said, wrapping her hands around the warmth. The smell was cirtusy and divine, helping further to wake Wynona up. The antioxidant help would certainly be a benefit as she wasn't getting enough sleep at the moment. Any healthy boost was more than welcome.

Fable settled next to his wife, sipping his own brew.

"Mr. Truall, are you also excited? Making a movie sounds like it will be less audience-based, like your wife is doing now." Wynona tried to act nonchalant, but she kept a close eye on the shifter. She was confident he didn't poison his wife, but the situation with Madam Ureo still seemed suspicious. Perhaps they were looking for two murders instead of just one? It wasn't an angle they had been investigating yet, but with as desperate as Wynona was becoming, she was willing to entertain anything at this point.

He grunted. "It should be less chaotic, for certain." He glanced sideways. "And more lucrative for sure."

Brell gave him an indulgent smile. "Making the movies will be stressful, but at least there will be breaks between them. Right now I'm on stage practically every night with no vacations."

Wynona whistled low. "That's a lot. You weren't ever allowed to take a break?"

"Only when I was in the hospital," Brell said softly, her head hanging down.

Fable set his mug down and wrapped an arm around her shoulders and kissed her temple. "No more. We're not tied to this place any longer. Life can only get better from here." He leaned back and used his free hand to tilt up her chin. "And maybe we can even start that family you wanted, hm?"

Brell's eyes were watery, but she smiled. "That'll be wonderful, won't it?"

Wynona tentatively sipped her tea, trying to act as if she weren't bothered by the little display. Right now she felt like a peeping tom and it was more than a little uncomfortable. Clearing her throat, she moved to set her mug down on the side table, but hesitated. Although there were already rings on the table, Brell had used a coaster and Wynona didn't want to assume anything.

"Here." Brell leaned forward to hand a coaster to Wynona. "I'm not usually sitting over there. Sorry."

Wynona smiled and took the offering, setting it down before adding her mug to it. "That's fine. I didn't want to risk staining the table."

"Any more than it already was?" Brell said wryly. She laughed. "You'd think with all the money Madam Ureo made, she could afford to purchase newer furniture for us."

Wynona nodded. Brell was definitely *not* one of the employees who was missing paychecks. And apparently, that meant she had a better idea of how much the theatre made. It was a wonder Madam Ureo's scheme went on as long as it did. Didn't the cast members talk to each other?

"It doesn't matter now," Fable snapped. "That harpy is gone and tomorrow, we'll be gone as well." His eyes moved around the room in disgust. "Good riddance."

"This is where I got my start," Brell gently scolded. "Without Madam Ureo, I would never have gotten a chance."

"Still..." he huffed. "I can't be grateful for a woman who was nothing but a menace to society. She was more worried about her bottom line than how she treated her employees." He growled low and took another drink.

Wynona watched the interplay, trying to discern if anything in Fable's demeanor could be interpreted as the actions of a killer.

"What are your thoughts?" Brell asked, surprising Wynona out of her study. "Would you be grateful for the person who got you started? Even if they weren't a good person?"

Wynona's mind automatically went to her family. If she had been born with her powers and treated the same as her siblings, what would life be like? It wouldn't include her tea shop, that was for sure. And it more than likely wouldn't involve Rascal. No...as hard as it was to endure the years she did, Wynona completely understood where Brell was coming from and it only made her like the siren more. "I think I would," Wynona said. "Sometimes the bad situations are exactly why we end up with the good ones. They shape us in a way that leads us to a happy moment that would have never happened otherwise."

Brell beamed and turned to her husband. "See? Wynona understands."

Fable grumbled into his mug, tipping his head back and draining it. "You two women believe what you want. But I'm glad she's gone." He stood and took the mug to the tiny sink, rinsing it out and setting it aside.

Wynona's mind churned. There was something...

"Did you have more questions for me?" Brell asked.

Wynona whipped her head toward her host. "Oh, sorry. I guess my mind was wandering."

Brell smiled. "Happens to me all the time." She blushed again. "Fable says I'm a dreamer." Brell shrugged. "I suppose it goes with the territory of being a performer."

"I suppose so," Wynona agreed. "You know, I wanted to ask you if you ever figured out who sent you those flowers?"

Brell stiffened and Wynona immediately felt bad.

"I'm sorry," Wynona said softly. "I didn't mean to upset you, but if we had any clue as to who tried to hurt you, it would help us greatly in figuring out this case."

"Don't you mean who tried to kill her?" Fable argued, his voice low and hard.

Wynona looked his way, noting the flash of his eyes. Just like Rascal, it was a warning sign that his animal was near the surface. "You're right," Wynona acquiesced. "Has anything come forward to give you a clue?"

Brell shook her head, her red lips pinched together.

Fable folded his arms over his broad chest. "Nothing we haven't already told the police."

Wynona took in a long breath. "I see." She smiled. "Well...I think maybe I should let you two get back to your work. It would seem that you have a lot of packing to do if you're going to be out of here tomorrow, and I don't want to stand in your way." Wynona stood and Brell followed.

"Thank you so much for stopping by," Brell said, walking around the coffee table to grasp Wynona's hand. "You've been so concerned and helpful. I appreciate you doing your best to solve this."

Wynona smiled. Brell didn't need to know that Wynona was invested because her best friend was the accused. "Helping the police catch the right criminal has ended up being sort of a hobby of mine." The statement was truer than Wynona wanted it to be, but true nonetheless.

"Must be exciting," Brell said eagerly as she walked Wynona to the door. "Finding the clues, putting them together." She shook her head. "I don't know that my artist's brain could ever be organized enough for that."

"It's not as crazy as it seems," Wynona said. "While I'm fairly analytically minded, it's mostly about watching for details." Her eyes drifted back to Fable for a second. His movements earlier had struck a chord, but Wynona couldn't quite figure out why. He'd been washing his coffee mug. Why was that significant? What was Wynona supposed to remember from such a mundane task?

"Still..." Brell continued. "I think it's wonderful." She leaned in slightly. "We don't have nearly enough women who insert themselves into that world. We all look up to women just like you."

The thought of anyone looking up to Wynona was laughable. She knew if anything, she was laughed at, not admired. When people looked at her, they either saw her connections to the royal family, or they saw her lack of magic. There didn't seem to be any in-between. Still, it was kind of Brell to try and make her feel good. The compliment was appreciated, if not quite accurate. "You're such a sweetheart," Wynona gushed. "Thank you so much."

Brell opened the dressing room door. "I doubt I'll see you again since we're headed out of town tomorrow, so good luck to you. I hope you find what you're looking for."

"You as well," Wynona said back. "I'll wait to hear about the movies. And I hope you two can settle down the way you've always dreamed of." Wynona truly wished the best for Brell, though she couldn't quite set aside Fable as a suspect. If it came to that, it would break Brell's heart and Wynona wasn't going to be happy about it, but she would absolutely sacrifice him for Prim's freedom if he proved to be guilty.

Stepping out into the hall, Wynona gave a little wave and walked toward the next dressing room. She had spent more time than she should have with the Trualls, but hopefully it wasn't wasted. She would figure out why Fable's mug washing was important and then continue to collect bits of information from other employees. This morning was it. Just as the Trualls were determined to be gone tomorrow, Wynona was determined not to let tomorrow come without answers. She just needed to keep going.

CHAPTER 25

Wynona nodded politely as Hamer, the gorgon, drolled on about how he meditated to get into character before a show.

"I close my eyessss," he hissed, tilting his head back and flipping both sets of lids closed. "Once I find peasssse in the darknesssss, I astral project mysssself to the ethereal plane...assss a vampire..."

Wynona covered a yawn with her hand. She had no idea how they had gotten onto this topic. Hamer was a chatty one. Just like the first time they had met, he had been eager to speak to Wynona as she was related to President Le Doux. Also, just like last time, he spent the entire interview speaking about himself, rather than answering any of the questions Wynona had about the case.

His eyes opened. "It takessss more work than you would imagine to pretend to be another," he said regally.

Wynona nodded and smiled. "I have no doubt. I've never even tried acting. I'll leave it to you professionals."

His beaming grin let Wynona know he enjoyed a good ego stroke. But before he could go on again, she pressed forward.

"Were you aware that Brell and Fable are leaving tomorrow?"

Some of the eagerness fell from Hamer's face and he pulled his gaze to the side, pretending indifference. "Yesss."

"Are you going to miss her?"

His nose flared. "I suppose the whole troupe will." He looked back at her sharply. "Much of the crowds were here to see her. Without Vampiria, our followers will greatly diminish."

"Doesn't that leave room for a new star?" Wynona asked, hoping to keep him talking. Apparently, he didn't love this subject, but she was trying to lead him around to the case.

Hamer sniffed. "I supposssssse, if our manager gives any of ussssss a chance to shine."

Wynona frowned. "Speaking of your new manager, has he given all of you the option of redoing your contracts? Weren't they void when Madam Ureo died?"

Hamer shook his head, his second eyelids blinking rapidly. "Only Brell's held that sssssstipulation." His lip curled. "I'm not sure how sssssshe managed it, truth be told."

"Brell said she didn't know it was there," Wynona responded.

Green eyes rolled to the ceiling. "I'm ssssure her husssband did. He would never have let her ssssign something without reading it first."

Wynona paused, her mind churning. Fable had been the one to sign the contract? He hadn't acted like it was him. She tried to remember what signatures had been on the document, but Wynona couldn't recall. She might need to bring that up with Rascal. "So everyone else is staying with the theatre?" Wynona clarified.

Hamer nodded. "Yesss. I have another two yearsss before I can look elsssewhere."

"Do you want to go somewhere else?" Wynona asked. "Are you hoping to move onward and upward?" She glanced at a wall clock and stirrings of anxiety and urgency began to build. It was later than she thought and she had hardly accomplished anything. She needed to kick this interview into high gear and get moving.

"Doesn't every actor wish for greatnessss?" Hamer asked. "To be dissssscovered would be the ultimate reward."

Wynona nodded. "Agreed." She slapped her knees. "Well, thank you for talking to me, but I really must be going." She had gained nothing from this little chat. Nothing. She couldn't afford to waste time like this if she was going to solve the mystery this morning. She still had a business to run and opening was coming up quickly. She stood and walked to the door.

Hamer jumped after her. "Wouldn't you like a drink?" he asked hurriedly.

Wynona closed her eyes for a second and took a deep breath in through her nose. Really, the man just seemed lonely. She supposed that constantly pretending to be someone else could cause that. And from what she had gathered, the actors at the theatre were more like competition than family. What a sad life. Forcing a pleasant smile on her face, Wynona turned around, her hand still on the knob. "That's very kind of you, but—"

"It'sssss no trouble at all!" Hamer shouted as he raced to the other side of the room. It was the same small drink station that Wynona had seen in the Trualls' room and the slightly larger office of Madam Ureo. A coffee maker and two mugs were planted in the corner while several extra containers littered the surface. "Do you like sugar or cream in yourssss?" he asked, smiling over his shoulder.

Wynona bit back the retort sitting on the edge of her tongue. She didn't even like coffee and yet she couldn't quite bring herself to break his heart. "I only have a few minutes," she tried.

Hamer waved away her worries. "That'ssss fine. I sssshould get ready soon anywayssss." He carried a mug to the sitting area and waited for Wynona while she replanted herself in the flowered wingback chair again. At this point she was going to have a permanent flower imprint on her backside from how many times she had sat on this pattern.

"Thank you," she said, doing her best to sound grateful and not frustrated. If Hamer caught onto her real mood, he didn't show it.

His green eyes glowed and he rushed back to the stand to grab his own mug. "I prefer lotssss of ssssugar," he said with a guilty expression. "I sssupose I never quite outgrew my sssssweet tooth."

"I think most of us are that way," Wynona said, her tight smile still in place.

Hamer sat down, sipping his brew and closing his eyes in apparent bliss. "Ssssssublime..." He opened his eyes and looked at Wynona expectantly.

She brought the cup to her lips and took the tiniest sip she possibly could, fighting a grimace at the flavor. It just couldn't compare to a good mint and lavender. "Mmm... " she said encouragingly. "Delicious."

"Have you ssspoken to your sssister lately?" Hamer asked, tilting his head to the side. "Perhapssss she isss looking forward to another interview with *Hex Haven Today*?"

How much worse could things get? Not only was Wynona wasting time, but now he wanted to talk about her family? Really? And Celia? Who wanted to talk about Celia?

The entirety of Hex Haven, that's who wanted to talk about Celia. The presidential family was worshipped like celebrities and Wynona hated it.

"I have no idea what Celia's schedule is," Wynona said with a fake sympathetic smile. She reached to put the mug on the side table, but bumped into something. Glancing over, Wynona remembered there was a large plant with a small watering pot taking up the extra space.

"Ssssorry," Hamer gushed, setting his own mug on the coffee table and lunging over it. He grabbed the watering pot and moved it to the coffee table. His pale cheeks flushed. "I don't get visssitorsss very often."

Wynona's smile was genuine this time. He really was sweet, if slightly awkward. She felt pity for him that he struggled so much with company. No one deserved to be alone. Glancing to the side, Wynona once again went to set down her mug, but she jerked to a stop, staring at the top of the table.

"Ms. Le Doux?" Hamer asked tentatively, when she didn't move for several seconds. "Isss ssssomething wrong?"

Wynona blinked herself back to the present. "Hamer..." She paused, her mind swirling. "Pretty much all these dressing rooms are the same...right?" She looked his way, forcing herself away from the table.

He nodded. "Identical."

She pointed to the pot. "Do they all have plants as well?"

He shrugged. "Assss far asssss I know."

Wynona's heart skipped a beat. "Did Mrs. Truall have a plant in her room?"

His two sets of eyelids blinked. "I think sssso....yesss..." He nodded slowly, then more confidently. "Yesss, it doesssss."

Wynona's breathing was starting to shallow out. "Do you know what kind of plant it was?"

Again, Hamer took his time answering, his eyes unfocused as he tried to recall. "No...though..." He tilted his head to the side. "It has spiky leavessss. I recall sssseeing it from the doorway onsssse. Perhapssss it was a type of aloe?"

"Shoot," Wynona grumbled.

"Was that not the right anssssswer?" he asked, sinking back into himself.

"No, no, no," Wynona assured him. "You did great." She stood. "But as fun as it's been, I need to run. I have some errands that are very important." Like saving her best friend, Wynona wanted to add. And right now, some ideas were swirling that just might be the beginning of doing just that.

"Musssst you?" he whined.

"I must," Wynona said curtly. "You've been wonderful, but I really have to go." She walked quickly to the door and pulled it open. A blast of cold air hit her in the face. "Whoa..."

"Ssssometimes they open the cargo door," Hamer said from right behind her, causing Wynona to jump.

"Oh...thanks," she said, stepping gingerly into the hallway. Her loose curls began to blow in the heavy breeze. Wynona tucked them behind her ear. She needed to get out of here. "Okay...bye," she said quickly, walking down the hallway.

In her hurry, Wynona ducked around several other actors, not bothering to stop and talk to them. Wynona had a lead, the first real one in this case, and she needed to go talk to Rascal about it.

The noise in the hallway got louder as she walked farther into the crowd and Wynona ducked into her shoulder a little. With the cargo bay open, the sound in the theatre really was obnoxiously loud.

"Excuse me," she said, ducking past a crew of men who were hauling in what appeared to be new stage props. "Oof!" Wynona pulled back, rubbing her shoulder. "I'm sorry..." She trailed off as she realized Ringer Doom was glaring down at her. "Excuse me," she said, trying to duck around him.

"Why are you here?" he growled, grabbing her upper arm.

Wynona paused and looked down at his hold. Her heart, which had already been beating harder than normal, took off faster than a centaur at a race.

His grip tightened slightly when she didn't answer right away.

"You're hurting me," Wynona said as calmly as possible.

"And you're trespassing," Ringer growled, bending down to get in her face.

Wynona tried to keep her shaking to a minimum and she was seriously regretting leaving Violet in the Vespa at the moment. The sun had been shining and Wynona had been worried the mouse would be a distraction, so the purple rodent had opted for a nap in the warm morning weather. "I have permission from the police to be here," she said carefully.

His growl started low, but grew.

"Mr. Ringer," she said. "Please let me go."

His hand tightened a moment before falling away completely. He straightened and looked down the hallway, Wynona suddenly forgotten.

She frowned. "Mr. Doom?"

He glanced down, but ultimately went back to the hallway.

Wynona turned, stood on tiptoe and tried to see what had caught Ringer's attention. There, just outside her dressing room door, was Brell. She was looking back into her room and speaking, but Wynona and Ringer were much too far away to hear anything over the noise...

Wynona paused. She glanced up at Ringer, who was still entranced, then back down the hall and concentrated.

"...we...van...party..."

Words that matched the movement of Brell's lips floated around Wynona's head like a spring breeze, dancing and tiptoeing around the multitude of bodies until it landed gently in Wynona's ear.

She gasped, a memory suddenly becoming clear. "No..." Wynona breathed. She slowly shook her head, completely dumbfounded how she had missed the obvious. It had all been in front of her the whole time. How could she have been so clueless?

Without bothering to look at Ringer again, Wynona dashed away, running to her Vespa and jumping in the seat.

Violet squeaked, shocked out of her nap and clung to the edge of her basket.

"Sorry, Violet," Wynona said over the noise of her engine. "But we need to do some quick research."

Violet scowled and chittered.

Wynona nodded as she pulled out into traffic. "Yes, I think I figured it out, but I need proof." She took a deep breath. "And for that...I need to see my family."

CHAPTER 26

Wynona sat on her scooter staring at the large castle in front of her. She knew it well. She'd grown up in it.

And she had never wanted to see it again.

Making it through the security gate had been easy. But getting inside without losing herself? That was a different story.

Violet whimpered and scrambled up the basket, carefully maneuvering herself over the handlebars until she had reached Wynona and her favorite nuzzling spot on her shoulder.

"Thanks," Wynona whispered, her eyes never leaving the massive home. "There's nothing for it," she stated after a moment of silence. "I have to go in." Turning her head, she leaned back, trying to see Violet. "Think I'll make it out alive?"

Violet shook herself all over and scrubbed her face.

"Prim is worth it though, right?"

At that, Violet straightened and nodded.

"Right." Wynona straightened her legs and swung one over so she was off the scooter. Then, forcing her legs to keep moving, she marched up the steps, noting the slight tingle as she passed through the magic barrier around the castle.

It was tempting to pause and examine the feeling. Until now, Wynona had never been able to feel it, since her connection to magic had been severed. But now she understood a little better what others felt when coming up to the door.

She debated whether or not to knock. After all, this was her family's home, even if they weren't on good terms with each other. "Think I could sneak in, get what I need and sneak out?" Wynona whispered.

Violet grumbled.

Wynona sighed. "Yeah...you're probably right." Raising her fist, she was just about to knock when the door opened.

"Are you insane?" Celia snapped, tossing her perfect hair over her shoulder. "Do you realize what Mom and Dad would do to you if they found you here by yourself?"

Wynona swallowed the rock in her throat. "I need to get a book from the library," she said as confidently as she could, which wasn't very impressive.

Celia rolled her eyes. "Let me guess. You're solving another murder."

Wynona's jaw dropped. "How—?"

Celia grumbled before yanking Wynona inside. "You're such an idiot. Do you really think I don't watch the ghost media? That ridiculous fairy you run around with has been accused of Madam Ureo's murder." Dropping Wynona's wrist as if it would give her a disease, she marched ahead in the direction of the library.

Wynona had to admit she didn't think Celia would watch such things. The paparazzi and latest social media, especially when it was about the presidential family, would be right up Celia's alley. But hardcore news? It just didn't fit.

Wynona stared at Celia's back while they walked through the home. The same feeling Wynona had had when she helped clear Celia's name from a crime a few months ago came rushing back.

Had she judged her sister too harshly?

They had never had a good relationship growing up. Celia, though younger, had always treated Wynona like she was a disgrace. No one cared that the curse wasn't Wynona's doing. She had been a baby for crying out loud! But when a culprit hadn't been found, the family had given up the idea of reversing the spell and instead had placed all blame directly on Wynona's shoulders.

It was a wonder she had gotten enough care to actually survive to adulthood.

But during the investigation of the death of a coven member of Celia's, Wynona had had the feeling several times that Celia wasn't quite as bad as she wanted everyone to believe. Like there was someone just beneath the surface that wanted to break free.

That glimpse, however, never stuck around long enough for Wynona to study it in detail.

Right now was an excellent example. Celia had led Wynona, without question, to the library, but had spent the entire time being rude and condescending. Plus, Celia hadn't called their parents, though Wynona figured they more than likely knew she was here.

"Where are Mom and Dad?" Wynona asked as she stepped into her second favorite place in the castle. The first being Granny's old greenhouse.

"They're out, lucky for you," Celia said with an amused snort. Her face grew more serious. "You do realize that if they were home, they wouldn't let you leave, right?"

Wynona shrugged, trying to act nonchalant. "I don't see why they'd care."

Celia huffed and strolled to an overstuffed wing chair, falling lazily into it. "Just because they don't want you, doesn't mean they enjoy you making headlines by solving crimes and working like a common para."

Wynona's jaw clenched. "There's nothing wrong with working. It's the support of working people that keeps Dad in his job."

Celia shrugged and studied her nails. "Just saying."

Wynona closed her eyes, rested her fingers against Violet, who had thankfully stayed quiet, and took in a deep breath. "Thank you for letting me come in. I'll only take a minute of your time." She walked confidently toward the section of the library that she knew would contain the book she wanted. Wynona had spent so much of her time here that she practically knew the books by heart. If she could just grab what she wanted and be on her way, her parents could be left out of the equation completely.

She squinted at the shelf the book should have been on, and stilled.

"They reorganized it."

Wynona's neck hurt from how quickly she jerked toward Celia. "What?"

Celia smirked. "Dearest Mumsy thought it would be much nicer to have the library organized according to color."

For the first time since arriving, Wynona really studied the shelves. She hadn't bothered to look closely because she thought she knew what was going on. She rubbed her now throbbing forehead. "Who in the world would do that?" she complained.

Violet grumbled.

"Someone who doesn't bother to read?" Celia offered.

A retort was on the tip of Wynona's tongue, but she bit it back. It simply wasn't worth the heartache and anger to argue with her sister. Her energy was much better spent gathering the book and getting out of there before her parents came home. "When are Mom and Dad due back?"

"Beats me," Celia offered unhelpfully.

"Good grief," Wynona said breathlessly. Closing her eyes, she recalled the book, then made her way to the red zone. The problem was, there were probably close to two hundred red books. How in the world was she supposed to find just one, when there was no other distinction for her to follow?

"Should I have lunch brought in?" Celia asked.

"No, thank you," Wynona said tightly. "I'm only going to be a minute." She studied the shelves. Now would be an excellent time for her to be able to use her magic. But between how unreliable it was and her audience, there was no way she could do it.

"Suit yourself." Celia pulled her phone out of her pocket and quickly began scrolling, obviously not about to leave the room.

Wynona once again pet Violet to try and help assuage her frustration. The weight of what she was doing was quickly becoming more than she could handle. She had no idea when her parents would be home, and it would definitely be in her best interest to be gone by then. Wynona was fairly certain she knew who the killer was, but she needed the book to prove it. And Prim was currently wasting away behind bars and if Wynona didn't get things settled quickly, it might all prove too late!

Not having any other choice, Wynona got down on her knees and began scanning the books one by one. There were several hundred and she knew it would take her a long time, but she couldn't afford mistakes.

After ten minutes, Violet must have decided things weren't moving fast enough and she climbed down to the floor. Rising on her back feet, her nose twitched as she looked at Wynona expectantly.

Wynona let her weight thump to the ground as she landed on her hip. "It's called *Natural Paranormals*," she said. "Red cover, gold writing."

Violet squeaked and quickly made her way up to the top of the bookcase.

Wynona let her friend go at it and went back to her own search. The minutes ticked by and the library was quiet, except for the tapping of Celia's nails on her phone screen.

"How long are you going to search?" Celia groaned, rising from her seat.

"Until I find what I'm looking for," Wynona snapped back before she could stop herself. She closed her eyes and pinched the bridge of her nose. "Sorry. But this book is important. In fact, it's the difference between life and death."

"Even your own?" Celia pressed, leaning her shoulder against the edge of the bookcase. "Mom could be home any time."

Wynona kept her face as emotionless as possible as she turned to her sister. "I'll just have to risk it."

Celia scrunched her nose. "You really are a bleeding heart."

Wynona went back to the books. "There are worse things in life than caring about people." Celia didn't respond right away and Wynona hoped her sister would decide the situation was too boring and leave. Another couple of minutes went by and she had no such luck.

Celia hung her head back. "Ugh. This is so stupid." She wiggled her fingers, red sparks dripping to the floor. "What do you need?"

Wynona narrowed her eyes. "You're going to help me?"

Celia made a face. "Consider this your one and only thank you for helping clear my name." She sneered. "Do you want it or not?"

While this was unexpected, it was definitely not unwelcome. Wynona jumped to her feet, dusting off her pants. "Absolutely. I'm looking for *Natural Paranormals*."

"A textbook? Really?" Celia shook her head. "Sometimes I wonder how we're related." Her hand twirled and those red sparks shot out, rushing over the books, combing and caressing until a book began to wiggle. Slowly, it began to push itself to the edge of the shelf.

Wynona ran over and was just able to catch it before it splatted on the floor. The edge of the hardcover cut into her hands, but Wynona barely noticed. The heavy book felt like salvation in her arms and she almost began crying in relief now that she was holding the very thing that should free Prim. But first...

She turned, hugging the book to her chest. "Thank you," she said hoarsely. "I don't know that I can adequately express how much this means to me."

"Whatever," Celia said curtly. "I'd suggest you get out of here before our parents return."

Wynona nodded and looked up to Violet, who was working her way down the bookshelves. Wynona held out her hand and Violet jumped on, scrambling up to Wynona's shoulder. "Again...thank you." Not leaving Celia time to respond, Wynona rushed out, practically running down the hallway.

With each step closer to the front door, she prayed a little harder that she could make it out before her parents got in. She rushed past servants, PR reps and a few bodyguards that she and Celia had managed to sneak past earlier, but now Wynona wasn't doing anything to hide. She just wanted out. With the book.

"Wynona Odessa Le Doux."

Without her permission, Wynona's legs stopped moving. She hugged the book tightly, even as she felt her mother's magic work its way through her system. Tears pricked her eyes. She had been so close. Prim was waiting and the clock was ticking to catch the true killer. This was the absolute worst thing that could have possibly happened.

"Nothing to say to your mother?"

Wynona slowly spun, forcing the emotion from her face and putting her chin in the air. "Hello, Mother."

Marcella was as perfect as ever. Her skin showed no sign of age and her black hair was long and silky, laying just right against her shoulders and back to look as attractive as possible. Red lips were curled ever so slightly at the corners and a single eyebrow was raised high on her forehead. Though Wynona didn't work so hard on her appearance, there was no way to doubt that they were related.

The perfect complexion, however, could do nothing to hide the dark heart that lay beneath. At least, not for Wynona, who had far too many memories at her mother's hands.

"What are you doing here?" Marcella asked harshly.

"Dearest," Wynona's father drawled, his body turned away from Wynona. "I thought we agreed not to acknowledge her anymore. She's no longer a Le Doux."

Wynona felt her heart clench. It didn't matter that they had treated her like dirt beneath their feet. It didn't matter that she went out of her way to stay apart. It didn't matter that she had had to escape in the middle of the night in order to find her own life. Having her parents speak about her in such a way still hurt.

"It's sort of hard to ignore the abomination when she's standing in my foyer," Marcella said tightly.

"Then have her kicked out," he said, walking away.

Wynona took a step backward, toward the door.

That eyebrow climbed a little higher. "No."

Bile churned in Wynona's stomach and Violet whimpered.

"I think it's time we have a mother-daughter chat." Spinning on her heel, Marcella crooked her finger over her shoulder. "Follow me."

"Mother, I—"

Marcella snapped her fingers and magic wrapped around Wynona's legs, force-marching her down the hall toward her mother's office. Wynona's heart began to pulse against her ribcage and her breathing grew shallow. Purple sparkles snapped in her periphery and the sight of it only caused Wynona's panic to skyrocket.

"Please, no," Wynona whispered, squeezing her eyes shut. She didn't have to look where she was going—her mother's magic would do it for her—but if she couldn't get her emotions under control, her magic would explode and an already bad situation would become catastrophic.

If she didn't stop it, this might be the end of her life as she knew it.

CHAPTER 27

Wynona forced her breathing to slow in order to keep her heart rate down. If she could manipulate her body into behaving nicely, perhaps she could convince her magic that it wasn't worth breaking free right now.

The clips of heels on the marble floor changed and Wynona knew they'd entered a room. She opened her eyes, tilting her chin up and forcing her shoulders back. Her confidence might be fake, but no one other than herself and Violet needed to know that.

Violet had stayed suspiciously quiet during this little parental showdown, but Wynona could feel her attached at the nape of her neck. Her small presence was soothing and was a great help in Wynona getting herself under control.

Despite her best efforts, however, there were still small purple flecks in the air when her mother spun and glared her down. "Why are you here?" she hissed, her poised presence diminishing now that they didn't have an audience.

In...out...in...out...

"I needed a book," Wynona said truthfully. There was no real point in lying anyway. Odds were that her mother wouldn't believe anything she said.

Marcella scoffed. "A book."

Wynona wanted to congratulate herself on knowing exactly what was going to happen.

"If that's the case, what book is it?"

Wynona turned the bright red book around. "It's called *Natural Paranormals.*" With her legs still tied up, Wynona couldn't do a thing when her mother marched over and grabbed it out of her hands.

"What would you want with a textbook?" she asked as she scanned the contents. "Especially one that has nothing to do with that ridiculous little tea business of yours?"

"I need it for a case I'm helping the police with."

Marcella's laughter was slow at first, then built into a full belly laugh. It was a sound that Wynona had rarely heard in her life. Most of the time her mother tittered in polite tones while schmoozing other powerful paranormals, or promoting her husband. She rarely let loose with actual amusement.

"You...helping the police." Marcella sighed and wiped a supposed tear from the corner of her eye. "It just goes to show that we should overhaul the entire system. If they need the help of someone like you, then they shouldn't be in charge."

For the second time that morning, Wynona's heart pinched. Would the pain never go away? Would she never be free from the desire to be accepted...just once?

Purple ribbons floated in her periphery and Wynona stiffened. No matter how much she longed for her mother to actually treat her like a real witch, showing her magic was *not* the way to do it.

"What is that?" Marcella asked, stepping toward the display.

Wynona hung her head, complete despair wrapping around her. She could never seem to catch a break. Life had looked so good when she'd gotten away from this castle, only to come face to face with a dead body.

After getting that out of the way, she tried again, finding a small pocket of happiness with Rascal before Celia interrupted it all with her cries for help. Fighting her family and the entire police force, Wynona had once again triumphed, thinking she would finally reach a point where she could rest and enjoy life.

Now her best friend was in jail, Wynona was trapped without a way to get the evidence they needed to free her, her father had disowned her for the second time and her mother was about to discover her magic.

All the courage Wynona had built up this morning was gone. Only a bleak prison sentence seemed to await her. Because that's exactly what it would be. When her mother figured it all out, Wynona would never be allowed to leave again. They wouldn't want all that precious power going to waste, after all.

"Ahh!"

Wynona's eyes snapped open just as Violet ran up Marcella's legs. "Violet!"

"What is that thing?" Marcella screamed, her magic shooting in random directions as she tried to zap the rodent crawling over her.

"Mom, stop! Don't hurt her!"

"This thing belongs to you?" Marcella said harshly. "Where in the world did you get a magical creature? It can't be your familiar. You don't have any magic!"

With the distraction, Wynona's legs were set free and she nearly collapsed on the floor in relief as she realized her mother thought the purple ribbons were from Violet. Dropping to her knees, Wynona held out her hand. "Violet," she said softly. "Come on."

Violet scurried over, taking refuge in Wynona's hold. When Wynona pulled Violet into her chest, the mouse turned and stuck her tongue out at Marcella.

Wynona bit her tongue so hard she was sure it would bleed, as she tried to contain her laughter.

"That *thing* needs to be put down," Marcella said, fluffing and restyling her hair.

"She's a mouse," Wynona said calmly. "She's not a thing and she's a friend of mine, not to mention a great help to me at the tea shop."

"You let that thing loose while you're serving food?" Marcella's lip curled and she sneered. "Your grandmother would never have been so careless."

Hit number three. The very thought of Granny Saffron not approving brought instant tears and remorse to Wynona, even though she knew her mother was wrong. Granny would have loved Violet. She loved all creatures. But her powers brought a great responsibility with them and Granny Saffron had been fierce in public while soft only with Wynona.

Keeping her shaking to a minimum, Wynona walked toward her mother, who paused in her grooming and tried to appear intimidating. After dancing around from fear of a mouse, the effect had lost some of its potency.

"Thank you," Wynona said, picking up the dropped book. "I'll bring it back when I'm done."

"Keep it," Marcella snarled. "I don't want anything you've touched and that book is as useless as you are."

Wynona had been facing the door when the words slammed into her back. She hesitated only slightly before continuing to move forward. If she managed to get to the door without dying of a broken heart, it would be a miracle.

"You're no Le Doux," Marcella continued, following Wynona into the hall. "Your birth was a mistake. Perhaps we should go back to the time when the weakest were put down so they didn't pollute the whole society." She cackled. "You and your little vermin could both be put out of your misery."

There was no stopping the tears that began to track down Wynona's cheeks. The hallway seemed to last an eternity as she marched toward the exit. She didn't know what her mother had planned to accomplish before Violet had taken over the show, but whatever it was, it couldn't have been worse than the words she was spewing at Wynona right now.

"This is for Prim," Wynona mouthed to herself. "This is for Prim."

Loud shouts and commotion came from up ahead and Wynona had to hold back a groan. Another confrontation was the last thing she needed. But when the howl of a wolf broke through the noise, her heart immediately answered the call. "Rascal," she breathed, breaking into a run.

The scene that met her eyes in the foyer was one for the record books. Rascal, in his wolf form, had the Le Doux family butler, Zysus, who happened to be a centaur and very large, on his back while Rascal snarled and snapped at his neck. Other servants ran around, random bits of magic hitting every which way as they all tried to figure out how to stop the wrestling match without actually hurting Zysus.

"Rascal!" Wynona shouted, skidding to a halt just a few feet away.

"What is the meaning of this?" Wynona's father called out as he entered from another hallway.

Marcella came in behind Wynona, still cackling. The sound fit her much better than the laughter had. "This is the life you wanted?"

Wynona glanced over her shoulder to see her mother smirking and waving a manicured hand carelessly. "I can see why you're so anxious to go back to it."

Wynona grit her teeth and turned forward again. "Rascal," she said more softly.

His ears twitched.

"Please come down."

Zysus took advantage of the distraction, throwing Rascal across the room and charging after the wolf like the bull he was.

"STOP!" Wynona screamed.

The room stilled. Every servant, creature, witch, wizard and animal froze in their tracks.

The change in noise level was jarring and Wynona shook her head at the sudden silence. "What just happened?" she asked in a shaky voice. A purple mist covered the ground, slowly moving through the area, weaving between people and furniture. It came to Wynona's feet, causing her to suck in a surprised breath. It curled up her legs and wrapped around her waist.

Instead of the cold wet she had expected, the mist felt warm and...welcoming.

Tentatively, Wynona reached down and ran her fingers through it. The mist seemed to jump for joy, delighting in Wynona's touch and playing off her hands like a sprite on a leaf.

"I'm hallucinating," she said breathlessly. "I have to be hallucinating." Her eyes traveled the room again, but still no one moved. "This is bad. This is so bad."

A slight stirring at her neck had Wynona reaching up. "Violet? Are you awake?"

Violet's eyes were still closed when Wynona pulled the tiny body down, but they fluttered open quickly. Violet shook herself, checked each limb, then put her hands on her hips and glared at Wynona.

"It was an accident?" Wynona grimaced, her explanation more like a question than a statement.

Violet rolled her eyes and waved to the room.

"I don't know how to fix it," Wynona admitted. "And I'm afraid if I do, Mom and Dad are going to lock me up."

Violet twisted her lips to the side in a considering look, then nodded firmly. She waved her arms and chattered for several seconds.

"We can try that, I guess," Wynona said uncertainly. Her heart was still pounding against her chest. Carefully, she walked through the still playful mist, heading toward Rascal. Once there, Wynona's hands began to shake. Rascal's fur was on edge and his teeth bared as he'd prepared to meet Zysus head on. "How did he know to come for me?" Wynona whispered.

Violet scolded her.

"Sorry, now's not the time." Wynona sighed and took in a forti-fying breath. "Here goes." Slowly, she reached her shaking hand out and laid it on Rascal's head. She kept it there as the fur began to lay down and slowly, the wolf body softened.

Teeth snapped shut as movement was returned to the creature and Wynona jumped back with a squeal.

Rascal immediately stopped his aggression and turned her way, his golden eyes widening. After a moment, he turned his head and studied the room, his hairy jaw dropping in shock.

"Yeah...I know," Wynona said softly. "But we need to get out of here before they come to, or I'm not sure my parents will ever let me leave."

Rascal shook his head hard and after a moment, grew back into the man. "Are you alright?" he asked, roughly jerking her into his chest. His grip was so tight she could barely breathe, but Wynona couldn't bring herself to ask him to let go.

Nothing had ever felt so good as his support and warmth right now.

"I'm fine," she said, knowing it wasn't the truth, but it would have to do for now. She leaned back. "But we really do need to get out of here and back to the station."

Rascal tucked her into his side and warily moved them through the room and to the front door. "Are you sure you did this?" he asked, awe still in his voice.

Wynona pointed to the floor. "Notice anything?"

He shook his head. "You and purple. I wonder what causes a witch's magic to be a certain color."

"I don't know, but I also don't think now's the time to find out."

"Agreed." Rascal ushered her out the door and quickly latched it behind them. "Okay. Can you set them free now?"

"I really don't know how to do that," she said, scrunching up her nose. "Maybe getting a little distance will do it for me?"

He blew out a breath and pushed a hand through his hair. "It's worth a shot, I suppose." He looked at her scooter. "I really wish you would ride with me. I'd feel much better about it."

"I can't leave it here," Wynona stated with a shake of her head. "Then I'll have to come back."

"We could have Skymaw come get it. They can't hurt him."

Wynona paused. "Do you think he'd mind?"

Rascal shook his head. "I'm his boss. He won't mind at all."

Wynona tilted her head to the side and gave him a look. "He doesn't need to be doing meaningless jobs just because his boss says so."

A slow smirk grew across Rascal's face and he opened his mouth to speak just as a shout came from the house. Both of them jumped into action. "In the truck!" Rascal urged.

Wynona didn't argue. She'd just have to give Daemon an extra treat the next time he was over. She scrambled up into the passenger seat, quickly throwing on her seatbelt. "Okay, Violet?" she asked.

Violet squeaked, her grip on Wynona's hair tight.

Rascal threw the truck into reverse and the tires squealed as he turned around. It wasn't until the house was far in the rearview mirror that either of them took a deep breath.

Wynona closed her eyes and laid her head back against the seatrest. "If I'm ever stupid enough to try and do that myself again, please remind me of this exact situation."

"Speaking of," Rascal said in a low tone, "what were you thinking?"

Wynona sighed. "I'm sorry," she whispered thickly, her emotions coming back to the surface. "I needed a book from their library." She opened her eyes and pulled her head upright. "I know who the killer is."

Rascal jerked his head toward her, then back at the road. "You what?"

Wynona shook her head. "Not now. I'll explain it all in time, but if you'll drive us to the station, I need to look something up." She made a face. "I'm gonna need it if I'm going to be able to convince Chief Ligurio that Prim is innocent." She settled the book in her lap and opened it to the table of contents, scanning until she found the chapter she wanted.

"You're sure that little trip was worth this?" Rascal asked, his voice still tight.

Wynona nodded, her eyes still on the book as she reached over and rested a hand on his thigh. "It will be," she said. "To prove Prim's innocence. But just the same, thank you for coming for me."

He grunted and shifted in his seat. "It was nothing."

"It wasn't nothing," Wynona assured him, finally turning away from her research. "And when this is all over, I'll do a better job of thanking you." She smiled when the tips of his ears turned red.

"It seems to me you saved yourself," he ventured, half asking a question, half making a statement.

Wynona closed her eyes for a long moment. "That might be something we need to talk about as well. I have no idea what I did and if my parents figure out it was me, I might have just ruined any possible future I have outside of the castle."

She started to remove her hand, but Rascal let go of the steering wheel with one hand and captured hers. He brought it up to his mouth and kissed the back of it. "Then we'll just have to make sure they don't figure it out."

"Easier said than done," she grumbled.

"I have no doubt that we can figure it all out," he said calmly. "But first...like you said, Prim. Let's break her free, catch a killer and then we'll keep you safe."

"Sounds like a plan."

CHAPTER 28

As soon as they were in the station parking lot, Rascal jumped out of the truck and rushed around to Wynona's door, pulling it open.

She held up a finger. "Just a second." Her eyes continued to skim the chapter she wanted. Her memory had been mostly correct, but some of the minute details were a little sketchy. Right now, she was setting everything back in place. "One more minute..."

"Take your time," Rascal drawled, then winked when she glanced sideways at him.

Her finger was on the page, guiding her as quickly as possible. Enough time had already been wasted with her family and it was time to break Prim free. "Got it," Wynona breathed. Using her finger as a bookmark, she snapped the textbook shut, double checked that Violet was secure on her shoulder, and allowed Rascal to help her down from the truck. "Thanks," Wynona said breathlessly. Her heart was still pounding a crazy rhythm from the run in with her family. A despairing panic kept knocking on the back of her mind, trying to insert the worry that her family was going to come after her because of her magic. Or that there would be something in the ghost report about Rascal attacking the presidential family. Neither one would help their cause right now.

It took more mental strength than Wynona knew she possessed to shove the worries back and keep her focus where it belonged. On Prim.

Rascal kept her hand as they walked inside, which Wynona was grateful for. She wasn't quite as strong physically as she was mentally and her body was still going through heavy tremors as the adrenaline from the fight worked its way out of her system. He pulled open the door and put a hand on her lower back, ushering her inside.

"Wy!" Officer Nightshade called out with a wide smile, which promptly slipped from her pale face. "Are you okay?"

Her red eyes roved around Wynona and Wynona realized she must look like a woman who had just gotten in a fight. Self consciously, her hand went to her curls, which were probably standing on end. "I'm okay," she tried to assure her friend. At Amaris's skeptical look, Wynona amended her statement. "Or I will be."

Amaris nodded. "Okay, but in the meantime, let me know if you need anything." She looked to her superior. "Anything specific you need, Deputy Chief?"

Rascal shook his head. "Just the chief."

"He's in his office," the officer assured them.

"Thanks." Rascal continued pushing Wynona forward.

She nodded at Officer Nightshade as they went past. The edges of the book pressed into her chest as they made their way through the crowded hallway to the chief's office. But the security of the pressure gave Wynona comfort and she tucked it in a little harder.

Violet let out a sound that was almost a purr as she nuzzled Wynona's neck. It made Wynona smile. Violet was becoming more like an emotional support animal than a friend. Whoever heard of an emotional support mouse? But the longer they knew each other, the more Wynona realized the tiny creature was perfect for her.

They were very much alike, she and Violet. Often overlooked, different from the norm, but with a determination to succeed at anything they did.

"Chief?" Rascal called out as he opened his boss's door.

Chief Ligurio looked up, the desk phone plastered to his ear. His eyebrows shot up when he saw Wynona walking in with Rascal, but he didn't speak to them. "Uh-huh." He looked down. "Of course... We'll do our best... I have no further evidence at this time.... Right....

Okay... Thank you." The phone was settled back in the cradle. "Strongclaw," he said. "What brings you in this morning?" One side of his lips curled. "Especially after that dramatic exit you made only an hour ago?"

Wynona frowned and turned to Rascal, who was rubbing the back of his neck uncomfortably. "Sorry, Chief," he said. "It was an emergency."

Red eyes flickered to Wynona before settling back on the deputy chief. "I see."

A lightbulb went off in Wynona's head. "You left because of me?"

Violet let out a sigh worthy of a Southern debutante.

One side of Rascal's mouth quirked up at the sound, but he nodded. "Yeah."

"How..." Wynona held up a hand. "Never mind. I mean, I want to know, but not right now."

Rascal cleared his throat and nodded. The tips of his ears were red again and Wynona had a hard time pulling her eyes away from the sight, until the chief interrupted.

"If we're not going to talk about that, perhaps we could get to the point of this visit?" He narrowed his eyes. "And why do you two look as if you had to battle your way inside?"

Wynona shook her head. "No time." She sat down in one of the chairs across from the front of the desk and set the book in her lap. "I know who killed Madam Ureo."

Chief Ligurio's mouth flapped open and shut a couple of times. "Excuse me?" he finally managed to choke out.

"I was at the theatre this morning and something happened that brought to mind a tidbit I had read when I still lived with my family," Wynona said.

Chief Ligurio leaned forward onto his desk. "And?"

She held up the book. "And I went there to get the book so I could prove to you I was right."

His red eyes rolled. "Let's have it, Ms. Le Doux," he said impatiently.

Wynona stood and turned the book around before setting it on his desk. "Read right here."

As the chief was reading, Rascal walked around and Wynona pointed to the spot again, allowing him to read the same passage.

Chief Ligurio's head jerked up. "You're sure?"

Wynona hesitated only slightly. "Yes."

"Why the hesitation?"

"Because I hate the fact that we have to ruin someone's life."

Chief Ligurio sat back, folding his arms over his chest. "You don't think they ruined their own life by committing murder?"

Wynona splayed her hands to the side. "I would never condone murder, but I'm starting to see that most people use it when they feel they have been left with no other options." She blinked a couple of times. "I know what it's like to feel that way. I didn't choose to hurt anyone, but those types of corners are places where dark choices are made and eventually carried out."

The room was silent after her little confession and Wynona shifted her weight. She didn't mean to give away so much information, but it was true. She hated the crimes being committed, but much of the time she felt only sorrow for the criminal.

Rascal's sympathy-filled eyes were almost too much to handle. He'd gotten a first hand look at how her family treated her, and it wasn't pretty. Even Chief Ligurio had heard some of the things her parents said, including the first time her father disowned her.

"Regardless," Chief Ligurio said in a low tone, "I agree this could be the exact answer we're looking for." He tilted his head to the side. "The most important thing is we need to see it in action."

Rascal pushed a hand through his hair. "Right there. The whole time." He shook his head. "How did we not see?"

"We do need to see it in action," Wynona agreed, "But I have other evidence that'll help clench it."

Chief Ligurio sighed. "Why am I not surprised?"

She gave him a look. "I'm sorry I didn't realize it was all relevant at the time, but I do now and we need to let Prim out of that cage."

"It's hardly a cage," the chief snapped.

Wynona closed her eyes and took a deep breath at Violet's urging. "I'm sorry. I shouldn't have used that word, but you agree that this," she jabbed the book, "points us in another direction. Please let her out while we go and set up the real killer."

He squished his lips to the side. "I can't just let her out. But I'll agree to let her sit in one of the interrogation rooms while we go make the arrest."

"You really think we can just rush in and slap on some handcuffs and call it good?" Rascal asked. "Isn't the DA going to want a little more than that?"

"What exactly did you have in mind?" Chief Ligurio snapped.

"A set up."

Both men looked at Wynona like she was crazy.

She shrugged. "What? We've done it before."

"Maybe so, but we're talking a new level of murderer here," Chief Ligurio argued. "I don't know that I trust my men not to get hurt."

"Then use me."

"Absolutely not!" Rascal shouted.

Wynona straightened and looked at him dead in the eye. They were glowing fiercely and she knew the protectiveness was still stemming from the earlier encounter with her family. "I can do this," she said softly.

He squeezed his eyes shut and cursed under his breath. "I know that," he said through a clenched jaw. "It's the other people I don't trust."

Chief Ligurio's pencil tapped the desk. "She's our best bet," he said.

Rascal cursed again and Violet scolded him...loudly.

Very few things amused the chief of police, but apparently a purple mouse calling out a wolf shifter for being a potty mouth was one of them. "You can take your little...friend along," he continued with a grin.

"And the squad will be close by," Rascal stated emphatically.

Wynona sat back down and patted the seat next to her. "Come on, Rascal. You know this needs to happen. And we better get to planning. Our time is running short."

CHAPTER 29

Wynona's heart was pounding in her throat as she approached the theatre from behind. She'd been through this door a dozen times in the last couple of weeks, but during none of the visits had she held the information she held now.

Knowing a person was a murderer made it much more difficult to address them or the people around them without acting suspicious. And Wynona couldn't afford to act suspicious. She was here to get a confession. Or at least enough of a confession that the real killer could be put behind bars instead of Prim.

Seeing Prim brought up and set in a conference room with some food and water had been one of the biggest boosts that Wynona could have received on an otherwise horrible day. Prim had cried tears of joy and eventually begun growling and shouting when they'd shared their information with her.

Seeing Prim all worked up and more like her usual sassy self had been perfect and Wynona was eager to get back and celebrate.

Her business might be struggling after ditching it today and dodging calls from her daily patrons, but at least her friendship was being cemented in concrete.

"Ready?" Wynona asked softly.

Violet squeaked from her pocket and poked out her nose.

Closing her eyes for a second and taking in a deep breath, Wynona willed her body to calm down enough to handle her role. "Here we go." She knocked, then folded her arms in front of her waist.

It took several minutes and a couple more knocks before Mr. Doom finally pulled it open. He immediately blew out a harsh breath. "How many times are you going to come around?" he snarled. "The police have a suspect, our cast is breaking up and there's nothing here you haven't already seen."

He started to close the door and Wynona lunged forward, pressing on the door. She knew the only reason the door stopped was because Mr. Doom chose to do so. She wasn't anywhere near strong enough to stop him, but she was grateful he didn't just knock her out of the way. "I need in," she said, her voice shaking slightly. His shifter ears were sure to pick it up.

Mr. Doom studied her, then sniffed, leaned closer and sniffed again. "You smell like fear," he said in a low, mocking tone. "What exactly are you scared about?" His eyes looked her up and down.

It was almost as bad as when her mother had held her legs with magic. Wynona felt violated and repulsed as he looked her over and she came up wanting. "I'm not scared," she stated, but the lie was like glass shards on her tongue.

He chuckled in a deep tone. "Try again, little witch." His eyes flared. "Do I make you nervous? Does your police boyfriend know that?"

"Please let me in," Wynona said, clenching her fists and forcing herself to stand her ground. How could she save Prim if she couldn't even get past the first obstacle? She needed to be inside for all this to work. "I'm here on official business."

His eyebrows pulled closer together. "What for?"

"We've found the killer," she hedged, purposefully being vague. Wynona might know who did the killing, but she wasn't exactly sure how deep the betrayal went. "Is Mr. Rujins here?" she asked.

Mr. Doom straightened. "Are you saying..." He trailed off, suddenly looking nervous.

"I'm not saying anything," Wynona said quickly, not wanting him to make assumptions. "I'm simply asking if your boss is in his office."

Mr. Doom nodded solemnly.

"Please let me see him," Wynona said more firmly.

When Mr. Doom hesitated, Violet must have decided she had had enough hiding and poked her nose out, giving the giant of a man a proper scolding.

Though Wynona struggled to follow Violet when she spoke so fast, the intent of the words was plain to anyone.

Mr. Doom scratched his chin and nodded. "She's right. Forgive me." He pushed the door wider. "My fight isn't with you." Wynona still had never figured out why the bear shifter had such a soft spot for the mouse, but tonight she wouldn't argue.

She nodded. "I appreciate it. Thank you." Slipping inside, she immediately went to Mr. Rujins office, gathering courage as she went. The first step was complete, now she needed to handle the next one.

She knocked on the door rapidly, moving before her fear could catch back up to her.

"Enter," came the gravelly demand.

She gripped the doorknob and marched inside. "Mr. Rujins," Wynona said by way of greeting.

"Ms. Le Doux," he responded. "I didn't expect to see you here." One side of his upper lip curled. "Still gathering evidence?"

"How would you like to help catch the real killer in exchange for a deal?" Working with the troll put a sour taste in Wynona's mouth. If he was truly the loan shark that Rascal described him as, then Wynona knew enough to understand that Mr. Rujins was a crook who knew how to stay out of jail.

He stiffened, letting Wynona know she had caught his attention. "You're here in an official capacity then?" His eyes darted to the door. "Where's your puppy?"

"Deputy Chief Strongclaw and Chief Ligurio sent this." Wynona pulled a card out of her back pocket and tossed it on the desk. She wasn't going to get any closer than she had to. The time it took the troll to read the offer was nerve-racking, but eventually those yellow eyes came up to meet hers.

"Is this for real?"

Wynona shifted her weight, then forced herself to stay still. "We have the evidence we need for our own convictions," she affirmed, "but my job here tonight is to get a confession." She nodded her head. "That's where you come in."

"And you think if I bring up the contract, Mr. Truall will react?"

Wynona nodded. "Yes."

The slimy businessman relaxed slightly in his chair, eyeing Wynona warily. "How do I know this isn't some kind of trick to catch me?"

"The fact that you're worried about being caught tells me more than it should," Wynona grumbled.

That hacking laugh burst into the room. "You're smarter than your father gives you credit for."

Wynona stiffened. What did her father have to do with any of this? Was he involved with people like Mr. Rujins? In what capacity?

Mr. Rujins's smirk was obnoxious as he watched the emotions which had to be evident on Wynona's face. "Didn't know he got his hands dirty, did ya?"

Wynona tightened her knees. "Are you in or not?"

He sighed and threw the paper down on his desk. "Fine. But I'm holding onto this." His finger jabbed the paper. "If anything goes wrong, I'll take down the entire police department."

Wynona nodded her understanding.

Mr. Rujins groaned as he stood and walked over to a stand alone safe. Once inside, he pulled out a stack of papers. "The police still have the original," he mumbled, "but I can make do with what we've got here." He waved a manilla envelope in the air.

"Great. Let's get going." Wynona turned to the door and pulled it open, stepping out into the hallway. Mr. Rujins followed, then stepped ahead to lead the way to the Trualls' dressing room.

"It's a good thing you came when you did," he huffed as they walked the few doors down. "They'll be gone by morning." He shook his head. "I wish I could say I was surprised by what you're telling me, but..." He shrugged.

Wynona stayed silent. She didn't want to hear anything this man had to say. At least nothing that wasn't an absolute necessity.

He reached out for the doorknob. "You're sure about this?"

Wynona nodded.

He shook his head, finally looking slightly forlorn at the duty ahead. "Here we go." He pushed open the door.

"Mr. Rujins!" Brell exclaimed. It was the loudest Wynona had ever heard the siren speak. Normally she was so reserved and soft spoken.

"What's going on here?" Fable snapped, surging toward the intruders.

Wynona had to work to keep from jumping backward. They needed to get this confession before an angry panther tore them both apart. Violet stirred in her pocket and Wynona put a hand over her friend. At least she wasn't alone.

Jumping straight into character, Mr. Rujins waved the paperwork through the air. "You two aren't going anywhere," he snarled.

Fable came to a screeching halt, his dark eyes wide.

Brell rushed to her husband and peeked around his shoulder. "What do you mean?" she asked breathlessly. "I thought the contract said we were free in the case of Madam Ureo's death?"

Fable put his hand over hers, shushing her. "It's alright, sweetheart," he said softly, though his eyes were glaring hard at Wynona and Mr. Rujins. "They don't know what they're talking about."

Mr. Rujins laughed harshly. "Actually, it's been pointed out to me that there's a clause we missed." He paused dramatically, looking completely calm with the whole situation.

Wynona felt as if she was going to throw up, and for the first time since this started, she was grateful Mr. Rujins was doing the bulk of the acting.

"That's not true!" Fable shouted, moving toward them again. "We're clear! I had our lawyer check it out!"

Mr. Rujins clicked his tongue in a condescending manner. "Obviously, they weren't as thorough as they should have been." He turned to a page in the folder. "It says here that if the theatre is continued under previous management, the contracts are to be honored." His grin sharpened. "I wasn't hired. I was already a manager, just a silent one."

"You wouldn't do that," Brell asked thickly, her voice almost inaudible. "Not after all we've done."

"Oh, but I would," Mr. Rujins drawled, slowly walking away from Wynona. "You see, I only invest when I smell a profit." He tapped the end of his nose and winked at the despairing couple. "And you, my dear, are definitely a profit."

"I won't let you get away with this," Fable snarled, stepping forward menacingly. He didn't get far, since Brell had a hold of his arm, but every muscle in his body was tight and ready to spring.

"Fable, don't," she said. "I won't let you."

Fable looked down, his face immediately softening. "It's your dream," he whispered. "I can't let them take that away from you...from us."

"Actually," Wynona inserted, drawing all eyes her way. "I don't think that will be a problem." Wynona folded her hands together, keeping the trembling from being visible. "Will it, Brell?"

Fable scowled. "What are you talking about?"

Brell tilted her head to the side. "I don't understand," she said in her smooth tone, giving a confused smile.

It was good. The innocent, demure look. She had to have practiced it for a long time for Wynona to fall for it. Every siren Wynona had ever known had been a little on the egotistical side. It was more than likely a natural reaction to being such a draw for men. They were beautiful and they knew it.

But not Brell. Her quiet, humble demeanor had been just as warm and welcoming as the siren had obviously planned. Wynona had fallen for it hook, line and sinker.

"I think you do," Wynona said, thrusting her chin slightly in the air. "You don't need Fable to save you at all." She raised one eyebrow. "You've saved yourself before. Haven't you?"

Fable shook his head. "Saved herself? Are you really suggesting that Brell killed Madam Ureo?" He barked out an incredulous laugh. "Brell wouldn't hurt a fly." He shook his head again and looked at Mr. Rujins. "Is this where you're getting your information from? Because if so, you have to see that she's certifiably insane."

Wynona ignored the jab and kept her eyes on Brell.

The room grew quiet and eventually Fable looked down at his wife. "Brell...?"

Brell straightened, and her eyes lasered into Wynona's. Slowly, she tilted her head to the side, as if Wynona was a puzzle she couldn't quite figure out. "How did you know?" she asked slowly.

Wynona held her ground and Violet stirred, ready to help now that they were reaching the climax. "It's your voice."

CHAPTER 30

A soft, tinkling laugh floated through the room.

Wynona shook her head, knowing exactly what the siren was doing and trying to remain strong enough to countermand it.

"We don't all have the power, you know," Brell said, stepping away from Fable.

He reached for her. "Brell, what are you talking about?"

Brell paused at his touch, but didn't turn. "Just an old wive's tale," she responded. "Something I thought was lost to common knowledge."

"Your wife has the ability to float her voice through the wind," Wynona explained, her eyes never leaving her target. "She can hypnotize, manipulate, and do just about anything she wants once she has a person under her thrall."

Mr. Rujins snorted. "I guess we now know why you were so good as a singer."

Fable shook his head rapidly. "No. That's not true. Brell wouldn't manipulate anyone."

"It's how she convinced Madam Ureo to drink the tea with the daffodil in it," Wynona said. She pointed to where their coffee maker had resided. "Did you not notice, Fable, that you suddenly had three cups in your room?" Wynona began to move, her steps hesitant, but she needed to make her point. "Or what about the plant that used to reside on this table?" She tapped the small wooden stand.

Fable scrubbed his hands down his face. "She said it died," he rasped. He stumbled a couple of steps back. "It..." His panicked gaze turned to Wynona. "It didn't die, did it?"

Wynona shook her head. "I'm sorry." No matter how possessive and harsh Fable had been, Wynona felt bad for him. He hadn't asked to be pulled into this. In fact, if her suspicions were correct, there were more unwanted revelations on the way.

"You...killed her?" he said hoarsely, turning to Brell.

Brell's eyes filled with tears. "Someone had to do something," she pleaded.

Once again, Wynona could feel the voice creeping through the air. She could practically taste the magic as it tried to wrap around her mind, coaxing her into believing everything Brell said. "Stop!" Wynona shouted, shaking her head hard.

The shout must have worked, because Brell stopped and the magic fizzled.

Mr. Rujins rubbed his temples before glaring at Brell. "How many times have you used that on me?"

Fable's breathing grew loud and labored, drawing Wynona's attention. "Answer him," he demanded, his voice filled with anger.

"What?" Brell's head jerked from one man to the other.

"Answer him!" Fable snarled. "How often do you use that on him?"

"I..." Brell put a hand to her throat. It was clear to see that her scheme was starting to fall apart.

"Have you ever wondered why she rarely leaves your side?" Wynona pressed.

Brell's attention snapped to her and the meek confusion began to slip away.

"It wasn't real..." Fable choked out. He leaned onto his knees, his lungs working overtime as he tried to catch his breath. Fur began to flash under his skin as his emotions grew too difficult to handle.

"Fable," Brell said immediately, reaching her hand toward him.

"Don't you dare touch me," Fable snarled, backing up. "I think you've spent enough time turning me to your will."

"Think of the story you told me about how you met," Wynona continued. "Think of how you fell for her as soon as you heard her sing. Or how she's always touching you, and her voice rarely changes. She's working her magic to keep you with her, no matter your own feelings on the matter."

"I did this for us!" Brell cried. "I killed her so we could be together forever!"

He shook his head. "None of this was real. My feelings for you weren't real!"

That was the last straw. Brell's face contorted and for the first time since Wynona had met her, wrinkles and a red flush marred her perfect face. "How *dare* you," she said in a quiet, low tone. "How *dare* you take what I've done and throw it away!" She spun on Wynona. "And how dare *you* come in here just as I was about to see it all come together and ruin it." She turned to Mr. Rujins. "The contract is fine, isn't it? There's no clause about management?"

He shook his head. "Ms. Le Doux thought it would help pull a confession."

A humorless laugh left plump, red lips and Brell threw her shoulders back. "Well, it worked. Maybe you're not as insane as Fable thinks." She took a couple of steps toward Wynona. "But now I think it's time for you to go." Brell slowly shook her head. "I'm too close to let this go." Opening her mouth, Brell began to sing.

Wynona immediately put her hands over her ears. She needed to find a way to block the sound until she got all the answers she had come for.

WIth a twirl of her finger, Brell caused a breeze to move through the room and even after she stopped singing, the sound continued to echo and carry. Both men immediately closed their eyes and smiles donned their faces. They looked to be in utter bliss as they were serenaded by Brell's precious tones.

Wynona countered the woman's footsteps, keeping the chairs between them. "Tell me...why the wand?" Brell didn't answer, just continued to walk toward Wynona. "Was it simply to throw off the trail?" Wynona asked, slipping one hand into her pocket. The song immediately began to infiltrate her head, but Wynona did her best to fight it internally. "Fairies don't use wands, so I'm not sure why you would use it."

One edge of Brell's lips curled up into a tiny smile. "I hadn't planned to frame Prim... She was a woman after my own heart, after all. She wasn't afraid to stand up for what she wanted." Brell's manicured fingers trailed along the edge of the couch. "But when she discovered the body, the opportunity was too good to pass up." Brell turned her head to look at Wynona. "You can't win, you know. Although you're lasting longer than most, my voice always comes out on top."

Wynona gritted her teeth against the unrelenting magic. It was small, but never backed down. Her thoughts were growing fuzzy around the edges as she grew tired of fighting it off. She needed to wrap this up. "So you poisoned yourself to add to the evidence against Prim."

Brell's grin was enough of an answer.

"When did you figure out the situation with the contract?"

Brell snorted, an unladylike noise coming from feminine perfection. "Madam Ureo liked to brag." Brell threw her head back, breathing in deeply. "She enjoyed keeping others under her thumb and my contract was the source of that for me." Brell brought her chin down and grinned. "Watching her kill herself was more pleasurable than it should have been. I never knew I had a killer inside me."

"Just a master manipulator?" Wynona began to work her way toward the men. She clenched her hand, praying Brell wouldn't notice what she held. "What about the money? The skimming? How did that come into play?"

Brell shook her head and tsked her tongue. "My timing couldn't have been more perfect," she purred. "First Prim falls into my lap and then Mr. Rujins shows up for the money scheme." She shrugged nonchalantly. "How many ways could the police be pulled?" Her face darkened. "But somehow you saw past all that."

"My best friend's life was on the line," Wynona said through gritted teeth. "What would you have done?" Wynona drew even closer to Fable.

Brell must have been very sure of Wynona's failure, because she didn't bother moving. "Doesn't matter now, does it? Any minute now," Brell said soothingly. "I can feel myself winning."

Wynona could feel it too. The voice was too unrelenting. As Wynona tired, the voice never wavered. Slowly, it inched forward, wrapping around her thoughts and trying to ease her into obedience.

"It won't work," Brell sang out as Wynona managed to get next to Fable. "Disturbing him will only bring him out for a second before my magic takes over."

"Unless he can't hear you," Wynona said through gritted teeth. She reached out and stuffed the earplugs into Fable's ears, then rushed over to Mr. Rujins to do the same.

"NO!" Brell screamed.

The sound brought Wynona to her knees, wincing as she covered her ears. She had been unable to reach Mr. Rujins in time.

Fable stumbled backward a couple of steps, knocking over a stack of moving boxes and essentially blocking Brell from getting closer. He shook his head and his hands went to his ears.

"Don't take them out!" Wynona shouted, still breathing heavily from Brell's scream.

As if the room wasn't in enough turmoil, the door burst open and Rascal lunged in, snarling and eyes glowing. Chief Ligurio, Officer Skymaw and several other police officers were there as well, along with Mr. Doom, standing a head taller from the back of the group.

Without missing a beat, Brell began to sing, only this time her voice was harsh and loud. Gone was the sweet, persuasive call from earlier and now the magic beat at Wynona's head like a sledgehammer. The room filled with groans from men falling to the ground, each grasping their heads. From her periphery, Wynona could see Brell climbing over the couch and begin marching toward the door, all while holding onto her final note.

Wynona shook her head. She had to get up. After all this, Brell wasn't allowed to win. She couldn't just leave. This wasn't how this was supposed to end. A movement in her pocket drew Wynona's attention and a cylindrical container began to push out of her pocket.

Violet was an absolute genius.

Without pausing to worry about the consequences, Wynona grabbed the container, pushed to her knees and ripped out the pull-pin, aiming the bottle at Brell's back.

A piercing scream broke through Brell's music and Wynona shook, but held her ground. The banshee scream echo was nothing compared to Brell's commanding call.

This time it was Brell who cried out in agony and held her head. Wynona was careful to keep the canister aimed directly at the siren's back. When Rascal had given it to her, he had promised it only incapacitated the person directly in its path.

Without warning, a large ball of fur leapt onto Brell, taking her to the ground, and Wynona immediately stopped the scream. She didn't want to hit Rascal. She was breathing so heavily, there were sparks in her vision and this time it wasn't out of control magic. Though, now that she thought of it, Wynona was surprised her own magic hadn't reacted to Brell's.

Snarls and a couple of squeaks could be heard before the entire room full of officers jumped to their feet and Brell was quickly contained with a hag's thread, negating all her abilities.

"Get her out of here!" Chief Ligurio shouted above the noise.

Apparently, their fight had drawn the eyes and ears of the entire building, and since the hallway was so packed with people, the officers couldn't move to take Brell to the squad cars.

Violet jerked on Wynona's shirt and she looked down. "You wonderful, little thing," Wynona cooed, reaching down to pull Violet out of her pocket. She kissed the purple head. "Thank you."

Violet chittered smugly and settled herself on Wynona's shoulder.

"Wy!"

Wynona closed her eyes in relief. She'd know that voice anywhere. "Over here," she called out, climbing shakily to her feet. Before she felt steady, arms wrapped completely around her and Wynona grunted before settling into the embrace.

"Never again," he rumbled. "Never again."

Wynona laughed softly and relaxed. "I think I've heard that before."

"I mean it this time."

She didn't respond, but her smile was bright. Clinging to his back, she decided now was not the time to fight. There would be plenty of time to figure out what they wanted to do going forward. If the future was anything like the past, helping with these cases might be something she did whether she wanted to or not.

"Come with us, Mr. Truall."

Wynona pulled back and watched as a very confused panther shifter was guided from the office.

"And you, Mr. Rujins," Daemon said, pulling the troll to his feet. To his credit, the theatre manager didn't even try to argue. His legs shook and his eyes still looked glazed over as Daemon led him out of the room.

"Daemon," Wynona breathed. She raised her eyebrows at Rascal. "I couldn't figure out why my magic didn't kick in when things started to go south. It's because Daemon was here."

Rascal nodded and tucked a piece of her messy hair behind her ear. "He almost didn't make it in here. We got stuck in the crowd, who were surging toward Brell's singing and couldn't get through." Rascal's eyebrows pulled together. "Skymaw nearly hit the floor when your magic kicked in." He leaned in closer. "He told Chief it was because of Brell, but..."

Wynona nodded as she blew out a breath. "Well, with Prim exonerated and Brell behind bars, we can start working on getting all of my magic under control."

Rascal nodded and tucked her under his chin again. "The sooner the better," he said.

"Agree." Wynona soaked in the affection before remembering Violet. "Oh!" She leaned back again. "Guess who saved the day?"

Rascal grinned. "Are you telling me my favorite mouse was the true hero?" He reached out and Violet sauntered into his palm, smoothing her fur as she went. Rascal gave her a gentle ear rub. "I knew you would be amazing. I just had a feeling you needed to go along."

Violet didn't even pretend to be humble as she accepted his praise like the true queen she was.

Wynona couldn't help but smile at the scene. Prim would get such a kick out of this. "Prim!" Wynona shouted. "We have to get back to the station and let her out."

Rascal handed Violet back. "I'm sure Chief is already all over that, but we need to go back anyway. We need all the evidence you collected during the fight."

Wynona rubbed her forehead. "Yeah. That wasn't pretty and she almost got away with it all."

Tucking her under his arm, Rascal began to work their way through the crowd. "I'll drive you there," he said.

"What about my scooter?"

"I'll send Skymaw back for it."

Wynona chuckled. "I think he barely fit on it." She poked Rascal's side. "I doubt he wants to crunch his legs up like that again."

Rascal's grin was nothing short of devious. "Good thing he doesn't have a choice."

"Send Amaris," Wynona said with a yawn. "I'm exhausted and I'm more than happy to let you do the driving, but give Daemon a little break."

"If you say so..." Rascal drawled, helping her into the passenger seat of his truck. "Buckle up, buttercup. We're off to save your friend."

CHAPTER 31

"You're the most amazing witch in the entire world," Prim gushed as she hugged Wynona.

Wynona patted her friend on the back, so grateful that this hug didn't have to end so Prim could go back to her cell. "You would have done the same thing," Wynona responded. She leaned back. "Plus, Violet was the real hero of the day."

Prim clasped her hands together at her chest. "Violet," she breathed. "You did that for me?"

Wynona couldn't see the little creature on her shoulder, but she was certain she could feel the mouse's eye roll. Prim giggled in her tiny fairy voice and the sound was music to Wynona's ears. It had been too long since the world had been blessed with such amusement.

Prim pointed at Violet. "You like me. Admit it."

Violet huffed and smoothed her fur. The relationship between the two was a delicate one. Sometimes Violet tolerated Prim and other times she wanted nothing to do with the quirky fairy. Wynona had yet to figure out the pattern Violet used to pick her attitude for the day.

"Ms. Le Doux," Chief Ligurio said as he walked into the room, laptop and papers in hand. "Ms. Meadows." He sat down heavily, looking weary for someone who never aged. "My apologies for holding you for so long."

Prim clenched her jaw, but Wynona elbowed her friend in the ribs. "It's fine," Prim said tightly. "I understand."

Wynona gave the chief a sympathetic smile. "Is everything wrapped up?"

He shook his head. "We're working on it, but it's going to be a long night." He growled. "And an even longer week, truth be told."

"I'm sorry."

Chief Ligurio waved her away. "It's all part of the job." He glared at Rascal, who was still standing behind Wynona. "Are you ready to get to work, Strongclaw? Or are you going to continue hiding behind your girlfriend?"

Wynona's eyes widened as Rascal tried to cover his laugh with a cough. She wasn't sure why he was laughing at the remark. It was more than rude, but apparently, Rascal didn't mind his boss's ribbings.

"Ladies," Rascal said, inviting them to the two seats across from the chief.

Just as they were sitting down, Daemon opened the door and stepped inside. After closing it, he stood just to the side of the opening and took a formal stance.

"Is he...standing guard?" Prim asked incredulously. "Are you serious?"

Wynona was also suspicious of the move, but Rascal shook his head.

"Skymaw and I did a lot of work on this case. He's here to see it finished."

Wynona relaxed, but Prim stayed stiff. "Thanks for your help, Daemon," Wynona said, having not had a chance to speak to him earlier.

Daemon nodded, his eyes darting to Prim before coming back to Wynona. "Just doing my job, Ms. Le Doux."

Prim folded her arms over her chest and flung herself back in her seat. "Can we get this finished?"

Prim," Wynona scolded.

Prim threw her hands in the air. "Can you blame me? My plants are almost to the point of no return. I'd kill for a pizza from the

Weeping Widow and if I don't get a hot shower in the next hour, I don't know how I'm going to react."

Wynona laughed softly. "Fair enough." She turned to the chief. "What do you need from us?"

"A run down of everything from the beginning." Chief Ligurio set his computer up. "What happened after you got to the theatre?"

Wynona took a deep breath and launched into her story. As she got to the point where she was provoking Brell in order to get a confession, he stopped her.

"Okay, let's back up a minute." Chief Ligurio took a deep breath. "What's all this about a plant and how did you know she had once had a daisy in her room?"

"Ah, yeah. I guess I never explained that." Wynona shifted in her seat. "I realized very quickly after being at the theatre that all the rooms were the same."

He nodded.

"But it wasn't until I remembered the tidbit about sirens using the wind to carry their voice that I realized Brell's room was different."

"You just said they were all the same," Chief Ligurio said.

"Exactly," Wynona said, pointing at the vampire. "Hamer was right next door and he had the same chairs, the same couch and the same table. But on his table he had a plant."

"Couldn't he have brought it in himself?" Rascal questioned.

Wynona shook her head. "No. Because there were water rings on the table in the Trualls' room." She turned back to the chief. "The same type of water rings I saw on Hamer's from his watering can."

Chief Ligurio rubbed circles on his temple. "So there was a missing plant and you knew it was a daffodil, how?"

"I didn't," Wynona admitted. "Until Brell admitted it."

Rascal whistled low. "That was a risk."

Wynona shook her head. "No. It all made sense because of the mug."

"A mug now?" Chief Ligurio asked.

Wynona nodded eagerly. "Yes. Remember how all the rooms are the same? Even Madam Ureo's office was the same. Obviously, they bought all the furniture in bulk because she had the same coffee station that the smaller rooms did. Each station had a coffee maker and two mugs. I saw a dust ring in Madam Ureo's room, but we only found one mug." She raised her eyebrows at Rascal, who nodded his confirmation.

"And..." Chief Ligurio pressed.

"And there were three mugs in the Trualls' room."

"So you believed that the missing plant was the daisy and the added mug was there because Brell brought it back after using it to poison her boss." It was a statement, not a question, but Wynona nodded anyway.

"And the voice clue was there the whole time," Wynona lamented, shaking her head. "Several times I thought in my head how Brell's voice was like a breeze, skipping and dancing through the air." Wynona huffed. "But I never put it together."

Prim rubbed Wynona's back. "Don't beat yourself up," Prim said. "No one else caught it either."

Wynona gave her friend a grateful smile.

"Were there any other hindsight pieces of evidence?" Chief Ligurio asked.

Wynona nodded while taking in a long breath. "Yes. How obsessed all the men were with her."

"She's a siren."

"I know, but even when they weren't in her presence, they had a hard time. Mr. Doom for example," Wynona pointed out. "He fell for her immediately. And her husband." Wynona felt her heart clench. "If you spent any amount of time with him, he always seemed angry and on edge, but as soon as Brell spoke to him or touched him, he immediately calmed down." Wynona tapped her fingers against her knee. "I took it as him being in love with her, but now I know she'd been manipulating him. She never let him stray far. He was always within reach of at least her voice."

Chief Ligurio scrubbed his hands down his face. "So this whole thing was about the contract. Not the embezzling."

Wynona shook her head. "No. That was just an unfortunate scheme found during the investigation. As much as it pains me to say so, I believe Mr. Rujins was telling the truth. He came to find out what was happening with the books. The murder and his arrival were simply bad timing for him, but good timing for Brell. It simply gave the police more paths to get lost on."

Rascal let out a low growl from behind her. She knew he wasn't happy about it. Rascal would love to see Mr. Rujins behind bars and Wynona couldn't blame him. The man was sleazy and creepy, but in this case, he hadn't committed the crime.

"And what did Mrs. Truall say about all these things?"

Wynona's heart beat a little faster as she thought about how close they had come to losing today. "It took a little prodding, but eventually she broke." She tucked a piece of hair behind her ear. "She admitted that Madam Ureo used the contract as a way to keep her under her thumb and one day spilled the fact that the contract ended with her death." Wynona shrugged. "At that point, it was clear that Brell felt she had no options. Her manipulation of Fable came out and Brell insisted she had done everything for them." Wynona sighed, the exhaustion pressing in again. "I believe she loved him, but didn't give him a chance to love her back. She took what she wanted with him and when the flaw in the contract came out, she did the same there."

Chief Ligurio sat back and blew out a breath. "Save us from crazy women," he grumbled.

"Not fair," Wynona argued, as Prim scoffed and Rascal choked. "Do you really want me to point out all the insane men who have been serial killers in the past?"

The chief nodded her the point. "You're right, of course." Sighing, he sat up. "Okay. I think you've given us enough to have the DA put her away for good." He looked at Rascal. "Call Grimcrest and tell her what to collect in order to substantiate Wynona's testimony."

"On it." Rascal took his phone out of his back pocket and walked out of the room.

As he left, Wynona caught Daemon's eye. His jaw shifted and he looked like he had something he wanted to say, but was holding back. When she raised her eyebrows, Daemon shook his head subtly.

Wynona turned back to Chief Ligurio. "Brell admitted to using Prim as a scapegoat, though that hadn't been her plan from the beginning. The wand was meant to put you off her path and confuse the investigators. When Prim showed up in the wrong place at the wrong time, Brell decided to capitalize on it."

Chief Ligurio nodded. "Makes sense." He let out another long breath then turned to Prim. "Thank you for your patience and again, I apologize for the inconvenience." He straightened. "You're free to go."

Prim nodded graciously, but didn't speak. Wynona knew that meant she was biting back a cutting remark and she couldn't blame her best friend. This had been a horrible experience and it would take a while to feel normal again.

Wynona took Prim's hand and they stood up. "Thank you, Chief," Wynona said. "Let me know if you have any more questions."

"We appreciate your work, Ms. Le Doux," he said, standing at his chair.

Wynona held in her shock at his show of respect. He might not be the jerk she had thought he was when they first met, but he hadn't ever truly been warm either. Especially since she had disagreed with him from the very beginning in this case. They had butted heads so many times Wynona was positive she had lost any progress she had made in their relationship.

"I'll walk you out," Rascal said from the doorway.

Wynona smiled and led Prim over there.

"Our apologies, Ms. Meadows," Daemon said softly as they walked past. "We hope you won't hold it against us."

Prim barely gave him a glance as she walked out, head held high.

Wynona, however, wasn't willing to let Daemon go. "Thank you," she whispered. "For everything."

He nodded, his black eyes still troubled when he looked at the back of Prim's head.

"Wy?"

Wynona turned to Rascal, who was waiting for her, and gave him a tired smile. "Let's go home."

He took her hand and kissed the back of it. "That's the best thing I've heard in a long time."

CHAPTER 32

Wynona winced as another rock crashed to the ground.

"Aye, yi, yi," Prim groaned, slumping to the ground in an undignified heap. "Nona. I love you. But you're a mess."

"Thanks," Wynona said wryly. "You're a big help."

Prim gave her a wide, sarcastic smile. "I'm here, aren't I? I haven't left you to figure all this out by yourself."

"I know," Wynona breathed out. "Thanks." She rubbed her aching forehead. "I don't know if I can do this," she admitted.

"Of course you can!" Prim jumped to her feet. "You can't give up now. We've only been working for..." She glanced at her phone. "Oh..."

"Yeah. Oh." Wynona shook her head. "It's been, like, two hours and everything I try to pick up still falls to the ground within two inches."

"Maybe we're starting with something too big?" Prim suggested. "Want to do, like, a leaf or something instead?"

Wynona shook her head. "No. That can't be it. When I've been upset, I've moved huge things, so weight can't be the issue."

"Hello, beautiful," Rascal said, walking up to the women.

He was still in uniform and Wynona's heart skipped a beat. After he gave her a sweet kiss for a greeting, it began to speed. "Hi," she said breathlessly.

Rascal winked, then looked around. "Making lots of progress, are we?"

Prim snorted and Wynona glared.

"I mean, the rocks look like they've moved two inches since I left you at lunch."

He was laughing as Wynona whacked his arm. "Be nice!"

"I'm always nice!" he argued back, still grinning. "Besides. I have an idea for you."

"Oh, yeah? What's that?"

Rascal held up a finger, then moved over to Prim. Nestled in the grass at Prim's feet lay Violet, taking a nap in the sunshine. "Vi." He rubbed her head gently. "Hey...Vi."

Violet sat up and rubbed her eyes adorably before looking up at Rascal and turning hostile.

He chuckled and put his hands in the air. "I know, but it really wasn't very nice of you to let her do this all by herself."

Wynona jerked back. "What?"

Rascal ignored her as Violet began arguing with him. "I know she needs to learn to do it on her own, but she's learning backwards." He listened and nodded to the scolding coming his way. "I get it, Vi, but still...she needs to learn to channel it first and there's too much power."

Violet opened her mouth, then snapped it shut and reluctantly nodded. Looking guiltily toward Wynona, she slunk over and climbed up to her shoulder.

"I don't understand," Wynona said, looking between Rascal and Violet.

Rascal smiled encouragingly. "Just give it another try."

Wynona tilted her head and looked to Violet, who nodded. "Okay, if you say so." Wynona closed her eyes and took a deep breath. Violet's fur caressed her skin and Wynona felt her heart calm down even further. A light breeze blew across her face and...she paused, tilting her head slightly. There was...something different.

It was as if the world had shifted. Wynona could *feel* the magic in the air. They were practicing behind her house, very close to the Grove of Secrets. Wynona had always known the grove of trees was magical, it had a terrible reputation for allowing creatures in, but not letting them out.

But now Wynona could feel it. The trees pulsed with a life that she had never felt before. "Is that—?" She stopped herself from asking the question. It would sound so ridiculous. Creatures didn't just feel life or magic that way.

Violet brushed a little harder against Wynona's neck and she brought herself back into focus. Without bothering to open her eyes, Wynona held out a hand and envisioned the rock in her mind. She planned to picture her work, then make it happen.

She saw the rock rise in the air, strong and confident in a way it hadn't been before. Turning her hand over, palm expectant, she beckoned the object to come to her. She followed it every inch of the way, persuading and coaxing until she saw it land in her palm. Oddly enough, a weight landed in Wynona's hand at the same time.

She opened her eyes and gasped. The exact rock she had imagined was now lying in her palm. "That's... I mean... I can't..." Feeling her eyes bug out of her head, Wynona turned to Prim and Rascal.

Prim was standing with her jaw nearly hitting the ground while Rascal appeared like a proud papa who was watching a child succeed.

"How did I do that?" Wynona rasped.

Violet did that purring sound again. *Because I helped you.*

Wynona screamed and jerked away.

STOP THAT! The voice screamed in her mind.

"Oh my gosh, oh my gosh, oh my gosh..." Wynona held still, afraid to look at Violet. "Is that...you?"

Violet rolled her eyes. *Of course.*

"Why can I hear you?" Wynona felt like she was going to throw up. She had known Violet for months. Why was she just now hearing her voice? Only witches with familiars could speak... "Are you my familiar?" Wynona squealed.

Violet put a finger in her ear and shook it. *A deaf familiar, if you don't calm down.*

"How did I not know this?" Wynona asked. "Why now?"

We've never actually connected to do magic. Violet glared at Rascal, who was still grinning. *I was trying to let you learn on your own, because using a familiar is advanced magic, but Wolfy boy over there said you needed some help.* She sighed. *And he's right. Just don't tell him I said that.* She sniffed and smoothed down her fur. *Your magic came on too strong. Without me, you can't wrangle it into submission. Hopefully after you've felt what it's like to use it properly, you can start doing stuff on your own. I won't always be around to help, you know. I have a life to live.*

Wynona closed her eyes, feeling slightly light headed. "This is all too much."

Prim rushed over and threaded her arm through Wynona's. "Let's go get some tea, huh? Then you can tell me why I was listening to a very detailed one-sided conversation between you and a mouse."

Wynona paused as they walked up to Rascal. "You knew," she accused.

He stuffed his hands in his pockets. "I suspected."

"Why didn't you say something?"

He gave her a half smile. "Sometimes you have to wait for the right time."

His words were still slightly cryptic and Wynona was positive he meant more than just Violet being her familiar. But right now her brain couldn't take any more. "I need that tea," she whispered, allowing Prim to pull her into the house.

She could sense Rascal behind them as they walked inside. Normally she adored having all her friends at her house, but right now Wynona felt on the verge of collapsing. She had no idea what was going on with her. First, her magic begins to appear in quantities so great she can barely contain them. And next, she discovers her mouse friend is her familiar, and they can speak to each other now that they've connected their magic. Her boyfriend, who she had trusted implicitly had suspected all along and yet had allowed her to stumble along, nearly getting herself killed in the process!

What else could be thrown at her at this point? Why was her magic breaking lose anyway? Curses were meant to last a lifetime unless the person doing the cursing broke the spell. And why did Rascal seem to know more about her than she knew about herself?

Wynona collapsed in a chair and let Prim take over the kitchen. Wynona simply didn't have the mental energy to play hostess right now.

Rascal sat next to her and warily took her hand, sighing when she didn't pull away. "Are you okay?"

Wynona shook her head. "No," she said honestly. "I need to know what's going on with me." She sighed. "Do you know more?"

He shrugged. "Nothing that will help us further with your magic."

"But there's something else?"

His eyes dropped to the table. "Yeah. But you're not ready for it."

She blinked at him. "Is it about my family?"

He shook his head.

"Violet?"

He shook his head again.

Inspiration struck. "Does it have to do with why you knew I was in trouble?" she whispered.

Rascal glanced up, then back at the table before nodding.

"You're right," she said, slumping. "I'm not ready."

He kissed the back of her hand, then leaned over and kissed her temple. "I know."

"But someday...I will be."

"And I'll be here to tell you."

Wynona gave him a small smile. "Thank you."

Rascal winked. "Always."

Ready for Wynona's next adventure?
Don't miss Le Doux Mysteries #4
"Sweet Tea and Murder"

Why does every answer just bring more questions?

Wynona is finally starting to get a handle on her newfound magic. With Violet's help and Rascal's tutelage she's beginning to find parts of herself she never knew existed. But the big question still remains...who cursed her in the first place?

Wynona's search for answers is interrupted when she's informed that another tea shop has been opened and it's eerily similar to hers, right down to the house made custom teas. When she decides to confront the owner, however, Wynona finds herself in a very familiar place.

The middle of a crime scene.

The tea shop owner has been murdered and with Wynona's business's reputation on the line, she must set aside her own wants in order to solve the case. But with every step she takes, Wynona's magic grows stronger and her questions and fears begin to mount.

Can she solve the murder while keeping her magic a secret and therefore preserving her freedom? Or will her lack of control catch the attention of all of Hex Haven?

Grab Your copy of "Sweet Tea and Murder" today!

CPSIA information can be obtained
at www.ICGtesting.com
Printed in the USA
LVHW080747191122
733589LV00031B/1499

9 781956 176193